BEAUTY'S SECRET

BEAUTY'S SECRET

Copyright © 2021 Brantwijn Serrah.
ISBN: 9781954031036

Written by Brantwijn Serrah
Edited by Celia Breslin
Cover design by Christian Bentulan
and Brantwijn Serrah

USA TODAY BESTSELLING AUTHOR

BRANTWIJN
SERRAH

DARK EROTIC ROMANCE

ALSO BY BRANTWIJN SERRAH

Short Stories
Right Where I Want You
Equinox
Hunting Grounds
Graveyard Games
Bad Dreams
The Holston Street Halloween Party

Standalone Novels
His Cemetery Doll

Chronicles of the Four Courts
Book 1: Goblin Fires
Book 2: Elfin Nights
All Mad Here (A Four Courts Short)

Shifter's Dawn
Book 1: Leaving Tracks in the Snow
Book 2: Chasing Ghosts in the Night
Book 3: Standing Tall at the Dawn

The Dark Roads Saga
Book 1: The Pact
Book 2: Into Nostra
Book 3: Shadowlands
Book 4: Fighting Dirty
Book 5: Path of Wolves

Beast and Beauty
Book 1: Beauty's Curse

Join Brantwijn's newsletter for a free book!
Get updates and special offers from Brantwijn and other indie authors.
https://www.brantwijn.com/newsletter

AUTHOR'S NOTE

Hello, my Wayfarer,

Welcome once again to the world of *Beast and Beauty*. I'm so glad to see you back, and if you're brand new, welcome to the party! You might wish to go back and read Book One, *Beauty's Curse,* before I go on and potentially spoil anything for you.

Beauty's Secret marks the second chapter in the adventures of Sadira, a warrior, submissive, and slave (in the parlance of power exchange), and her barbarian Master, Bannon Sha'kurukh, the Red Bear of Sanraeth. In Book One, these two found themselves thrust together by cruel law and harsh circumstance and discovered a passionate connection through bondage and domination.

The story you are about to read contains intense sexual situations and strong themes of power exchange, including mild knife play. If such situations are upsetting for you, you may not enjoy my *Beast and Beauty* series, but I do have several other steamy romances you can certainly enjoy, such as my reverse harem trilogy, *Shifter's Dawn.*

You'll notice most instances of the word "Master" are capitalized in this narrative. This is a purposeful choice, symbolizing the submissive's deference to a specific Dominant (commonly known as a Dom). If not capitalized, the word is being used in a more general sense, specifying no master directly.

Within these pages I have taken poetic license to weave elements of the BDSM lifestyle into the fantasy world my characters inhabit. You won't find any explicit discussion of a contract or see the same terms you might see in a modern BDSM romance, but I hope I have managed to convey the importance of safewords, well-communicated limits, and the tenet *safe, sane, and consensual,* at all times. Anywhere I may have failed to accurately address or represent the lifestyle or consenting members within it, I beg your forgiveness. I hope you will please consider the wider library of excellent informational material on BDSM and power exchange, should you find yourself drawn to it. And I promise to keep learning as well.

As always, my darlings,
Read, write, and be merry

Brantwijn

Dedication

With love, for my love.

Special thanks to Ashley Harper, of my reader group, who christened the country of Sanraeth, and for whom the character of Ashe is named.

PROLOGUE

SOMEWHERE AHEAD, IN a sea of blue light, my mother calls.

Seren! Time to come home, your dinner's waiting!

"*Madrēn?*"

So, I wade toward the light, shielding my face with an upraised arm. Soft green creepers and dangling tendrils of fern brush my head and shoulders. The smells of crisp, clean water and wet soil invite me deeper down the passageway. A sense of sweetness, of peace and blessing, awaits me ahead.

Yet even as my heart leaps, a cutting sting jabs at my gut.

"*Madrēn!* I hear you!"

Blue light, pulsing like a heartbeat. Drawing me deeper in. A fire in the heart of the earth. So, I push on, bare feet silent on moss-covered stones. Rough, gray stones, the colors of a thunderstorm, not the familiar, sandy yellow of Vashtaren dwellings or the ochre hue of Alaric's castle.

Yes, the castle. I am not this little girl. Not Seren. I am—

Something slithers in the darkness.

I am Sadira. The soldier. The slave.

"*Madrēn*, are you here?"

Seren! Where've you got to, my silly face?

A low, dry hiss rises from the shadows. The hollow rattle of a sidewinder's tail. Around my ankles, long, winding coils grow tight. Like the tattoos, red as blood, spiraling over my skin.

No. No, you can't keep me here. You can't keep me from her!

"*Madrēn!*"

But the snakes drown out her voice. In a rising chorus of hisses and slithering scales, they tangle around my limbs.

Has the light grown weaker? Or are these hideous reptiles pulling me away from it?

The light is dying. Somewhere buried beneath the earth, the light—the Light—*is dying.*

And my mother. My mother, left behind in some unknown land.

Is she still calling me? After nearly thirty years, is she still waiting for me to come home?

There is no black morass of shadows—no writhing snakes. This is a dream, and dreams hold no *real* enemies, no tyrant kings, no great serpents. Whatever lies ahead, it *belongs* to me—part of the life Alaric Khan stole away—and I will go to it!

With each resolute step, though, the snare of the dream tightens.

I've been here before. I've dreamt of this all. Yet I have never—made it—

"Let...go of...me..."

I must reach...that...light!

BEAUTY'S SECRET

BEAST AND BEAUTY, BOOK TWO

by Brantwijn Serrah

CHAPTER ONE

I JOLTED FROM the bed, hands flying up in thoughtless reflex. For an instant, I was *sure* someone meant to grab my arms and snatch me away into empty blackness.

Just a dream, I assured myself. *That sense of attack... or was it falling?*

The spartan bedchamber around me stood silent in the gray pre-dawn. The desert heat had already begun to rise, and the thin sheets, damp with sweat, tangled around my legs. I kicked them aside before lying down again, naked.

Beside me, my barbarian warlord Bannon Sha'kurukh reached out and caressed my arm. "Trouble sleeping?"

"No..." I ran a hand through my hair. "I dreamed, is all."

"What did you dream of?"

Brushing my fingers across my lips, I murmured, "I... I don't remember."

He looped his arm over me and drew me close to his body. In the heavy heat, I would have preferred to simply lie next him, twining fingers instead of limbs, whispering instead of sweating in his arms. I allowed him to squeeze me tight against his chest, however. Especially in moments like these—moments so tender and loving—I found it hard to object.

Bannon had moved us into a lesser bedchamber, far from the grand suites of King Alaric, my former master. This new room was far smaller and had no adjoining baths, and certainly no pleasure room where one could find tools, toys, and harsh implements of sensual discipline.

I didn't mind, though. At first, sleeping in Alaric's bed with my new paramour presented a thrill: submitting to Bannon's desires on the very blankets where Alaric had owned me; sharing the opulent baths once reserved only for Alaric's pleasure; kneeling in the wooden stocks of the torture chamber awaiting the harsh sting of Bannon's hand instead of the sadist king's. Acts of defiance stoking a wicked and sweet and satisfying release; a brazen, vicious infidelity to my tormentor.

Since the culmination of Alaric's last act of evil, though—possessing Bannon's mind and raising a gruesome, undead abomination from the sands—I had no wish to return to those places. I didn't need a soak in his sauna, most of which had collapsed during the final battle, anyway. I had no interest in any of Alaric's possessions.

But today, I must go back, regardless.

I tilted my head up to the small window high on the wall. The pearly silver gleam of morning brightened, little by little. My last day in the castle of King Alaric Khan.

The first day of the search for a homeland and a people I didn't remember. I didn't even know if they still existed.

Seren! Come home, silly face!

Bannon's soft, sleeping breath drifted over the back of my neck. Though I'd started to sweat, and his huge frame practically covered me in his body heat, I closed my eyes and wound my fingers with his.

Stay calm. There is nothing in those rooms to harm you. Not anymore.

My free hand drifted up to my neck, where my slave's collar used to be. The smooth metal ring I used to twist and fiddle with was no longer there. The familiar weight of the embossed black leather, likewise gone. Alaric had used it to mark me in more ways than one: he might have died on the battlefield, leaving me free of his earthly power, but he'd tied up one final, nearly fatal claim in the lines and glyphs around my neck. He'd fashioned the collar into a phylactery to protect and carry his wicked soul, even after his body was cast to the scavengers.

But I destroyed the collar. I broke his power. There's nothing left he can do to me.

Why should a return to his quarters intimidate me now?

Perhaps because it would be the last time in my life. Once I selected whatever final items I wished to take with me, it would be time to bid farewell to those rooms, to Alaric, and to Vashtaren altogether.

I don't belong to this desert. Yet it has crept into my bones. What do I know of other lands or other people, except what we took on the field of battle? I have never seen the sea, or any of the countries beyond it. Barbarian lands might as well be the distant surface of the moon, for all I know.

Bannon had been teaching me to think of his people, the Sanraethi, in more suitable terms. I tried to remember and correct myself. While Bannon didn't seem to mind being called *brute* or *barbarian* in the throes of rough, passionate play, the rest of his people weren't amused. If I meant to join him, and them, and wanted to find a place in their ranks, I couldn't continue to think of them as savage foreign soldiers. Especially when they were really my liberators.

I lay awake in Bannon's arms, stifling hot but consoled, as the light from the window strengthened by degrees. It turned from a soft, muggy gray to a brightening rosy glow, and then a crisp, hot gold. Bannon stirred again, sleepily planting kisses along my cheek and jawline before rising and stretching his long, muscular body in the early beam of light. Beautiful lines of sunny splendor limned strong, hard, tawny limbs.

I admired him, and my lips quirked into a smile. His eyes caught mine, and he eased out of the stretch to lunge at me and swat my bottom.

"Get up, you wicked little wretch." Gathering me in his arms, he lifted me from the mattress and swung me around. "Lazing about in bed, are we? I might have to heave you into one of the horse troughs for your morning bath and see how you smirk at me then!"

"No, Sir!" I begged, wriggling in his grasp. "Wouldn't you much rather I bathe *you* as my punishment?"

Bannon set me on my feet and stroked his beard. "Well, then, *that's* a good idea. Yes, I think I shall. Stand ready, my girl, while I call up a tub."

I assumed my usual stance of patient obedience: chin up, chest out, hands clasped behind my back. Bannon donned breeches long enough to step out into the hall and send a courier for the wash basin, and I had time to privately hope it wouldn't be his daughter, Ailsa, tasked with bringing it up. Ailsa was old enough to be married herself, but still, she didn't much approve of the circumstances which led Bannon and me to share a bed.

"First smirking, now daydreaming?" Bannon's amber eyes glittered as he closed the door behind him and rubbed his hands together. "Goddess Sherida, what am I to do with such a cheeky girl?"

A delightful heat rose to my cheeks and stirred in my thighs. "You could take me over your knee, Sir."

Bannon ran the backs of two knuckles down my cheek. I resisted the urge to look up into his eyes while his hand drifted down to my neck and then to one flush breast. He seized it with a gentle but possessive greed, squeezing softly, the pad of his thumb circling my studded nipple. I swallowed the moan fighting to rise. He then stepped closer, squaring his body to mine, and his other hand came up to take my right breast, too.

"Look at these brazen little tits." He gave each pinkened nipple a tight tweak. "And that pert ass. That wicked look on your face. I'll bet your pussy's just as wet and ready as a bitch in heat."

I closed my eyes, arching to his touch as he groped and squeezed my breasts together in slow circles, pinching and tugging the stiff peaks, rolling the gold barbells piercing each tip. Every rough touch stoked a sweet, illicit joy, the thrill of exposure and indignity.

"Come then!" He released me, taking a seat on the edge of the bed patting his lap, beckoning me. "As you suggested, kitten. Over my knee."

"Yes, Sir."

5

I lowered myself over the tops of his thighs. He seized my wrists in one big hand, and with the other caressed my naked bottom. I fidgeted, teasing him, and shot a childish, mocking look over one shoulder. He caught me—I'd meant him to—and his palm came down on my ass with a swift and stinging slap.

"You impertinent brat!" he scolded, though he smiled. I stuck my tongue out and wiggled my rear, daring him, until another solid slap struck my other cheek, and a shiver of delight ran through me.

"Wicked! Little! Tart!"

Bannon punctuated each word with another spanking, bringing a wonderful red heat to my bottom and stoking the deep yearning in my belly and loins. I couldn't help a laugh, which Bannon answered with another slap and a hard, possessive grab.

"What has gotten into you?" he growled. His words were hard, but still playful. "You mark me, kitten, I'll whip these naughty cheeks until they're red as plums and you can't sit straight for a week. Then I'll have you on all fours while I *fuck* that sweet, sore ass. Is that what you want?"

"Maybe it is."

Just why did I play with him so? I'd challenged him before, spirited and daring, prompting him to punish me in firm, but passionate, ways. This morning, though, I'd found some lustful mischief inside, something I would never have *dared* to act upon when Alaric disciplined me.

Because Bannon is my Master now.

And my Master hasn't taken me in weeks.

A knock on the door put an end to our game. The wash tub had arrived.

I fell into a pout. As Bannon helped me off his lap, he patted my cheek and gave me a soft chuck under the chin.

"No worries." He rose and crossed to the door. "I won't forget what a wicked girl you've been."

He retrieved the washtub and the tray of bathing implements with one quick word of thanks to the deliverer, then carried it in and kicked the door shut again. "You're in for a very thorough punishment later, Sadira."

Yes. Please. Show me you still want me.

I clasped my hands behind my back and gave him another taunting smile.

Shedding his meager clothing, Bannon sank into the tub and gestured for me to join him. Retrieving a waxy cake of soap and washrag, I obeyed, sliding into the water atop him so we faced one another, my needful pussy pressed conspicuously to his rigid, standing cock. Like this, I bathed him as promised, running the rag over his broad chest and shoulders, then down his arms. The sweet scents of jasmine and patchouli bubbled up from thick lather. With a long, leisurely sigh, Bannon leaned his head back over the rim of the tub and accepted my doting. Yet when I pressed my slippery wet breasts against him, he gave no sign he noticed.

At last, I set the cloth aside and instead worked both hands between us, over the shaft of his cock, palms slippery with soap. Bannon uttered a groan as I kneaded him, my hands moving gently in a measured, pumping rhythm. While I stroked, I rocked my body to his with a needful whimper.

Bannon opened one eye and peered at me. "I know what you want."

"Do you?"

"Oh, yes." He slid a hand around the back of my head and tilted me close, so our foreheads touched. "You want a good, hard fuck. Isn't that right, my sweet slut?"

"Yes, Sir." I relinquished my grip on his erection and rested against him. Unable to meet his eyes, I added, "It... has been some time."

Neither one of us had to say, *since the battle with Alaric.* Or whatever tainted, twisted abomination Alaric had summoned and empowered with his last, dying magic. We hadn't spoken about the matter or discussed any thought of abstinence, but since the fight, we'd spent nearly four weeks in quiet celibacy.

Why, though? I'd wondered more than once. Had it been the deep violation of Alaric possessing Bannon's body? The brutality he promised me while *in* that body, wearing the face of my new Master, whom I'd come to trust?

Or that eye. That horrible, green, pulsating eye at the heart of his revenant monster. That eye which held everything left of him... and something even darker, even more sadistic, within.

Those things seemed likely, even obvious. It didn't ease my worry, though, when I imagined I'd done something to chill the passion between Bannon and me. Perhaps my barbarian had satisfied his curiosity about Lord Khan's personal consort and her strange lust for pain. Or perhaps having his body stolen and used by a madman had changed him. Made him resent all the prizes—or problems—he'd inherited when he struck Alaric's head from his body.

As long as he held me at night and showered me with affection, I left things where they stood. I, too, had my reservations. All was well if I had eyes on him, could watch his movements and not be surprised. Now and then, though, when he caught me off guard or moved somewhere on the periphery of my vision, my heart skipped a beat and adrenaline flooded my veins. I recalled Alaric's voice in my ear, whispering *I have always been stronger than you.*

It had been that dark sorcerer, not Bannon, who promised to hurt me worse than ever before. And yet—

They were Bannon's hands on my wrists. Bannon's fingers closing in on my throat.

So, we didn't speak of it. We didn't speak of our spontaneous bout of celibacy over the last month, either.

Well, he's got a raging cockstand right now, doesn't he?

Yes, and he'd administered vigorous spankings and fondled my breasts with wicked greed. Still... why hadn't he demanded me in full?

Bannon tucked a lock of my hair behind my ear and leaned close to kiss me. "Soon. I promise. First, we must prepare for the journey. Our caravan leaves this afternoon."

"Yes, Sir."

I schooled my reaction, donning a mask of polite obedience. Of course, it couldn't only be the morning I finally found the courage to bring up the conspicuous lack of sex between us. It was also the day I left the desert behind.

The day I threw aside everything I knew, to follow Bannon into—

What?

CHAPTER TWO

RETURNING TO ALARIC'S chambers sent my heart into a painful, piercing ache. The moment Bannon swung open the doors to the opulent master suite, I caught my breath, hands clenching into fists.

The master bedroom hadn't been touched since the final battle with Alaric's revenant golem. The earthquakes predicting the monster's rise had shaken the pitcher of drinking water from its place on the bedside table, leaving it shattered on the floor, and knocked the small pots of paints and kohl from Alaric's vanity. The bed had been spared any real damage, but the canopy above it sagged with small chunks of stone fallen from the ceiling.

Relief filled my chest at the sight of Alaric's personal shrine to Akolet, the sacred serpent. He'd stored it in a wooden tabernacle set against one wall, and now the doors hung open, one of them dangling precariously by a single hinge. The stone centerpiece of the altar within—a statue of the seven-headed serpent—had broken into pieces.

Bannon rested a hand on my shoulder. "Are you all right?"

"Yes," I replied, though my heart still ached with each beat. "I... I feared it would still smell like him. Bergamot. How I *hated* that smell, and it haunted me in these rooms, even after he was gone."

Only he hadn't been gone. I touched my throat, forgetting again that I no longer wore any collar. The cursed sigil protecting Alaric's soul after death had been destroyed.

Perhaps I will never have to bear that wretched smell again.

Behind us, a pair of workers entered carrying two large, wooden crates. I recognized one of the girls: a Sanraethi slave who had also belonged to the sorcerers of Akolet. When our gazes met, at first she glanced away, avoiding eye contact. I was used to that. So many people believed me a witch and feared the power I might wield. Before I could lament the gesture, though, the girl looked up again, and a faint red chagrin colored her cheeks. She offered me a smile before she and the other worker retreated into the hall.

I blinked. My hand came to my lips, and I half expected to find some strangeness there, some odd bit of food stuck at the corner of my mouth or an unexpected wart on my chin.

Did she genuinely just smile at me? Me, *Alaric's supposed* queen?

Beside me, Bannon chuckled. He crossed to the fireplace mantle and picked up a polished wooden figurine sitting at one end, turning it over in his hands.

"Are you surprised?" he asked. "The whole castle watched you strike down the seven-headed serpent. Akolet himself, I've heard them say, returned to punish us all. I think you might have put to rest the rumors of your 'evil witchcraft' at last."

"Really?" I tilted my head, trying to read his expression, then moved to examine Alaric's shrine. I stared at the broken statue, picking up one of the monster's viper-like heads.

"You're a war hero now, Sadi. Maybe soon, instead of Alaric's witch, they'll call you the She-Bear of Vashtaren."

She-Bear. Mate of the Red Bear, not the dark magician.

I dropped the fragment of stone back with the other remnants and shut the tabernacle doors, adjusting the broken one into place to hide the altar altogether.

Facing Bannon once more, I stood at attention. "What do you need from me, Sir?"

"Need?" He glanced over the room, rubbing his chin. "Everything I want from these rooms, I have already. Since you agreed to travel on with me to my homeland."

He flashed me a smile and I returned it, warmth rising in my chest.

"But if there's anything you still wish to claim," he continued, "now is the time to do it."

"Me?"

My hand fluttered up to my throat again, and again I found no ring. *I must stop doing that!*

"Nothing in these rooms ever belonged to me," I told Bannon. "Even the dog pillow on which I slept could be taken from me, if Alaric willed it. Nothing is mine."

"It is now."

Bannon took a seat at the round wooden table set by the fireplace. "When I claimed my victory, all of Lord Khan's possessions became mine, didn't they? Castle, servants, treasures... even you, according to the customs of the Vash. Well, for all I care this castle can crumble to the sand, the servants have their freedom, and I have no desire for Khan's treasures. Save one, and she has chosen me."

He waved a hand at the room. "You dwelled here, Sadi, as awful as it may have been. If anyone has the right to claim something out of these rooms, it's you."

I pursed my lips. Rubbing my chin, I looked over the master suite in which I'd served so many years as Alaric's personal pet. *Did* I want to take any of it with me?

"Not the dog pillow," Bannon amended when I spent a long moment staring thoughtfully at it. "You'll never sleep on anything so demeaning again."

Dropping my gaze to the floor, I hid a grateful smile. "Thank you, Sir."

I paced the grand room for several minutes, still uncertain. The workers brought two more crates while I pondered the little, everyday things of Alaric's life. Things I'd been forbidden to touch unless he instructed me to retrieve them. Clothing he'd selected for me. Makeup he'd demanded I wear.

"I can't," I declared at last. "It's all his. I'll always think of it as his and won't be able to touch a thing without cringing."

"You took his swords," Bannon pointed out.

Yes, I did. I sat on the end of the bed and tapped my fingers noiselessly on the blankets. Alaric's khopeshes were mine now, and it brought me a deeply gratifying feeling to wield them. A mad and

13

empowering defiance. I liked swords, of course, and appreciated the elite craftsmanship and beauty in the blades. Alaric had never deserved such beauty. That made it easy to take them from him.

I glanced around the room again.

"These furs," I said finally, lifting a corner of the plush, thick pelt atop the bed. "I've always loved the way they feel. Especially when my barbarian pins me down and holds me against them."

"Indeed." He nodded his agreement. "Anything else?"

After another moment's hesitation, I pointed at the mirror over the fireplace. "And that, too. I quite like it. I suppose it might be broken along the way, though."

"Maybe, maybe not." Bannon rose and took hold of the mirror, lifting it from its brackets on the wall. "We'll wrap it in the furs and hope it survives."

As he lay the mirror across the table and came to my side to gather the pelts, he tipped a nod in the direction of the inner rooms, where Alaric's saunas— and his pleasure chamber—waited.

"Anything from there you'd like, kitten?"

I hadn't even considered taking anything from the pleasure chamber. This time I didn't argue, though, and rose to my feet to peruse the vault of illicit pleasures while my barbarian packed away the items I'd already selected.

The smooth smell of clean leather and richly oiled wood, sweet with hints of orange, greeted me in my favorite room of the castle. It made my heart soar to see nothing in the chamber had been harmed or broken in the earthquakes, save for a few hanging tools of discipline which had fallen harmlessly to the floor. Hardly thinking about it I gathered them up and returned them to their places.

For a little while I forgot the task at hand, and basked in the comfort of the space, running my fingers over the hard wood and firm leather of the devices, soothed by the quiet serenity around me. Yes, each tool of torture had been used to inflict pain on my flesh, but to me, pain became a twisted, tormenting pleasure, wringing orgasmic bliss from my body.

Alaric had hurt me, yes. In many ways. In here, though, the hurt always led to something greater, something momentous. Release. Relief. Catharsis. There'd been no true punishment within this chamber—though there had been moments when play had pushed far beyond my desire and left me injured. There'd been no *fear*, though. To me, each visit meant reward. Or at least, carnal indulgence.

The furniture couldn't come with me. I sat on the edge of a bench where Alaric had perched me, bent over with my bottom raised up and my arms bound from wrist to elbow in rope. He'd struck me with paddles and strops, even a light, whippy cane. The bench would be too big to transport, though, and so would every other piece in the room. I sighed.

Perhaps I can show Bannon how to build similar devices once we've reached our destination.

"Look here." Bannon had appeared in the doorway. "I let you off on your own for three minutes, and you're daydreaming again instead of doing the work I assigned you."

I hopped to my feet, beaming. "I'm sorry, Sir. Would you like to punish me?"

He strode into the room, grinning and stroking his beard. His gaze roamed over the torture devices, and I imagined he must be choosing which one to strap me to.

"So many of these we never had the chance to explore," he lamented, giving voice to my own thoughts. He ran a hand along the top of an elegant pillory, then fingered a set of shackles hanging down from the ceiling. "Show me your favorite."

I brightened. Without hesitation, I took him by the arm and escorted him to a large, standing wooden cross in the shape of an X. The dark, gleaming beams had metal restraints bolted at top and bottom, and crossbars, too, turning the X into something closer to the shape of an hourglass. It stood upon a base which propped it up at an angle, and at the intersection of the beams—where my body would rest—a small, smooth, vaguely pear-shaped protrusion had been carved.

"You bind my body like this," I told him, stepping up to the device and positioning myself upon it with my back against the wood. I raised my hands so they fit in the upper restraints and spread my legs, so my ankles met the lower ones. "The knot in the wood presses against me, well..."

I flashed him a wicked smile. "Somewhere *sensitive*. When I stand like this it can be painful and leave a lovely bruise. When I stand like *this*—"

I turned to face the cross, demonstrating the wrist and ankle placement again, and rested against the beams. Touching my tongue to my upper lip, I moved my hips against the wood to show him how the wooden bulge would press and rub between my legs, providing a firm, hard shape to grind against.

"You may whip me, or spank me, or run a wheel of spurs over my flesh." I writhed suggestively against the wood. "With each stroke, I squirm, pressed against the knot, rubbing and teasing... but never enough to carry me to orgasm."

"I find that hard to believe," Bannon chuckled, stepping up behind me. "My sweet slut comes so easily and so shamelessly. I bet you could work yourself into a trembling, wet climax on that thing without much trouble at all."

"It's not like a cock, Sir." I spoke in a breathless whisper. "But you *can* fuck me against this cross yourself."

"Can I?"

His hands moved up to meet mine, and he closed the restraints over my wrists. He pressed his body to me, forcing me against the wooden knot, and I gasped. Even through my sarong, the hard shape of it teased my cleft; against my bottom, the powerful jut of Bannon's erection strained beneath his breeches.

"Just like this?" He slid his hands around my torso and cupped my breasts beneath the loose silk wrapping I wore. "Seems like a fine position to take your ass."

"Yes." I closed my eyes. "Yes, that is one way to enjoy this particular piece."

"Ah, I *knew* my pet slut would be wanton enough to give me that pleasure."

His voice poured over me like sweet, dark liquor. I shivered. "Any part of me that can be fucked, I believe we agreed?"

"We did." He kissed the back of my neck and glided one hand down between our bodies. A beautiful dawning relief spread through me at the click of his belt buckle.

He was fumbling between us when a voice called out from the master bedroom. "Captain? The ladies down the hall said you'd be in here."

Rayyan!

I cursed under my breath as Bannon moved away. He reached up to release me from the restraints and I eased down from the cross, straightening my sarong.

Oh, Rayyan, of all the times for you to come looking for us, why now?

My friend poked his head in from the darkened passageway, brightening as he laid eyes on us. "Ah, Captain. Mara asked me to find you."

Rayyan stood slightly shorter than me, a native of the Ruined Sands. Unlike Alaric's people, the serpent worshippers, who were all bizarrely pale in this sun-drenched desert, Rayyan had smooth, beautiful brown skin and dark, tightly coiled hair, which he'd shorn to a single strip down the center of his scalp. The Order had stolen him from the river colonies in the south and forced him to live the life of a woman—his anatomical sex—for over twenty years. As soon as he'd attained his freedom, Rayyan discarded every vestige of that life and presented himself to his rescuers—and his former friends—as the man he was.

I'd thought I understood my dear Rayyan. But I'd known a different person: a shrinking violet, awkward, struggling and demure and obedient. In the scant weeks since our liberation, though, the woman I'd thought I'd known had disappeared and passed into distant memory. A shadow, a paper mask blown away on the wind.

Now, only the true Rayyan remained. He no longer flinched when given attention or stared at the floor when he spoke. He spent his days outdoors, rebuilding vital parts of the castle or studying the fallen stonework as I might study a book of lessons. He carried a spear and had taken up one of the Sanraethi shields, and the soldiers of the morning guard welcomed him, training him in their ways of warfare.

The change took me by surprise at first. These days, I wondered how I'd ever mistaken him for anybody else.

"Soldier," Bannon greeted Rayyan. "What does Mara want?"

"There is a dispute over what's to be done with some of the relics from the solarium."

Bannon rolled his eyes heavenward and gave a weary sigh. "Cordelia, I assume?"

Lady Cordelia Shan, the niece of Bannon's king, had assumed regency over Vashtaren after the death of her father, the king's brother. A shrewd and intelligent lady, if still somewhat young to be ruling in her uncle's stead. She had an unfortunate habit of crossing Bannon's lieutenant, Mara, though, and this would not be the first time Bannon had been called to intervene.

Bannon joined Rayyan at the entrance to the torture chamber and the two of them fell into discussion. With a sigh, I crossed to the collection of playthings displayed along a section of wall and perused them for anything worth taking along on our journey.

I selected a short whip comprised of soft suede strands and struck it against my palm. Not a painful sensation, but a firm, sweet caress, for gentle arousal and teasing torment.

Bannon will like this. I set it aside to be stored in one of the crates and took down a wooden paddle next.

After several minutes Bannon appeared again at my side. I tried hard not to jump as I caught his movement out of the corner of my eye, but he seemed not to notice. He reached for one of the toys, lips pursed into a fine, hard line as he turned it over in his hands. A knife, handle brazenly carved into suggestive, sexual figures, with a keen, deadly blade.

He met my gaze over the toy. "I know you enjoy pain, Sadi, but *this* is a damned murder weapon."

"Yes." I brought my fingers up to play along the triple scars above my collar bone, raised lines Alaric had specially inflicted to contrast and complement my tattoos. They weren't the only scars he'd engraved me with. "Knives can become intense tools for mastering and branding one's slaves."

When he didn't say anything, I stepped closer to him, taking his hand in mine, and guiding the very edge of the blade lightly across my skin. I held his gaze, staring deep into his ferocious eyes.

"Remember, my barbarian," I whispered. "I am well-trained, and pain is my pleasure. Don't worry. I can take it."

I stole the knife from his fingers and flipped it in my grasp, pressing the blunt side against his naked chest, drawing it across his skin in a simple pattern and leaving a flush, pink line in its wake. Bannon gave a hiss through his teeth, grabbing my wrist.

"There's no need to draw blood," I assured him. "Just the kiss of the blade on skin brings delight... it summons up the rush of sensation and threat of danger. It focuses the mind and body in the moment. In the flesh."

Bannon's eyes, sparking with deep heat, burned into mine, and his grip on my arm tightened. After a brief, hot moment, though, his gaze shifted to other implements hung on the wall: wooden paddles with fat, stubby spikes; wooden rods for caning; harnesses, restraints, and chains. I tilted my head to the side, trying to read his expression.

Releasing me, he selected a leather mask meant to buckle tightly around a slave's head, covering mouth and nose. "And this. How would you breathe?"

"There are slits cut into the leather." Taking it from him, I turned the mask over to show him. "See?"

"And do you find pleasure in it?"

I considered. Alaric had made me wear this mask, and others like it. I'd never had the power to say no, but if I had, would I?

Shrugging, I set the mask aside. "If it does not please you, I do not require it."

He searched my expression. After a moment he took a half-step back from me and crossed his arms, and a cold sense of worry trickled down my spine. Had I upset him?

"Remember what we talked about?" he asked. "How you must say *atala* any time you wish me to stop? That I will not allow you to endure any punishment or pain beyond what you agree to endure?"

"Yes. I have done as you asked. I have spoken the word when I needed to."

And you have always done as you promised and relented the instant I did. Except for... in the sacred shrine...

I bit the insides of my cheeks, rebuking the thought. *Alaric. That was Alaric, not Bannon, who refused to yield.*

"Why do you ask, Sir?"

Bannon raised a hand in gesture to the toys and tools on the wall. "The same is true for all of these, and the acts for which they are used. I'll give you the discipline you desire. I'll work that beast inside you into submission and I'll temper your wild lusts with my own. Together we'll draw pleasure and fulfillment from the exchange. I'll even trace a knife's edge along your skin *just* enough to tease and torment, but there are some lengths, Sadira which are too far for me."

Pointing at the mask I'd set aside, he said, "I don't wish to suffocate you. I don't wish to crush your beautiful breasts in a vice or thrust you in an animal cage. Do you see what I mean? *I* may also say *atala.*"

I blinked. "Oh. I... yes, Sir, I do see."

Turning to face the display of tools, I touched a finger to my lips. "Traditionally, a Master and his slave may forge agreements regarding such details. Acts which are desired, and those which are refused."

"Yes." He smiled, as though it relieved him to know I'd read of such agreements in our book of sensual mastery. "I assume Alaric did not bother?"

"He didn't." I reached up and selected a large, smoothly carved implement resembling a hook. "If he had, though, I can think of plenty acts I'd have refused. I did not enjoy *everything* he did."

Bannon's tone softened. "Will you tell me what?"

I returned the hook to its place—I had no intention whatsoever of taking it with us—and picked up an obscenely oversized bronze phallus, another plaything I'd come to despise. A painful tightness coiled in my chest.

Bannon waited for my reply without prodding me. Once I'd tossed the phallus disdainfully to the floor, I took a deep breath.

"Trading me to the others. Like a... like a tool to be borrowed, used, and returned. Allowing *them* to be master over me when I wanted nothing to do with them."

I hated discussing Alaric's practice of giving me to his followers. It made my skin crawl, and a nauseating shame brewed in my gut. Bannon knew by now, of course, but even so, I couldn't shake off my disgust and disgrace.

"Please do not ever do that to me," I whispered, avoiding his gaze. "Please."

Bannon touched my shoulder, then drew me into an embrace.

"Never, dear heart. Put it out of your mind."

I rested my head on his chest, savoring the warmth of his body despite the muggy desert heat. After a moment of quiet intimacy, I straightened, stepping out of his arms, and offered him a smile.

"I never liked the mask, either."

The hour neared noon, and Bannon had already made clear his intention to leave the castle before the sun hit its apex. Together we selected a small collection of playthings—only those I found irreplaceable and to which Bannon did not object—before tucking them away in the crate along with the furs and the mirror I'd claimed.

Everything I want to keep, relegated to one single crate. I smoothed the last of the blankets over the top of my new belongings. *Everything I inherited from a life of slavery.*

Of course, I'd never imagined I'd inherit anything at all in my whole life.

Bannon settled the lid over the crate and one of the workers came in to seal it with nails. He and Bannon hoisted it up between them and carried it out the doors.

I remained behind, gazing around the room.

"Time to leave you at last," I whispered, fingers brushing the base of my throat. "Everything you did to me. All the hateful evil you spread, to all of us, and everyone around you."

No answer. Had I expected one? Perhaps, even now, I did.

"Goodbye. Good riddance."

I turned my back on the master suites, on Alaric's grand bed and his shattered shrine to Akolet, on the bittersweet memories of the torture chamber and the ruined beauty of the baths. Taking a deep, steadying breath, I exited into the hall.

Then I gasped as a freezing cold passed over me like a malevolent shadow, and the heavy, iron doors to Alaric's bedchambers slammed shut of their own accord.

CHAPTER THREE

THE PORT CITY of Olyb marked the end of the desert, and the gateway to the bright, sparkling expanse of the sea. It stood at the mouth of the river delta, a teeming hub of travelers, merchants, tradesmen, and treasure hunters. Not as large as the capital city of Vashtaren—and yet, it threatened to crush me.

I'd never been to Olyb before, nor anywhere even like it. My pulse raced and my chest tightened as we rode through the busy streets. No one else seemed bothered. Beside me on the bed of the supply wagon, Ailsa, Rayyan, and two Sanraethi refugees gazed at the bright market pavilions and bustling people with interest, as calm as if they navigated such volatile seas daily. I, on the other hand, thought I'd never be able to pick through all the activity or wade through the tide of different faces and bodies all around.

Thank goodness I'm up here. I gripped the wooden bench beneath me until my knuckles ached. Most of Bannon's soldiers flanked the wagon on foot; if it had been my turn on the ground, I'd surely get lost in the mania. Underneath the cloak I wore to stave off sunburn, a nervous shiver traveled through my limbs.

What is wrong with you? You lived in the capital of the Cursed Sands! These streets are no different than those of Vashtaren!

They were, though. Vashtaren had been a royal city with cobbled streets, buildings erected from the same ochre yellow sandstone, and pale, sharp-eyed loyalists living tidy, ordered lives under the custom of the Khan dynasty. Olyb had never belonged to Alaric's family, and the Vash people here were easily outnumbered by other desert natives, not to mention foreign visitors and pirates.

No carefully cobbled streets here. The boots of the soldiers and the hooves of the horses leading our wagon beat up a red cloud of dust from the unpaved road. Soaring banners bearing wild colors flapped in the wind overhead, and the cries of merchants, like cawing birds, filled the air. The whole city seemed in a state of constant, winding, undulating movement. It made my chest grow tight.

"Aren't you a soldier?" one of the Sanraethi asked when he noticed me rubbing the heel of my hand against my chest. "Were you never sent onto a battlefield? Far more chaotic than this."

"I served as bodyguard," I replied, staring out over the crowd. I had a feeling I'd said it too softly for the man to hear, but Rayyan spoke up for me.

"It's different," he said. "Except for the final days of the war, Sadira remained at Lord Khan's side to protect him personally. He rarely ventured far from the capital city, except to cull more harem girls and slaves. He'd never bring Sadira to any port or trade hub like this."

"His enemies would have far too strong an advantage," I murmured. A long, undulating banner

26

of bright sky blue stretched across one of the side streets we passed, and I quirked an eyebrow at the unfamiliar language written across it.

The Sanraethi man gave a soft, curious huff, but said no more. I caught sight of a young woman standing before a market display of fruit and flowers, leaning forward to pick ruby red pomegranates from a basket.

"*Oh,* pomegranates." Rayyan put a hand to his heart and turned his eyes heavenward. "It's been ages since I had one. Do you want to come with me to select some before we reach the docks?"

I faced him, frowning. "There are so many people."

"It won't be bad. I'll be right there with you."

At that moment, the wagon came to a stop, and from his place atop the buckboard, Bannon called down to exchange words with a person on the street.

"Come on." Rayyan took me by the arm. "It won't take long."

"You're safe to go," Ailsa put in. "I'll let the captain know. Just report straight to the docks when you're done."

I threw a glance up to where Bannon sat. His back was to me as he and the driver of the wagon conversed with whomever we'd paused for. I hated to go without his express permission, but Ailsa waved me along.

"You don't need his approval for every little thing," the healer told me.

My first instinct told me to argue. Bannon himself had said as much before, though, hadn't he?

You're only clinging because the crowds frighten you, said some unfamiliar and serene part of my brain. *But your Master wishes you to face your anxieties, and* grow, *silly face.*

I blinked. Silly face? Why did *that* phrase slip so easily into my mind?

Rayyan tugged on my arm again, and I relented. Together we slid down from the bed of the wagon to the dirt road, and Rayyan led the way into the crowd.

The smells of frying seafood, sweaty bodies, and exotic perfumes pelted me from every side. A scrappy dog bounded past and gave a bright, happy bark as Rayyan paused to pat its head. A man perusing a cart of wares bumped into me and muttered a soft apology without even looking up. I had just enough time to be grateful no one could see my telltale piercings and tattoos underneath my cloak when a flash of gorgeous sapphire color caught my eye.

I came to a halt, jerking Rayyan back. Rayyan spun, startled by the abrupt stop, and I took hold of his wrist to pull him toward an open shop display.

Spread out on a shelf below the store window lay a dozen folded bolts of cloth, in an array of rich gemstone hues. I ran my hand over a smooth cotton length, finding it light and cool, gliding through my fingertips like water.

"These are *beautiful.*" Folding and replacing the first, I turned my attention to one of striking gold and orange hues which darkened to deep, midnight blue at one end. "I've never seen such lovely sari before."

The dressmaker smiled her thanks. She'd been arranging one of the bright, draping dresses over a young customer on the other side of the window and returned to her work without saying anything, but a young, skinny boy who appeared to be her helper rose from his seat and approached. When he peeked underneath the hood of my cloak, though, he blinked with surprise.

"You aren't one of the river or desert tribes. I've never seen eyes your color before."

"She was one of the captive people under the rule of the Khan dynasty," Rayyan replied before I could. He squared himself beside me, his expression careful. The dressmaker and the boy both resembled Alaric's people, pale and sylvan, with dark eyes and fine features. They could easily be loyalists.

Neither one appeared bothered, though, and the boy—after a poorly-disguised attempt to get a better look at the tattoos on my face—held out his hand to me.

"Oh, I'm sorry." I quickly re-folded the cloth and returned it to its place on the table. "I can't buy anything. I just saw how bright and fine the dresses were and came over for a closer look. I shouldn't have touched it."

I thought I might anger the dressmaker, but the woman's smile remained. Finishing the final wrap of the sari over the shoulder of her customer, she called the boy to finish the sale and took his place at the window instead.

"You really *are* a foreigner, aren't you?" the woman marveled as she tilted her head to get a look under my hood. "I thought you might be one of the red-haired Sanraethi we've seen in town lately, but you don't look like them either. Where do you come from?"

A prickle of unease crept over my shoulders. I shied away, taking Rayyan's hand, when a tall figure moved close beside me. Bannon.

"I thought the two of you were off to claim some pomegranates." He rested a hand on my back and scanned the table of bright saris before us. He offered a genial tip of the head to the dressmaker, who returned it.

"I apologize, but I'm afraid I have to cut the shopping trip short. My soldiers are needed at the docks."

"Ah." Rayyan rubbed at the back of his neck. "Sorry, Captain. We'll go there now."

"Go on, then." Bannon waved us along. "I have supplies to procure. If you move quickly enough, maybe I'll buy those pomegranates you were after, and they'll find their way into your pack."

"It was very nice to have met you, foreigner," the dressmaker told me. Her smile widened, eyes sparkling. "Thank you for your compliment on my sari. I'm sorry you weren't able to purchase one."

I nodded and muttered a soft thanks of my own. As we turned away, Rayyan put a hand on my shoulder and gave me a tiny squeeze.

"Strange, isn't it? To have someone speak to you, even be kind to you, never knowing who you used to be?"

He wore a bittersweet grin. I put back my hood and scratched my head as we made our way to the docks together.

Mara had begun assigning tasks by the time we arrived. As Rayyan and I reported back to our wagon, the lieutenant pointed to a set of large crates already unloaded and set to one side of the dock.

"Those are too heavy to carry up the planks," she explained. "So, you two work with the deck crew to hoist them aboard by rope and pulley."

I marveled at the enormous ship before us. The gleaming flanks rose almost straight up, the slender curve of the hull almost too subtle to be noticed, making it resemble a floating fortress more than the sloping, canoe-like fishing ships I'd seen in the river colonies. Dozens of long oars angled down from an open gallery along its sides, and from my place on the dock I could just make out what seemed to be a large tower atop the deck, where a pair of Sanraethi archers stood chatting, their bows set carefully to one side. The rear of the ship swooped high into a curl like a fish's tail.

Eye of Akolet!

I had to take a step back to get a clear view of the prow, which seemed to hunch low and solid over the water. A long, jutting promontory thrust forward across the surface as though to cut through the waves, and a regal, gilded carving rose over it in the shape of a massive, snarling draconian beast.

"Sadira?"

Mara tapped her foot, one eyebrow raised. I collected myself and turned my attention to the deck above, where a crew I didn't recognize—the sailors of the ship, no doubt—assembled a pulley. Rayyan had already moved down the dock to the crates we were meant to move.

With a quick salute to Mara, I hurried to my work.

Rope nets had been laid aside in a pile for us, and Rayyan spread the first one out flat before the crates. Together we lifted the first of our cargo over the net and set it down, then wrapped the ropes over it and tied them at the top. Rayyan showed me how to secure the net with a strong workman's knot before the deck crew swung their pulley over the side of the boat and lowered a thick steel hook. I attached it to the net, and the crate was hoisted into the air.

Rayyan dusted off his hands and gazed at our work with pride. "Right. Just like that."

Not so long ago, he'd asked me if I'd ever worked with my hands and done good, physical, invigorating labor. Trained as a bodyguard and consort, of course, I hadn't, and I hadn't expected my friend—also a consort most of his life—to have done any, either. He took to it easily, though, and it gave him an obvious pleasure. I smiled at him and followed his lead as we moved on to the next crate.

"We're lucky," he told me as we worked. "One of the ship's crew said they've been loading cargo for days. On a ship this big, they've probably stored thousands of pounds of food and livestock. And look, they're loading horses down at the end of the dock. There's a whole stable on board. And we've got just these last few supply crates to manage."

The briny smell of the sea invigorated us, and the buzz of activity from the market and the city streets now seemed far away. They no longer suffocated me. Perhaps, out on the dock, I'd managed enough distance to appreciate the pleasant energy without drowning in all the noise.

From here the sound of the criers and the merchants is actually pleasant. Pausing between crates, I put my hands to my lower back and arched, basking in the warmth of the sun. *I can smell the spices and cooking meats from here... I didn't realize I was so hungry.*

"Sadira." Rayyan tapped my shoulder, interrupting my thoughts. "You've got an admirer."

I glanced back and forth, but no one had approached us. Then Rayyan pointed down. There, by my feet, a small, skinny gray feline crouched, staring up at me with wide, soft green eyes.

"A caracal?"

As I met its gaze, the creature brightened and came to its feet, tail standing straight in the air. Most caracals had a tawny, auburn coat, but this one—just a cub—had shabby fur like old pewter. Like others of its species, though, it had large, pronounced ears with long, sleek, dark tufts. It wound around my ankles with a high, raspy mew.

No animal had ever shown interest in me. Not like the beautiful songbirds tamed and kept by the other consorts, or the loyal, slender black dog which had adopted one girl and followed her everywhere. Many cats had gathered in the corners and crawl spaces around the castle kitchens, and helped keep pests away, but none had ever come to me or played for my attention.

"She must be hungry." Rayyan gathered up the cat and looked it over. The mangy creature squirmed in his hands, though, working its way free to pounce onto my shoulder instead.

"But... why?" I plucked the cat up stared at it. It stared back, placid and perfectly behaved, with no hint of struggle now that it was in my arms.

Rayyan's right. She must be hungry—I can see her ribs!

"Where did she come from?" I asked. But before Rayyan could answer, the sound of an argument caught our attention.

We turned back toward the pier. A crowd of people had gathered there, arguing with a pair of female Sanraethi standing watch at the head of the pier. My heart dropped as one man stepped out from the agitated mob and stabbed a finger in my direction.

"Oh, no..." Hardly realizing I did it, I clutched the cat to my chest.

The Sanraethi had certainly been stationed before the dock to shoo away beggars or stowaways, not to repel an altercation. It didn't appear the crowd would be easily dissuaded, though: angry shouts rose from their ranks like the chorus of cawing seabirds, and a few raised their fists, spat at the soldiers, and tried to push them out of the way.

"I don't suppose it's the foreigners they're mad at." I looked from the mounting disturbance to the remaining crates Rayyan and I had yet to load. Only three left, but it would take another half hour at least to get them all tied in the nets, secure for transfer, and up over the railing of the deck.

I glanced toward the end of the dock and the gangplank leading up to the ship. Mara, Ailsa, and a handful of sailors had taken notice of the disturbance, too, and paused in their work to watch with furrowed brows and curious expressions.

The cat gave a rumbling, inquisitive noise and struggled in my hands. When I relaxed my grip, it slipped through my fingers and up to my shoulder. There, it hunkered down, and a low, gravelly growl ticked away in its throat.

I grasped for it again, but the cat ducked my hands. "What is this thing *doing?*"

Rayyan didn't answer. He crouched to retrieve the spear he'd set aside when our work began, and as he rose back to his full height, he positioned himself between me and the crowd.

"You should get onto the boat, Sadira. I don't know if—"

Before he could finish, something came sailing through the air and struck me on my left shoulder with a sharp, solid pain. Startled, I fell back two staggering steps, clutching at the spot with my right hand.

"Sacred serpent!" I hissed. A smooth, white stone the size of a bread roll lay on the boards at my feet.

I had just enough time to realize what the angry crowd meant to do before another flying missile struck me square on the forehead. Not a rock this time, but some foul, fermented fruit with bruised red skin, soft and cotted with mold. It splattered when it hit, sending stinging juices down into my eye and over my cheeks.

"That's right, whore of Alaric!" yelled a tall, pimply boy who must have been no older than fifteen. "We know who you are!"

"When is this going to *end?*" I snapped as I wiped rotten fruit from my face.

One of the Sanraethi grabbed the boy by the arm and shoved him back. A squat, hunched older woman darted past the guard and pelted me with two eggs, and another stone fell just short of hitting my kneecap.

"The ship," Rayyan told me, moving between me and the group.

People jostled and pushed aside the Sanraethi. Over my shoulder, Mara shouted instructions to two of her warriors, ordering them to join the guards and keep the mob at bay.

"The *ship,* Sadira!"

"No." I sank into a ready stance of snake and scorpion, a pose of power in the dance-like martial art of *chorremachi.* 'I'm not running, Rayyan. Let them try and bury me in their rotten fruit. I am *through* with this!"

The caracal kitten on my shoulder arched its back and hissed.

Three of the mob managed to push the first guard off the side of the dock and into the water. The second guard lifted and spun her spear, leveling it at her attackers, but she could no longer hold them at bay: several sprinted past her toward me.

Rayyan and I readied ourselves. The caracal spit and growled.

One of the men lifted his arm to send another rock my way, when a wild, savage howl sounded from the pier.

Slinking out from between buildings, moving like oily shadows, a pack of wild dogs prowled toward the crowd.

CHAPTER FOUR

THE DOGS SNAPPED and barked at the mob as the came near, and one lunged at a man who tried to kick it, tearing off his boot with a snarl.

"What now?" I whispered at Rayyan.

Rayyan stared at the dogs, wide-eyed, but kept a firm, brave expression on his face.

"This city seems to have a problem with wild beasts." He leveled his spear at the lead dog, the biggest of the pack. "A caracal kitten is one thing, but jackals?"

The dogs strode right past the mob, snapping at their ankles or giving a short, sharp bark at any people in their way. They, too, seemed intent on me, focusing dark, shining eyes in my direction, bearing vicious teeth.

On my shoulder, the caracal gave a strained, curious sound. I backed away from the dogs, careful not to move too suddenly, as I raced through the options in my mind. My khopeshes were stored in one of the crates with my other belongings. I hadn't claimed one of the soldier's spears like Rayyan—I hadn't expected to need it. Human attackers could be dissuaded with a few quick strikes and a throw sending them into the water. Hungry beasts, however, were another matter.

Hungry? Don't be stupid. They're not here for food. They're here for you.

Dark harbingers.

The alpha stopped right before Rayyan, baring its teeth, hackles raised. Rayyan lunged, thrusting with his spear, but the dog ducked to one side and caught the shaft in its jaws. Two of the others bounded forward, flanking Rayyan and lunging for the big muscles of his legs.

I didn't have time to think. I darted at the nearest of them, putting my fingers to my lips and letting out a high, sharp, whistle. Just as I hoped, all five turned their heads toward me, dark eyes glittering and pointed ears alert.

The alpha dog released its hold on Rayyan's spear and came at me instead. I sunk back into a fighting posture and raised my hands to strike—then, though, to my astonishment, the jackal relaxed, sitting back on its haunches.

Eye of...

I narrowed my eyes. The dog held my gaze, sitting still as a stone. The others—every one of them—locked on me as if scenting prey. But then each sat down, staring at me with the same eerie, waiting expression.

"Sadira?" Rayyan, still holding his spear up and pointed at the lead dog, shot me a cautious glance. "What did you do?"

I opened my mouth to say I didn't know, when one of the mob shouted. "See! She commands the black dogs! Sorceress!"

The man wound up and pitched his stone at me, striking me in the belly. I doubled over clutching my middle, and the caracal leapt down from my shoulder. Heedless of the jackals, it streaked at the rock thrower and bounded up onto his thigh. He screamed as it dug in with its wild claws and sunk its teeth into thick muscle.

He hardly had time to pry the feline from his leg, though: the alpha dog had spun around and barreled at him the moment I'd been hit, and it knocked him to the planks and pinned him down. Its lips curled back from its teeth and strings of saliva dripped onto the man's face.

The other dogs got back to their feet to join the attack, but I put a hand out and, on instinct, gave a second ear-splitting whistle.

To my amazement, the alpha backed down. It moved off the man, still rumbling with a wet, vicious snarl, and placed itself between him and me, shoulders lowered, ready to attack.

The caracal kitten had dropped from the man's thigh when the jackal knocked him down. It came bounding to me again and wound around my ankles.

"I don't understand." My gaze shifted from the jackals to Rayvan, down to the caracal, and to the swarm of people. My heart pounded in my chest and the day seemed to grow dim around me.

Alaric did this. The beasts outside the castle—the creatures he summoned to keep us trapped within the walls—

The dogs bristled and growled, hackles raised as more people shouted at me, jabbing accusatory fingers at me, throwing eggs and fruit. The lead dog had them frightened enough to stay at a distance, though, and their missiles fell short, splattering or bouncing off the dock several feet from me.

Bannon's voice boomed over the crowd.

"What in the name of Goddess Sherida are you people *doing?*"

The crowd parted, most of them turning to meet the towering Sanraethi captain. Others kept their eyes on the dogs and me, as though expecting an attack as soon as they looked away.

Oh, thanks be. I straightened, as did Rayyan, and gave Bannon our salute: right fist held over the heart. The jackals, however, hunched low to the docks, mad black eyes flashing with warning.

Bannon stalked through the mob, eyeing them. Behind him came the two Sanraethi women, one of them still dripping and bedraggled from her unexpected swim.

"I don't suppose there's someone among you who wants to explain why you're attacking my soldiers?"

Bannon bent to peer at the man knocked on his back by the dog. "You, maybe?"

The man scowled and rolled onto his stomach to climb to his feet. As he did, Bannon planted his boot square between the man's shoulders and shoved him back down to the boards.

"I asked you a question."

"Are you blind?" The man tried to point toward me and the dogs, though his awkward, sprawled position made it difficult. "Alaric's witch called the black dogs to her side! In our *city!*"

Rayyan pointed at the man with his spear. "Captain, the dogs only appeared *after* these agitators started throwing rocks at us."

"Not at *you*," sneered a woman at the head of the mob. "At *her*. Alaric's pet!"

"*My* pet," Bannon corrected. He lifted his boot off the man's back, and the man scrambled back to his group.

"I know Olyb has kept itself more or less independent from the Cursed Sands and the rule of the Khan dynasty," Bannon said to the crowd. "But I'm sure you know enough about desert politics to know who I am, and how I staked my claim on Alaric Khan's defeated kingdom."

"By the right of victory," barked an older woman, slim and willowy but startlingly loud. She folded thin, bony arms over her chest. "And you took his consort by right of claiming. Everyone knows, Red Bear of the Highlands. What *you* don't understand is that we *know* how to deal with scorpions and snakes. You crush them under your heels before they get close enough to sting you!"

"She touched the fruits on my market wagon, and they spoiled before my eyes!" shouted a young man, waving a hand with a browned, foul-looking dragon fruit.

I brought a hand to my mouth. Speeding through the day's events in my mind, I remembered the young man. He'd manned an old produce cart with an elderly man dressed in the manner as he.

"But I didn't touch anything on his wagon. Not one thing!"

Had the fruit spoiled after mere proximity? No, the vendor must be lying. Looking for an excuse for bad wares.

"She spooked my chickens and my ducks!" another merchant claimed. "Two of my hens nearly pecked each other to death!"

"*Pah,*" Bannon spat. "Your hens only scuffled, as animals do. Don't try and put the blame on my woman."

The crowd seethed, and more voices cried out over each other. Some shouted complaints of their own misfortunes, while others called Bannon an idiot and a whoremonger. When the willowy woman in the lead tried to step forward, though, raising an oozing, rotten tomato to cast at Bannon, the big, black alpha dog sprung forward at her with a loud barrage of barks.

Both Bannon and the woman staggered back, but Bannon recovered his balance. She, on the other hand, fell against the others in the crowd, knocking two others with her to the ground.

"Get out of here!" Bannon roared at them, cutting a hand through the air. "Take your poisonous accusations elsewhere and let my soldiers do their work. We're setting sail soon enough anyway."

With grumbling, nasty displeasure, they started to disperse as he'd commanded. As the first few dropped off from the edges of the mob and sulked away, some of those who'd been right at the front, storming down the dock and pelting their missiles, lingered and glowered. The woman who'd taken a tumble hawked and spit in Bannon's direction, before her colleagues helped her up and led her from the port.

Bannon waved them away, sneering. As they broke apart and wandered away, he approached me and Rayyan.

I raised my hands to stop him, shooting a pointed glance at the dogs still surrounding me. Bannon hesitated, but in the same instant, the pack all lowered their ears and gave a strange shudder, as though shaking water from their coats. Dark, canine eyes glanced back and forth, and one of them uttered a low huff.

The alpha male barked twice. The others trotted to him, moving past Bannon without so much as a sniff or a nip. Soon all of them had retreated to the shoreline and disappeared again in the dark space between two buildings.

Bannon watched them go, then checked me, searching me from head to foot.

"Are you hurt?"

"No, Sir." I assumed my submissive pose, and all at once remembered the caracal kitten at my feet. It wound between my ankles and mewed, shining green eyes gazing up at me.

Bannon rubbed his chin. "New friend?"

"I don't know." Crouching, I scooped the caracal into my arms. "It showed up while we were working. I thought it might be hungry."

"There are fishermen only a short way down the pier," Rayyan pointed out. "And no shortage of pests in the alleyways, I'm sure. The kitten—*and* the dogs—came to *you*, Sadira."

"Why?" I spun on Rayyan, a bolt of sharp guilt piercing my chest. "Why would they do that?"

"They looked ready to defend you to the death," Bannon said.

I rubbed at the back of my neck. "I know."

I didn't mention how the jackal's focused glares and strange, shining intelligence had reminded me of the wild beasts arranged outside Alaric's castle during the cursed siege. I brought my hand back down to scratch at the caracal's chin, and the cat reached up with both paws to seize my wrist and rub its silvery-gray face against my palm.

Bannon eyed the cat for a moment, stroking his beard. When he reached out to touch it, it shied from him, hissing, and climbed back onto my shoulder.

"Strange thing," he muttered, his tone unreadable. A flush of chagrin crept up my ears.

Bannon frowned, gazing from me to the pier where the angry protesters and then the animals had disappeared.

"You should get on board," he said. "I'm tired of Alaric's legacy following you even now. Once we're on our way at least we can leave it behind."

He might as well have slapped me. My mouth dropped open and I wanted to retort, but I schooled my reaction before Bannon turned back to me.

"Sir?" I asked. "Respectfully, I'd like to finish my task loading crates with Rayyan."

"One of the other soldiers will help him." Bannon glanced at Rayyan, who gave him a nod. "Onto the ship, Sadira."

I hung my head. With a heavy sigh, I gathered the caracal from my shoulder and set it down on the dock.

"On with you. There's fishermen all over who'll have something to share."

She offered a strange chirruping sound, something curious and bright. I gave her one last scratch of the ear before following Bannon to the gangplank, where Mara and Ailsa stood waiting. They both looked at Bannon with questions in their eyes.

"Go on ahead," he said to me, gesturing up the gangway. "I'll join you after I've explained what just happened, and Mara's given me a report of where we stand in terms of setting sail."

"Yes, Sir."

Before I stepped onto the gangplank, he reached out and gave my shoulder a gentle squeeze. When I met his gaze, he stepped closer, pulling me into an embrace.

"Kitten, walk with your head held high." He kissed my cheeks, then my lips. "You're not to blame."

His reassurance did little to cheer me up. I glanced back at Rayyan, now fitting the loading net over the next crate along with one of the other spear carriers. Being stripped of my duties thanks to a mob of people whom Alaric had wronged—*Alaric,* not *me*—brought a sour, aching pain to my gut.

I want Bannon's people to know I am not some spoiled pet, afraid to work and favored with special privilege. They thought I was Alaric's queen, some slavish, pampered bitch. I don't ever want to be called that again.

I met Bannon's eyes and straightened my shoulders, giving another obedient nod and bringing my fist over my heart in salute. He released me, and I climbed the gangplank without a word.

A bright, booming voice called out as soon as I ascended to the deck.

"Well, what've we here? Is it the famous desert witch everyone's been on about?"

My spine stiffened and I bristled, ready for another spat of curses and accusation. *At least since we're on the boat they won't throw rocks...*

45

To my surprise, though, the stout man striding toward me across the deck regarded me with a cheerful, sparkling grin. A thick, blonde beard arranged in long braids poured down his front almost to his stomach, and one leg ended in a thick, ornately carved wooden stump. The smell of something spiced and robust emanated from him as he came right up to meet me, evidently unperturbed by my appearance.

"Welcome aboard the *Drekakona!*" He gave the same salute as Bannon's soldiers, and on reflex I returned it.

"Are you the captain?" I asked.

"Nay, the quartermaster. Call me Torv." Clapping a hand on my shoulder, he gestured over the broad deck before us. "Shall I show you the ship, then? She's a proud *dhalut* warship. She's been too long here in port, though, waiting on Bannon and the army to return. She needs to be out on the open sea again. Oh! The king's witch has brought her familiar, too!" "

I gave a start, shaken again by the word. I glanced back and forth, hoping nobody else heard him, and then noticed what Torv meant.

The caracal kitten had followed me up the gangplank and sat at my heel, twitching its short tail back and forth. Its green eyes locked on Torv, sharp and suspicious, its tufted ears alert.

"You again?" I crouched, curious, and the kitten promptly leapt onto my shoulder. It rubbed its cheek against mine, then shot another glare at the quartermaster. A flat, quiet growl rumbled in its throat.

A witch's familiar?

But then...who's the witch?

CHAPTER FIVE

AN HOUR LATER, I sat on the floor in the quarters assigned to Bannon, arms propped up on the edge of the single, meager captain's bed. I stared at the caracal. It had tucked itself into a comfortable position on the quilts and returned my gaze with its misty green eyes, purring.

"Why are you following me about all of a sudden?"

The caracal—a female kitten, I'd determined—continued to stare back, offering a tiny, mysterious grin in response.

"Are you some kind of omen? A harbinger of bad luck?"

I didn't want to say out loud what I really feared. More black magic shadowing me. Another foul curse of the serpent god and his minions.

Or perhaps the first curse never ended at all.

The caracal rose and padded across the mattress to butt her soft head against me. I stroked her silvery fur, and again considered the strange coloring. A gray caracal wouldn't survive long out on the open sands; she'd stand out against the pale white landscape and tawny rocks much too easily, and predators would spy her in an instant.

Like me? I scratched the kitten's ears. *A standout among Alaric's pallid people* and *among the other slaves? Now among the highlanders, too?*

The kitten didn't *seem* dangerous. Of course, she had launched herself at an armed human man and nearly tore a small chunk of flesh from his thigh. Not to mention the tense, coiled aggression she showed everyone else.

"And just where are you going to stay?" I asked. "We'll be at sea for months, you know. You can't sleep in this cabin as long as you're hissing and growling at my Master."

Torv had already told me the captain welcomed cats aboard the *Drekakona*. "They keep the vermin out of the food stores," he'd said. "Useful animals, and smart. No one'll bat an eye at one more."

One more street cat, maybe. I stroked my thumb across the velvety back of the kitten's ear. *Caracals can grow big as hunting hounds, and they're feral. She might eat the other cats sooner than the rats.*

The sound of boots outside the door caught my attention. I straightened and looked up toward the door. To my delight, it was Bannon who entered, hauling a trunk under one big arm.

"Good, you're already here." He shut the door behind him and set down the trunk. "We set sail with the tide in just a few hours. Is that thing still here?"

I gathered the kitten in my hands and gazed down at it, nodding. "She followed me onto the ship and won't leave my side. She doesn't seem to like Torv or anybody else who gets close to me. See?"

As though to prove the point, the caracal put back her ears and glowered at Bannon, giving the same low, flat growl as before.

"Well, if she stays, she'll be earning her keep in the galley." He gestured around the small room. "And you'll have to find her a bed, if you're keeping her."

"I think it's more like she's keeping me."

I set the kitten down and rose to my feet. "I'm sorry for the trouble earlier, Sir. I, too, wish I could discard the bad blood and burnt bridges Alaric left for me to bear."

Bannon lifted his foot and pushed the trunk over to rest at the end of the bed. We had extraordinarily little space around it: hardly enough to stand side by side. The sea lapped at the side of the ship close below our one porthole, a quiet, lazy afternoon sound, but I wondered what we might hear in a rainstorm or on rough waves.

"Torv called this a dhalut." I crossed to the porthole and stood on tiptoe to peer out of it. Nothing but wide, placid blue seas. "What does it mean?"

"It comes from an old language, meaning 'father'." He ducked down to take a seat on the bed and reached out to stroke the kitten, ignoring her growling. The kitten hissed and jumped down, bounding over to me to hide behind my ankles.

"More specifically," Bannon continued, "it means 'great father', or 'father of fathers'. Before the dhalut was designed, our people relied upon longboats, mostly good for short sea voyages but not transport such as this. The dhalut is built to carry a battalion of soldiers, along with supplies and horses.

It's the biggest ship we have, and we brought three with us to wage war on Lord Khan."

"Three?" Scooping the caracal into my hands again, I sat beside my barbarian. "Then where are the others?"

"Docked across the river, closer to our outpost. You're on the *Drekakona,* the Dragon Maiden. There is also the *Drekamodir,* the Dragon Mother, and the *Drakadrottnig,* the Dragon Queen. They won't set sail for a few days, yet, while the last of our forces prepare to return home."

"What about our group?" My gaze drifted to the ceiling, and the distant pounding of boots on the deck and crew calling out to one another.

"Our cargo is loaded, but the captain and his people still have work prior to departure." He took my chin in his hand and kissed me. "Mara has charge of our soldiers, but they're at leave to go back into town and make any last purchases before the tide goes out."

The caracal hissed and swiped at him when he came close. Bannon narrowed his eyes at me and wrinkled his nose.

"I think you should name her," he said. "How about 'Schala'?"

"Why? What does that mean?"

"She was the beautiful princess of an ancient land in our lore. Unfortunately, she met an untimely end. Just like this one will if she doesn't—stop—biting!"

He toyed with the kitten, punctuation each word with a quick ruffling of the fur on her head, prompting her to nip and growl even more. Finally, I rose to my feet, putting the caracal up on a secured shelf above the bed.

"I'm worried this sudden adoption is a bad omen," I admitted.

Bannon stood as well, slipping an arm around my waist as he also studied the kitten. "Why would you think so? She's not *that* troublesome, even if she is a brat."

"It just feels... strange."

He didn't say anything immediately. Turning me to face him, he looked into my eyes, and caressed my cheek with the back of his hand.

"Sadi," he soothed. "You are safe here. No more black magic. No more vengeful ghosts. No more sorcery."

I bit my lip and looked away. "The dogs, though. And this caracal—"

"Whatever happened on the dock, you aren't to blame. You didn't draw those people and you didn't call those dogs. Did you?"

He curled a knuckle under my chin and guided my face back to his. He quirked one brow and frowned in a comical exaggeration of concern. I couldn't suppress a smile.

"No, Sir, I didn't call any dogs."

"Maybe cosmic forces are conspiring to keep you safe then." He kissed me, then hugged me. "Sadira, when I asked you to come with me, back to my homeland and on to wherever we must go to find your people, I asked if you would trust me. I know it must be difficult to trust, after—"

"Please, Sir." I shook my head. "Don't talk about it."

"I think we must," he said. "At some point."

"I trust you. The rest doesn't matter."

Bannon grimaced, and released me. He stroked his beard, and his gaze moved to the trunk he'd carried in moments before.

"Will you trust me now?"

"To do what?" I asked.

Bannon opened the trunk and pawed through it, until he found something wrapped in a bold orange cloth. I recognized the fabric: one of the scarves from the torture chamber. Scarves Alaric had never seemed to have any use for, as his tastes never seemed to run toward gentle binding or soft sensations.

My heart gave a flutter. "Oh?"

"Come with me. I want to show you one of the things that makes a dhalut a special kind of warship."

We left the caracal behind, and she seemed content to curl up on her own and sleep for a while. Bannon led me past the senior crew quarters and across the gangplank that ran above the rower's gallery. Below, several well-muscled sailors loitered. Some stretched across the rower's benches, catching a nap before departure.

"The gallery takes up two full decks, the second and third decks," he explained to me as I paused to stare down at the leveled benches and bright, open sides. "We're one deck above, on the middle deck. Below us is the orlop, where the livestock and supplies are held—"

"And the stable?" I asked, still uncertain whether a full stable could truly have fit on the ship.

He tipped me a wink. "Aye, the stable, too."

The *Drekakona* was huge. We passed dozens of soldier and crew quarters, storage holds for crates of treasure and personal cargo, even a carpentry workspace and leatherworking shop. He led me nearly

53

to the back of the ship, to a staircase leading down. We descended past the first level of the rower's gallery and to the second, and Bannon—growing visibly more enthusiastic, pulled me into a dim compartment beyond the rows of benches.

A great, iron anvil took up most of the room, with a metal contraption I took to be a small, movable smithy. It had been modified and perched on a flat stone platform.

I studied the strange additions to the device. *To avoid fires,* I thought. *It's meant to guard against sparks spilling out and setting light to the wooden ship.*

"A weapon forge?" I asked.

"Not only for weapons. Plenty of tools and rigs on the ship require the attention of a smith. Though it's used as sparingly as possible, given the circumstances. Does the anvil remind you of anything?"

It didn't take me long to see what he meant. A sweet thrill shot through my core. "The spanking bench. In the torture chamber."

Bannon grinned. "Very good, kitten. Now... are you ready to trust me?"

We stood alone in the compartment. No door to close behind us. We were far enough away even from the few rowers at their benches, though, and if we were careful, no one would hear us. My eyes darted from the anvil to the open passageway, then back to Bannon.

"Strip," he commanded.

I closed my eyes and drew in a deep breath, letting it out again with a soft, nervous chuckle. My hands shook, anticipation making me giddy, as I removed my simple soldier's jerkin for him.

Bannon stood back, crossing his arms over his chest, smirking as I removed my clothing piece by piece. His gaze electrified me, roaming over every inch of skin I bore to him, until I stood stark naked before him. If anyone *did* happen by this section of the lower decks, on their way to or from the cargo storage or the rower's gallery, I'd be fully exposed. They could feast their eyes upon me as Bannon did, their hungry stares burning me up with wicked delight.

"Bend over the anvil," Bannon instructed.

I turned my back to him and obeyed. Bannon reached out to snatch a coil of rope from the wall and came to me, bending and wrapping the length of it several times around me, binding wrists and feet at the base of the anvil. I stood before him, bent double over the hard, cold iron, buttocks raised.

"You have a choice, Sadi..."

Bannon strode around the anvil so I could look up and see him. In his hands, he held the wrapped orange scarf, and he slowly unfolded it to reveal the torture implement he'd hidden within.

"Do you prefer the smooth, soft side?" He held up a long, leather strop. One side had been lined with velvet, a sweet and sensual undertone to a fierce flogging. I knew what would be on the other side before Bannon even showed me.

Spikes. I licked my lips. Tiny spurs in starry clusters of four, barely big enough to do damage... unless the spanking was especially hard.

"They'll turn your ass pink as a pomegranate." He moved behind me once more and I lost sight of him. Then I gasped as the bold orange scarf came down around my face and Bannon pulled it tight into a blindfold. His hand gripped my buttocks and he squeezed me hard.

"Well," he prompted me. "Which do you want, my beautiful pain slut? The velvet?"

He ran the smooth, soft side of the strop over my buttocks, caressing me with a loving desire.

"Or the spikes?"

CHAPTER SIX

THE FIRST STROKE of leather across my skin sent a bright, tingling shudder through my body. In the space of a breath, I reverted from soldier to slave again, biting my lip against a cry of pleasure.

Bannon caressed me. "That's my girl. Let's work out all this tightness you've been carrying, yes?"

The strop came down again, and I caught my breath in a harsh gasp. "Yes, Sir. Please."

He'd started out using the soft, velveted side of the strop, but he wouldn't stop there. He only meant to prime me for the more intense pain to come. Pain I welcomed. Pain I needed.

Bannon brought the strop down on my rear again, alternating it across both round, pink cheeks, following it with a warm palm circling over the place where he'd struck me.

"Are you comfortable?" he asked.

"Yes, Sir."

Another strike, making me jerk and twist against my bonds. He'd tied me tight and the rope chafed my wrists, unyielding. I pulled as hard as I could and found no give. When the next strike came, I couldn't help a soft moan.

"Do you want the rowers to hear?" Bannon taunted me. This time when he ran his hand over my hot, flush skin, he squeezed, and I drew in a shaky breath.

"No, Sir."

"Then *keep quiet,* little kitten."

Two more swift, stinging slaps with the strop, first on my left cheek, then my right. I bit my tongue to still my cries, and he leaned over me, pressing himself against my tender, upraised haunches, fisting his free hand in my hair.

"That's better." His breath at my ear sent a beautiful shiver through me. "Good girl. Now let's see how long you hold that tongue while I have my way with you."

"Mercy, my barbarian!"

I knew very well *mercy* wasn't the word to stop him, and *barbarian* would only excite him. The sweet surge and release of tension in our play filled me with joy, and each smart slap of the paddle took me farther and farther away from dread and fear.

"Don't think you can do it?" He brought the strop down again and I choked on a cry, turning it into a shuddering, eager whimper. "Come now. Where's my ferocious she-cat? My bloody tigress, conqueror of desert golems and revenant kings? Surely you can endure a paltry little tanning of your hide?"

"Happy to endure it," I assured him with a soft huff of enjoyment. "I can't promise I'll manage to do so quietly."

"We'll make a deal, then."

He flipped the strop in his hand, turning it to the naked, studded leather side and sliding it back and forth against my flush skin. The spurs prickled and rasped; I writhed against my ropes.

"The longer you endure without succumbing to cries of pleasure, the longer I will drag out the torment." Tightening his grip in my hair, he tilted my head back to whisper his hot, rumbling promise in my ear. "I'll treat you to *hours* of pain if you like. Assuming you can keep all those wild, wanton outbursts to yourself. What do you think? Shall we test your limits here in the hold, where the entire crew might hear your shameless harlotry?"

"Yes!" I hissed, stirred by the wicked threat of exposure. If I failed his test and gave into my urges to moan or call his name, I could bring strangers running, and we would be caught in the middle of our little game. My body, naked and flush with the heat of his spankings, helplessly displayed.

A twisted wish brought a tingle to my skin and sent a brief shock of pleasure through my breasts and down to my core. *And would he stop if someone did come upon us? Or would he continue my punishment, leaving me totally revealed in my yearning?*

For just a second, Bannon's tone changed. It softened and lost the firm edge of play.

"It's your decision, kitten," he whispered. "Remember what you must say if you wish me to stop. Do you remember?"

"I do."

"What is it, love? If you wish to stop—if you wish to be unbound—what do you say to me?"

"I say *atala*." I licked my lips. "But I don't wish to stop, Sir. Please. Keep going."

Releasing his grip in my hair, he stroked my cheek, then planted a kiss on my temple. "Very good, kitten."

After a gentle beat, he straightened. I caught my breath in anticipation, and then the leather came down again, dealing a sharp, sweet, raw slap across my buttocks. I choked back a cry, though my body lit up with excitement.

"Like that?" Bannon taunted.

"Yes, Sir."

"Say it again."

Oh, he will make *me beg even as he orders me to keep quiet!*

An impossible challenge. Yet one I would relish in its torment. "Yes, Sir."

The strop came down again. I drew in a long, shuddering gasp and let it out in a breathless moan, writhing hard against my bonds. It came down again and then again in smooth, rhythmic strokes as Bannon murmured rough, rumbling encouragement over me.

"There's my girl... my good, strong girl. How beautiful your sweet ass looks! All flush and pink for me..."

I tugged and stretched against the ropes, gritting my teeth. Cool iron against my breasts and belly could hardly relieve the warmth building within me. The swift, stinging prickle of the spurs—too small to break the skin, yet sharp enough to bite—made me jump, and made my skin twitch.

"Maybe you can keep your tongue after all." Bannon paused in his spanking to run the soft, velvety side of the strop over my sore cheeks. "If you can handle your challenge even when I use the spurs, maybe something harder, and hotter, will break you."

I gasped as he slid two fingers into my entrance and tempted me, stroking.

"Do you want to keep going with the strop?" he asked. The tone in his voice told me he knew exactly what I wanted—but also what I would choose.

"I can endure harder spanking, Sir," I murmured, breathless. "Please, let me prove myself."

"You really think so? You think you can withstand a longer beating before I fuck you?"

Oh, how I wanted him to fuck me. How I longed for the rigid shape of him inside me, the rock and sway of him filling me at last, ending our awkward time of celibacy.

But I can take more. I know I can. And if I can't... it only means I might be witnessed as the Red Bear's hungry plaything.

"Yes, please. Let me prove myself. I am far from finished."

I lost count of the strokes soon, and the beautiful pain lured me into the swell of perfect surrender. I nearly lost my focus and gave the cries he wanted to wring from me. I caught myself, biting my tongue and the inside of my cheeks. Once or twice, I caught the sound of crew members nearby, moving back and forth between cargo holds or joining the waiting rowers. Each time an unfamiliar voice seemed close to our hideaway, I held my breath, skin tingling with anticipation.

Bannon laughed under his breath and teased me. "So close... *someone* is going to find us and see your pretty pink pussy and ass on display..."

A terrible thought rushed me from my bliss then.

If someone does *catch us, he'll stop. It'll be over, just like before, and without any fucking at all—*

"You're doing so well," Bannon mused. "I've never had the chance to *really* push you to your limits before."

"Sir," I pleaded, forgetting to whisper. Shame bloomed in my chest—did I really mean to cave in just when he'd praised me for my endurance?—but the fear we would once again miss our chance overpowered it.

A moan fought to break free, like air held too long underwater, and my heart picked up speed. "Please, no more. My barbarian... Sir... I need you so badly right now."

"Oh?"

He hesitated. The surprise in his voice only made me more anxious. I writhed against my ropes.

"It's been so long," I nearly whimpered. "Please, take me, Sir... please let me feel—"

Let me feel your lust and love again.

He kept silent for a beat. I almost worried he'd change his mind, or he'd be unable to do it. Maybe he'd lost his passion for me after all. Maybe, faced with Alaric Khan's inherited memories, standing before Alaric's prize whore, Bannon could no longer—

No longer love me after all.

The threat of tears overwhelmed me. I closed my eyes tight and swallowed, ready to apologize, and ready for him to withdraw from the play altogether. Just as I opened my mouth, though, Bannon lay the leather strop down on the anvil beside me. I thrilled at the sound of his belt buckle being undone.

A second later, he slid one hand possessively over my hip, and the rigid, rock-hard cock pressed up to my sore cheeks.

"Ah, yes..." I breathed. "Barbarian... how I have longed for you."

He bent over me, teasing me with the tip of his cock along my wet, hot entrance. His free hand slid along my body, looping under my left arm, as he crooned in my ear.

"As I have for you, sweet kitten. I can't tell you how deeply."

His hand closed around my throat.

I can't tell you, kitten...

I choked.

How infuriating it's been to have to crawl my way back to power.

My heart gave a panicked leap. My bound hands jerked against the ropes hard enough to hurt, desperate to claw at his grip. I smelled it—cinnamon and bergamot—and my whole body grew cold.

You have no power! I've always been stronger than you.

I was in the serpent's shrine again. With Alaric. Alaric glaring at me through Bannon's eyes. *Taking over* my barbarian, holding me down, strangling me to cut off my breath.

Nowhere left to go, pet...

"Atala!" I screamed. Bucking under Bannon's body, I pulled and twisted against my ropes, all my sweet pleasure burned away in a flash of horrible fear. "Atala! *Atala!*"

Bannon jerked away as though my skin had turned to fire. His sudden withdrawal stabbed at my heart, still so unused to denying my Master anything, but a second later he'd moved around the anvil to crouch in front of me, cupping my face in his hands very gingerly to make me look him in the eye. *His* eyes, amber and warm, wide with concern.

"What's wrong, Sadira? Did I hurt you?"

Footsteps came toward us from the passageway, and Bannon lunged to one side to snatch up a length of burlap lying over a workbench and used it to cover my naked body. A trio of crew members, none of whom I recognized, appeared in the entryway, but Bannon raised a hand to stop them coming closer.

"I'll handle this. Go back to what you were doing."

The three crewmates exchanged glances, befuddled. I couldn't keep looking at them, so I closed my eyes in shame. My chest ached with every breath and my shoulders shook. No titillating thrill of exhibitionism now. Mortified, I tried to shrink under the burlap.

As they left, Bannon returned his attention to me, touching my face again with careful fingers.

"Are you hurt?" he asked again.

"No."

My voice came out small and tight. I couldn't even look at *him*. I couldn't admit how it relieved me to see his own eyes looking back at me, not red with tears of blood, and not *green,* like Alaric's.

I told him I trusted him. How disappointed he must be now.

He began untying the ropes at my wrists. "Tell me what happened."

My skin stung with rope burn. I'd jerked too hard against the restraints in my panic, and as Bannon freed me, I rubbed tenderly at the reddened impressions, flinching. He moved around me to untie the other twists and knots.

"Your hand at my throat," I managed to say, weak and miserable. "It took me by surprise, and... and I thought of what happened in the shrine. The way Alaric tried to—"

"Strangle you." Bannon unlooped the last of the ropes and uttered a soft growl. "Of course. I'm sorry, Sadi. I should have realized."

How could he have, though? I'd never balked at that primal, possessive gesture before. I'd embraced it. I'd enjoyed it!

He touched me carefully, going slow as he helped me to my feet. Afraid of frightening me, I thought. *Delicate,* as though I were some fragile little girl.

But I feel like a fragile little girl. My chest... oh, and my stomach...

How I wanted to cry. This time, *I'd* ruined our play. I'd wanted so much to be with him again, and then I'd broken down like a feeble idiot.

"Come here." Bannon enveloped me in his arms, stroking my hair. "Let's get you dressed and back to our cabin, where you can relax. I have something for you, anyway. A gift."

I don't deserve a gift. I wrapped my arms around myself as he scooped up my clothing and handed it to me. I dressed in silence, avoiding his eyes, replaying my outburst over and over in my mind.

Bannon rested his hand on my upper arm and gave me a soft kiss on the brow.

"It's all right," he soothed me. "You're safe. I promise."

AS SOON AS we returned to our shared cabin, the caracal kitten—Schala—bounded down from the bed and wound herself around my ankles. I scooped her up and crossed the room to the porthole, sitting on an old wooden bench before it to look out at the sea. The caracal rubbed her face against my chin, purring, and despite myself, I relaxed.

Bannon bent to return the scarf and paddle to the trunk. Then he joined me by the porthole, taking a seat beside me. I noticed he kept a respectful distance, and gently rested one palm on my knee, offering me a reassuring squeeze.

His tenderness eased my worry. We sat for some time watching the sea, with Schala purring in my arms, until at last I found myself able to scoot closer to Bannon, resting my head on my shoulder.

He looped an arm around me. "Do you feel better?"

"Well enough," I murmured back. "I'm sorry."

"It's not for you to apologize, my treasure."

He kissed my head again. I closed my eyes and took a long, deep breath. A deep weariness dragged on me.

Funny, though... no headache. I'd have expected a real monster of a migraine, after such an attack.

"Would you like your gift now, my kitten? A reward for your strength and bravery this morning on the dock."

I blinked and straightened in my seat. "What do you mean? I did nothing on the dock beside get hit by a few rocks and rotten eggs."

Schala gave a soft rumble of a mew and dropped from my lap to the floor, sauntering toward the bed.

Bannon gave me another kiss and rose from the bench.

"You composed yourself admirably, and thanks to your caution, neither any of my people nor the locals came to any harm. Well..."

He shot a smirk at Schala. "No *great* harm, in any case. A few bites from a feral kitten should heal without any trouble."

He returned to the trunk and withdrew another length of cloth from within. The sunset-colored sari I'd examined in the marketplace earlier. I came to my feet, biting my lip.

"I saw you admiring it." Bannon beamed as he handed the sarong to me. "Put it on, love. I can't wait to see how it looks on you."

I stared at the cloth in my hands. The sharp tension in my chest worsened. All at once, the air in the cabin seemed thin, hard to breathe.

"I... Bannon, I..."

Too many hard, cutting emotions jabbed at me at once. My fingers turned numb; the sarong slid to the floor, and seconds later, I followed it, crumpling to my knees.

Bannon's expression turned anxious. "Sadira?"

A storm of tears overcame me. I folded my arms around my stomach, nauseous and dizzy, and started to sob.

CHAPTER SEVEN

AGAIN, I FOUND myself cradled in his arms, like a child. Again, he rocked me and soothed me, saying my name over and over, and I couldn't find my voice to tell him to stop. His attention made me feel so *stupid*. So senseless and infantile. At the same time, his warmth grounded me, and I clung to him, grateful for his solid presence.

"What did I do this time?" he asked with a small, apologetic smile. "I honestly thought you liked it, Sadi."

"I do." I ground the tears from my eyes and reached for the sari, gathering it to my chest. "Truly, I do, Bannon. I'm only overcome. I... I've never had such clothing before."

"Come now, I've seen what you had in your trunks at the castle."

I shook my head. "No. Those... all those costumes and garb, Alaric chose. He delegated my daily appearance, left the matter of selecting garments to his pages and seamstresses. And those outfits? None of them *belonged* to me. Should he have wished it, at any time he could give them away."

"Ah." He ran a hand through my hair. "No wonder you didn't choose any to bring with you, then. I thought it somewhat strange."

"They weren't mine." I shuddered. "It was like wearing another woman's clothes. And always so much *green*."

He touched the sari, smoothing his knuckles over its bright, cool folds. "I think these colors will suit you. If you do like them, of course. Will you put it on for me?"

Steadier now, I nodded. I held the sari up to my body, examining the glittering gold embroidery worked into the design. Despite the clash of emotions overwhelming me, my heart gave an excited flutter. Could this lovely possession really be *mine? All* mine?

I lay it upon the bed and began to undress. When I'd shucked my simple soldier's garb, though, Bannon touched my shoulder, making me pause.

"Wait just a moment."

He took me by the arm and guided me to stand in front of the room's long, rectangular mirror, anchored to the wall beside the bunk.

"Look at yourself." Standing behind me, he gathered back my hair. "Sadira, my beautiful, beautiful love."

Am I?

I knew men desired me, at least. The men of Alaric's retinue, the Order of Akolet and the noble Vash lords he did business with. Men like them were aroused by anything, though. Any person or object that made them feel powerful. Had they ever found *me* beautiful? Or had they simply nursed a constant erection of the ego because I was a low, helpless slave in their kingdom?

Bannon slid his hands down my sides in slow caress. "You are like a fierce desert lioness. Golden and strong, magnificent under the sun."

He'd called me lioness before, but I knew he had it wrong. I was a serpent. Alaric's monstrous beast, full of poison.

"Hear me now." Bannon took my chin in one hand and tilted my head up, making me look in the glass. "Look at your grim face. I can tell you're not listening to me. Full of dark thoughts and sorrow. That isn't what I want for you, Sadira. Leave those old ghosts and torment in the past, back in the dark magician's crumbling castle. The lioness does not listen to the laughter of craven hyenas."

He ran the backs of his knuckles over my cheek—the cheek marked by the intricate tattoo that surrounded one eye and wound down my jawline.

"Do you know how many women I've met with such a daring design upon their faces?" he whispered. "Not a one. It sets you apart and draws me to your eyes. Such beautiful gray eyes... like a waiting storm."

He followed the tattoo down to my shoulder, kissing my skin.

"Your neck... so smooth and slender. Your arms... so strong. Look at your breasts: perfect and rosy, and your nipples decorated like pretty pink jewels in a gold setting."

Wrapping his arms around my waist, he hugged me close to him, kissing my hair. I closed my eyes and inhaled a long, deep, cleansing breath, relaxing in his embrace.

He continued, his voice warm, enumerating the ways in which he admired my body. Even without looking at my reflection, I could picture myself, letting him describe his vision of me. The tight knot in my chest—which had sharpened and waned since my moment of panic before—finally released its grip altogether.

"All right," I whispered to him once he'd started his exploration of my legs. "I understand what you mean to show me. Thank you, Sir."

"I want to hear you say it yourself, Sadira. Tell me."

"I am beautiful." I turned in his arms, laying both my hands on his chest. "Like a lioness, not a snake."

He narrowed his eyes. "Why *ever* would you think you were a snake?"

I stepped away from him, taking the sari again, running one finger down an elegant swoop of embroidery. "Because I grew up among snakes, my barbarian. Because I was raised and trained by one. These vicious, venomous desires in me—the *need* to indulge such deep and deviant poison."

Holding the sari to myself, I spun back toward him.

"I did tell you I was a monster." A weak smile came to my face. "What sort of woman—what sort of *lioness*—lusts for subjugation and pain?"

"You also told me your *true* desires were for a lover who would master you and still the chaos within," he pointed out. "You are full of energy and pride and power, kitten. You *teem* with it. And it fulfills you, to have a mate who can cool your fire. Hold you steady. Help you burn away the hardest and wildest of that energy."

For I fear I will shatter to pieces without it.

Somehow, despite my senseless breakdown and the humiliation of it, and despite the dark, angry doubts swirling in my head, Bannon soothed my heart.

Not a snake, but a lioness. Not poison, but full of power.

Well, maybe I wasn't quite as magnificent as he painted me... but I managed a real smile, and the last of my shame slipped away.

"Now," he said, coming to me to also put his hands on the smooth, cool fabric of the dress. "Please put it on."

I did as he asked, wrapping the sari around my hips as I'd seen Vash noblewomen do for sacred gatherings and celebrations. I'd worn a few in the past, when I accompanied the king to certain feasts attended by the highest nobility. None of those had been so beautiful, though.

I wrapped the sari around my waist to form the skirt, tucking and folding it neatly, altering the length on the subsequent round to allow two embroidered borders to show. I gathered several pleats at one hip, wrapped it once more, and finally draped it over one shoulder, securing it with a styled gold pin.

In Vashtaren, it wasn't out of place to wear the garment with one or both breasts bared, but I'd learned the Sanraethi had a different sense of modesty when it came to that particular part of the body. I plucked and fidgeted with the fabric to cover myself, but Bannon's hand came down on mine.

"I like it like that." He lovingly touched the side of my naked right breast. "I knew you would look radiant in it, Sadira. You chose the perfect one."

A spark of joy filled my chest. I wrapped my arms around his neck and kissed him. All at once, I believed him, feeling more beautiful—really, uniquely beautiful—than I ever had before.

The *Drekakona* set sail at the height of the afternoon, her sails full of sun and her rowers raising a lively chant that could be heard even on the deck. Bannon took me to the prow of the ship—Schala following at my heels—and we stood with the salt breeze welcoming us and the seabirds calling overhead. Though the Sanraethi soldiers shot a few startled glances at me in my sari, still wrapped in the Vashtaren style, the sailors looked upon me with smiling appreciation.

A fierce note of pride returned, nourishing me like something savory and sweet, as I allowed myself to bask in the pleasure of being someone of importance, a princess or a noblewoman, instead of the slave who'd slept on a dog pillow at the foot of Master's bed all her life.

BANNON AND TORV both cautioned me that the first few days aboard a ship could stir up bouts of seasickness and foul temper. Ailsa had stocked up on ginger root in port, and her foresight paid off when many of the soldiers, including Bannon himself, required ginger tea or light broth spiced with ginger to settle their stomachs in the first few days.

I did not take ill, to the surprise of many. The rocking of the ship only made me sleepy, and if I wasn't helping break out the tools and supplies we'd brought aboard and stocking them in their places, I found myself drifting off, and yearned to return to our cabin for a long, deep nap.

Rayyan, meanwhile, needed no time to adjust. Brimming with excitement, he reported for duty every morning before the two roosters in our livestock pens had crowed. The fishing boats he'd worked on intermittently as a child had been much different than this Sanraethi warship, but when it came to tasks like hauling nets and preparing supplies, he knew his work.

Several days into the voyage, once he'd adjusted to what Torv called 'his sea legs', Bannon called the horde to him and declared all the soldiers now able crewmen under the assignment of the *Drekakona's* captain, Arne.

"It's routine," Ailsa told me as we all stood before Bannon on the mid-deck and he made his announcement. "Not all Sanraethi warlords ask their hordes to work alongside the sailors transporting them, but my father expects it. It keeps the fighters in shape and eases the workload on everyone."

Bannon assigned me to join Rayyan and the other Vash refugees, to receive instruction from one of the crewmates named Ashe. I received the orders with a flutter of keen anticipation and made quickly for the huddle of people gathered before the main mast.

"The cat's still following you, is it?" Rayyan glanced down at my side, where indeed, Schala sat, looking back up at him with wide, watchful green eyes.

"I don't know why," I replied. Crouching to scratch the caracal's tufted ears, I added, "I'm coming to like it though. I just hope she doesn't cause any trouble."

"Good morning!" a bright-faced young woman greeted me from the center of the group. Her russet hair had been twisted into tight, long spirals and pulled back with a leather tie, and her smooth copper skin was dappled with freckles. "You're Sadira, then?"

I folded my hands behind my back in neutral pose and nodded, deciding this must be Ashe.

"Right, then." She planted her hands on her hips. "First thing's first! I'll be showing the lot of you how to move about the ratlines and secure the sails. I hope you're good at tying knots."

I nearly laughed out loud, buoyant with glee. *This* I could do in my sleep.

Ashe delivered a slew of instructions to us, pointing out the main rigging and the key guide ropes, explaining how to manage the masts and sails. Then she assigned pairs of the refugees to join a crewmate at each post, directing Rayyan and me to follow her to the forwardmost one.

She took hold of one of the rope ladders anchored at the railing. "Climbers, either of you?"

I looked up, surprised at how excited I felt at the prospect of moving across the great webwork overhead. "No," I admitted. "But I'm up for the challenge."

Rayyan wrinkled his nose, one side of his mouth twitching. He shook his head in answer to Ashe's question.

"You'll learn by doing, then. Let's go on up."

The rope, rough and heavy, felt good in my hands. Not the sort used for play, of course, but still I enjoyed the taut, twisted cord and the buoyant spring of it beneath me as I hoisted myself up. I'd worried about being clumsy—I'd almost fallen from the castle walls into a howling sandstorm the last time I tried climbing—but this latticework of knots and rungs seemed easy.

The harem slaves of the Order of Akolet had been suspended by ropes in tests of endurance and stylistic display, usually for Alaric's amusement. I'd had my body posed and tied, turned into a hanging piece of art, and shown off like an expensive ornament at gatherings, to demonstrate the king's power and decadence. The harnesses and coils hadn't been designed to allow movement, though—we weren't swinging performers, only objects, set pieces. The Masters took care not to cut off circulation to our limbs or wrap our throats in any way which could lead to strangulation, but maneuverability had never been their concern.

Well... most of them had taken care.

I rubbed at my throat, steering my mind away from thoughts of Alaric, who never seemed to mind if his hogties and suspensions posed the threat of strangling me. For him, of course, the threat was always the point.

Pulling myself up a few feet into the rigging, I gave a bright little laugh, exhilarated. This was nothing at *all* like the rope suspensions of the Order. The *ratlines,* as Ashe had called them, bowed and swung under my weight, tricky but amusing. As I found my balance on them, a confident satisfaction filled me. The breeze off the surface of the water danced through my hair and a pair of birds swooped down right off the bow, sniping and cawing at one another, close enough for me to see the stubborn glints in their eyes.

Ashe shimmied up the ropes with ease, and I did my best to hurry after her. Rayyan moved more slowly behind me, more careful as he checked his footing and scanned his next handhold.

When we'd made it halfway to the top of the first sail, Ashe pointed up at of the central mast. "See there? That's the lookout. Lead watch-station for the ship."

The lookout—a square catwalk built around the mast just above the topmost sail—could have held three crewmates easily, though at the moment only one was stationed there He leaned on a thick wooden rail, gazing down at us as we navigated the ropes. Our gazes met, and he tipped me a small salute. Torv.

He seems friendly enough, even though he calls me witch. I lifted my hand in a tiny wave back at him. *Is he mocking me? Or has he not been told the stories of Alaric's cruel and evil sorceress?*

Of course he must. *Everyone* knew the stories. The tales of the king's loyal accomplice and her perversions had reached most corners of the northern Vash continent and even across the seas. I still hadn't convinced most of the soldiers or even the refugees that I wasn't the woman people had heard about.

He must be mocking me. He must find it amusing, or he wants me to know where he stands.

"Here's where we reef the sails."

Ashe had come to the first spar, and Rayyan had joined her there. I shook off my thoughts of Torv and his teasing and moved to join them.

Ashe mounted the spar and showed us how to move along it, using guide ropes to hold a steady balance. I followed without even thinking about it, and she pointed out the arrangement of rigs and stays. She'd already started explaining the assembly when I noticed Rayyan had not come up onto the beam.

I looked back at the mast. My friend clung to the rigging, body coiled and tight. The color had drained from his cheeks, and his mouth twisted in a tight grimace.

"Ry?" I started back toward him. When I reached the mast again, I crouched down on the spar, reaching out to put a hand on his shoulder. "What's wrong, dear heart?"

"I didn't expect it to... to be so high." He closed his eyes, shaking. "I mean... the deck seems so far below now..."

I peered down. "It isn't so bad. Just be careful—"

He gazed at me, expression full of fear. I shut my mouth and glanced over my shoulder. Ashe seemed to understand immediately and climbed her way back toward us.

"If you come a little higher, you'll reach the crosstrees," she assured Rayyan. Indeed, a short way above us was a platform of crisscrossing beams, broader than the spar and supported by struts.

"I don't want to go any higher," Rayyan said through gritted teeth. He'd only been a soldier a short while, but I'd never known him to balk at any of the tasks he'd been given. Even when ordered to clear the rooms of his former Master, where he'd been victimized and humiliated, *I'd* been the one to interject and request a different assignment.

He's terrified. He hasn't looked this awful since Bhrune still kept him as slave.

Again, I checked below us, gauging the distance. "Can you climb back down? I'll come with you."

Rayyan shook his head violently. "I can't move. The ropes... I can't keep my balance on them."

"Don't be silly." Ashe gave up her grip on the guide ropes and stood unassisted on the spar, crossing her arms over her chest. "You made it all the way up here."

"If you climb onto the beam here, you can get to the mast, and climb the ladder back down," I coaxed him.

"No." Rayyan shook his head again. "I can't move. I just can't!"

I pursed my lips. "Okay. I'm coming back onto the ropes with you. Don't worry."

He gave a frightened yelp when the rigging shifted under my weight, but I quickly laid my hand over his.

"It's all right, Ry. We'll climb together. If anything happens, just grab onto me."

He made a strained sound but nodded. Taking his hand, I moved it down along the ropes, guiding him.

"Come on, brother," I coaxed him. "You can handle this. Remember how the Order would suspend us with ropes just like these? You managed that fine."

"That was different," he retorted, though he moved with me a few more feet down the rigging. "I was a slave. I couldn't refuse. Bhrune would have broken my arms and forced me into the harnesses if I did."

"Bhrune was a stinking, foul-mouthed pig, and I killed him just for you," I said, trying to make my voice light and conversational. As I hoped, it brought a smile—though it was an uneasy smile—to Rayyan's face, and he uttered a soft, shaky laugh.

"You didn't kill him. We both know that."

"Sure I did. Haven't you heard the Sanraethi talk about it? They *still* think it was me, even after everything that happened."

By now we were about halfway to the deck again, and Rayyan had lost some of his stiffness and moved more easily, though he still trembled from head to toe. I led him along, reminding him how much he'd already endured and how he'd survived the worst of the Order's brutal Masters.

"You've faced much worse challenges than this and survived, Rayyan, you'll be back on your own two feet in no time. It's just a little farther, now."

At last, his foot came down on solid, stable wood, and Rayyan dropped from the rigging. He heaved a great sigh of relief, wiping sweat from his brow, and then hugged himself. Schala came trotting up beside him, gazing up at me and uttering a soft miaow.

"Thank you, Sadira," Rayyan said.

Still hanging from the ropes, I shifted, looping my arms through the latticework so I could face him.

"Of course, brother." I grinned at him. "You know I'll always—"

A loop of rope fell from above, cutting me off. I glanced up to see where it had dropped from, when a second rope tumbled over me. It coiled itself around my neck, like a serpent, just as the first one slung itself around one of my arms.

The sharp heat of adrenaline flashed through my veins as the ropes constricted, holding me bound in the rigging, choking off my air.

CHAPTER EIGHT

MY HEART PLUNGED. The rope around my neck jerked upward, sending a jolt of deep pain through me, and driving me in to a breathless, coughing fit. I fought the coils along my arms, struggling to get my hands free and pry the tightening noose away.

"Captain!" Rayyan yelled, spinning to search the deck for help. The rigging bounced and swayed as someone swung onto it above—Ashe, probably, climbing quickly down after us.

I twisted one arm nearly free when a fresh rope whipped into action. It wrapped around my wrist and bent the arm backward, against my spine, into a position eerily like those I'd just been thinking of: the suspended poses our Masters tied us into.

But that was different! I strained, tears stinging my eyes as the edges of my vision turned fuzzy and gray. *I prepared for those contortions... I had to stretch and be limber! And they* never *wound the ropes around my* neck!

Except Alaric. Alaric, who broke all the rules.

A sharp pain shot through my shoulder as the rope forced my arm into place, a reverse-prayer position. I couldn't scream; I couldn't even choke out a desperate whisper, and my vision had started fading to black. Somewhere far off, the ropes were now trying to force my other arm into place along with the first, and I'd lost the strength to struggle.

In the darkness of my mind, the flickering, pulsing blue light replaced all other thought. A heartbeat. A life. Slowing... fading...

Then, the ropes let go in abrupt surrender. I toppled from the rigging in a clumsy heap, gasping for air. A frigid cold swept over me and I curled into fetal position, shivering.

A soft, warm presence nudged at me, chuffing and *miaow*ing with low, mournful worry.

"Are you all right?"

Bannon's voice. My vision hadn't cleared, but his wonderful scent of fiery autumn immediately reassured me. I groped for him, and his hands reached out from the darkness to gather me against his crouching form.

A thump on the deck sounded nearby. "Is she okay? I saw her get tangled up, but I couldn't get down fast enough."

Ashe. Tone full of fearful astonishment. Somebody put a hand on my back. I had a feeling it was Rayyan.

"I'll be fine..."

It hurt to talk. My throat burned, each breath like sand scraping and grinding on soft, vulnerable muscles. Schala butted my hip with her head, uttering another nervous rumble, so I dropped a hand down to scratch her ears.

"Bring her water," came Ailsa's voice. Wonderful. I'd made a fool of myself in front of the whole ship.

No. The ropes moved. I didn't get tangled up, they wrapped around me of their own accord!

They'd tried to tie me up just as I had been before. In Alaric's court.

At last, I could make out Bannon's arms around me, and I lay my hand on one, giving him a grateful squeeze. "You cut me down?"

"Yes. It was just that rope around your neck that really had you. Once I severed it you slipped out of the others easily. You must watch more carefully when you're climbing, kitten. There are always loose lines between the rigging shrouds."

"But I didn't... the ropes—"

I blinked and looked for Rayyan in the haze. "Didn't you see it, Ry? They did it themselves. They *wrapped* around me."

Rayyan's mouth twitched. He ran a hand over his scalp. "I don't know, Sadira. I was trying not to look at anything the whole time."

Had nobody witnessed the attack? Did they really believe it had only been clumsiness on my part?

Somebody put a cup in my hand, and I drank, thankful for the fresh water as it coursed down my burning throat. My heartbeat slowed to normal at last, and as I passed the cup back to the crewmate who'd brought it, I let Bannon help me to my feet.

"Do you need to return to the cabin?" he asked me.

"No," I protested without hesitation. "I'm already recovering. I want to keep working with the crew. I don't wish to be coddled, Sir."

First the mob on the docks and now an incident with the rigging? The Sanraethi would certainly think me useless and a coward if I couldn't manage to pull my own weight.

Bannon looked me over, grimacing, and touched my throat where the reddened marks of the rope had left my skin raw and stinging. He checked my shoulder next, and I flinched. It still stung from being jerked and maneuvered into awkward, unyielding angles.

He rubbed at his chin. I took his hand in mine and spoke softly, respectfully.

"Bannon... let me do this. I want to do this."

"Very well." He clapped his hand gently on my upper arm, careful not to be too hard. "But I'll have your word you'll be more careful in the shrouds."

Bannon had no reason to suspect foul play, but the implication hurt, nonetheless. I bowed my head in a nod.

Then again... if no one saw, maybe it really was an accident.

The small knot of onlookers around us began to disperse, leaving him, me, Rayyan and Ashe. Schala wound around my ankles, offering a slow rumble of a purr.

"Well." Ashe crossed her arms. "Rayyan will need a new assignment if the heights bother him. Might as well show you the other work we've got on board."

I'd wanted to climb up to the lookout and see the view from above, but Ashe didn't offer me any chance to disagree. With a gesture to me and Rayyan, she started off down the deck.

Before I followed, Bannon tilted my face up to him, and pressed his lips to mine.

"Careful," he reminded me. "I'll be conferring with the ship's captain, should you need me."

I'm not a child, I almost told him, but bit my lip at the last second, obediently nodding instead.

OVER THE NEXT few days, during the morning shifts Ashe took Rayyan and me around the ship, enumerating our potential working tasks for the voyage. She showed us the archery defense towers rising at the bow, center, and stern of the ship, which could be crewed by up to six archers each in case of attack, and the heavy ballista stationed at the very front of the bow. No one had any reason to manage the mighty weapon for now, but whole teams were assigned to respond the instant an alarm bell rang out.

She demonstrated how to secure the ropes and pulleys along the siderails of the deck; when and where the livestock were allowed to roam, and how to return them to their pens on the orlop at the proper time; how to work the anchors; even how to judge oncoming weather and read the lay of the sea. The deck was to be cleaned each day, a task usually assigned to cabin boys, but Ashe assured us if the captain grew displeased, *we* might very well be given a mop and bucket for the job.

"Captain Arne and the Red Bear keep their meeting rooms and war council in the stern." She pointed to the sheltered portion of the ship below the stern deck and the wheel. A single door with a porthole led into the rooms beyond, but Ashe opted not to include them in our tour.

Leading us to the prow one morning, she hailed a trio of sailors tending to the rails and the gleaming figurehead. Using resin and waxes, they treated scuffs and chips in the wood.

"Purely maintenance, for now," Ashe explained. "Repairs from the last journey were all made while the

Drekakona docked in port. But every voyage will take its toll, and the soft woods need proper sealing and restoration."

"Especially here," one of the others put in. She gestured over the railing down toward the water, where the ship's fierce promontory cut through the waves. "Don't expect to run into enemies on the trip home, but if we do, that battering ram's our best weapon, 'sides a team of boarders. So, we never skip the upkeep."

I tried to pay attention but the youngest of the three, a short, skinny adolescent with long, shaggy hair, distracted me. Their eyes ran over the winding tattoos along my arm. A frown tugged at my mouth, and I rubbed at the back of my neck—still sore, even now, from the incident with the ropes—and sidled behind Ashe.

We descended to the gallery deck and the steering oars, handled by a broad, smiling Sanraethi oarsman and his partner, a skinny crier who called directions down to the rowers. Then Ashe took us to the first level of the gallery, and we watched the crew at work. Today their boisterous chanting had been replaced by a steady drumbeat, provided by a fair androgyne sailor at the very center of the space. Bodies shone with sweat as they flexed and pulled, heaving the great oars against a stymying current.

Rayyan observed the rowers with a far more comfortable, even interested expression on his face. His gaze roamed over the hefty oars, and he rubbed at his leanly muscled forearm, studying the difficult, demanding exercise.

"To the galley next!" Ashe announced. "There's other work to be done below decks, like tending the chickens and the pigs in the livestock pens. We'll go over those after we've eaten, though. The cook's got fresh crab meat from port and by the smell, I'd guess it's near ready to serve."

I'd had an early meal of milk and bread, but the moment she mentioned food, my stomach gave a deep, hollow ache, as though I'd been fasting for days. Rayyan broke into a broad grin, evidently also hungry, and we followed Ashe to the galley with an eager bounce in our steps.

Twenty minutes later, we'd found ourselves a place on deck where we could sit on supply crates, out of the way of workers, with rough tin plates of crabmeat and biscuits on our laps.

"Have you eaten this before?" I asked Rayyan, inspecting one spindly armored leg with uncertainty.

He reached out to take it from me, drawing a small blade from his belt and wedging it under one of the joints. He split the shell open to expose gleaming white flesh and handed it back to me.

"We had rock crabs on the river." Cracking open one of his own, he pried out the meat with his fingers. I hadn't been brave enough to accept one of the large red claws when the ship's cook offered it—I couldn't shake the image of a giant scorpion as I beheld it— but Rayyan had taken one gratefully, and he cracked it next, offering me half.

I took it, amused by the way the soft meat held the curved shape of the claw even when extracted. "How much do you remember of the river valley?"

"Oh, quite a lot," he replied. "I had brothers, like I told you. My mother and father managed the mill, and I had an uncle who worked a fishing boat."

Schala wound around my calf. I bent to slip her a piece of the crabmeat, and a loud, thrumming purr rose from her scrawny frame.

"I'm glad you've decided to come with us to Sanraeth," I said. "But did you not think of returning home, like the other Vash slaves did?"

Rayyan waved a hand. "That life is long gone for me. I don't know if I could stand to look in the faces of my family again, after..."

His face grew dark. I understood what he intended to say, even if he couldn't make himself say it. After being made into a whore.

"I'm not sure what I would do, even I did go back." Dropping the shell of the claw back onto his plate, he leaned back, looking up into the sky. "I have no desire to be a fisher, like my uncle, or a miller or shepherd. Maybe a builder, but..."

His gaze returned to the ship, and he glanced toward the quarter-deck where Bannon, Mara, and the ship's captain, Arne, stood supervising a group of soldiers preparing nets.

"Before I started serving with the Sanraethi soldiers," Rayyan murmured, "I'd never held a weapon in my hand. They taught me how to use the spear, how to defend myself. And others. So many of the slaves had no one to protect them. That is something I can do now. I am no miller, no fisher. I am *definitely* not meant to be a bride or bear children."

I smiled at the brighter tone in his voice. In my heart, I knew what he would say next, but still it overjoyed me to hear it.

"So, I'll be a soldier. The Red Bear has welcomed me into his horde. The others have accepted me well enough. Most of them don't even know I was ever part of the harem at all. I like that."

Slipping Schala another piece of crab, I nodded again. For all he sounded as though this had only just come to him, I expected he'd known it, deep inside, for some time.

I'd known Rayyan as a timid person, a meek little mouse in the claws of a fierce, cruel cat, always toying with him and humiliating him. Working with the Sanraethi, and bearing the mantle of a *guard,* had brought out his thriving inner strength. I recalled the way he'd looked at the rowers and their hard, physical labors, the way he'd perked up with interest.

"I am glad," I said to him again. "And I am glad we will be together. From one life to the next. You are so very important to me, Rayyan."

He smiled at me. I picked up another of the crab legs, dug out my own small knife and worked it under the joint, as he had.

"And what of you?" Rayyan asked. "Now you are free, and on your way to a strange foreign kingdom, what will you do?"

I caught another one of the sailors staring at the crimson ink and taut, white lines of my scars and tattoos, and hurriedly glanced away.

"Hard to say," I mumbled. "I hoped leaving Vashtaren would mean leaving behind all the infamy and gossip. I keep forgetting, though, how all my sins and *perversions* are marked right on my skin for all to see. Anywhere I go—even across the sea, apparently—I'll still be the dark magician's witch."

I thought of Torv and the jovial way he'd said it, so casual and unconcerned. "That's not who I wish to be. It's not who I've *ever* wished to be."

Rayyan wiped one hand clean and gently touched my wrist. He held my hand up, showing me the cryptic symbols and lines inked across the back of it.

"You may not be able to erase what's been done to you," Rayyan replied. "But you *do* have the power to change other things. Things Alaric never would allow you to change."

Gently I tugged away from him. I closed my eyes and thought of the sunset-colored sari Bannon had brought me. A gift, but also something of my own choosing. A symbol of my freedom to change.

A symbol which had brought on a wild, emotional attack.

Rayyan brushed a hand through my blonde mane. "How long has it been since your hair was cut?"

Maybe a whole year. I combed my fingers through it. "Do you think I should?"

"I think when I sheared my hair, it felt even more liberating than shedding my collar."

I touched the base of my throat, where the absence of my own collar still struck me as painful, odd, and *wrong*.

But when I'd worn the sari, walked out among the sailors and soldiers and refugees wearing something Alaric would never have chosen, something *I* had desired for myself, it had filled me with such powerful joy.

My hair had been dyed and damaged, always styled in the straight, flat sheet favored by the Vash. It had taken hours for me to uncover its natural blonde shine again, once I had been free to, and days after that to coax it back to any sort of body and life.

I like my hair. I genuinely like it, and it never did look right in that lank, straight fashion.

My gaze roamed over the women on deck, considering their colorful, complex styles.

As much as I disliked Mara, I'd always admired the way she kept one half of her dark locks tightly braided against her scalp, while the rest of it tumbled free and wild. Some of the other Sanraethi women wore it similarly, sometimes with close, neat braids on either side and a wave of free tresses along the top, all coming together to be tied back and tumble down between their shoulders. Some, like Ashe, wore it all in braids, and others left it totally unbound, adorned with beads and metal charms and wild bird feathers.

"Do you know anyone who can style it for me like the Sanraethi women?" I asked Rayyan. My voice came out quiet, even shy.

"Calla." Rayyan picked up his plate and stood. "She served one of the Vash women as a handmaiden, but she's Sanraethi by birth. I think I know what bunk she's been assigned, too. It will be a wonderful surprise for the captain."

I hesitated before rising also. An unexpected twinge made me rub at my chest, where the first tight twinge had started.

A surprise? He means to do this right now, before I speak to Bannon?

I touched the place where the ring of my collar should be, wishing I could worry its familiar smooth curve, spin it in its shackle, as I intoned, "A slave does not preen or pretty herself except as her Master orders."

Rayyan snorted. "*Old* rules, given by old, dead men. Bannon will have no objection."

I swallowed. Rayyan still didn't understand my desire to embrace my servitude and give myself over to my Master's guidance. Bannon may not object to me altering my appearance, but I wasn't *supposed* to without speaking to him first. He might not object, but it ought to be discussed.

A slave serves Master's *desires. Her dress, her jewelry... her hair.*

Bannon had learned a lot about his role as Master from our book. He *could* punish me if a careless decision displeased him. What if he didn't appreciate my adopting his people's fashions? If I somehow offended him by styling myself like one of them? Like his own wife, maybe?

I'd be giving him the right to do it.

He is not *like Alaric. But he is* my *Master.*

"He will be pleased!" Rayyan insisted. "I saw the way he beamed at you in the dress you chose. Whatever else you decide to do with your appearance, he will adore you even more."

My heart gave a throb. My fingers searched for the collar and the ring that weren't there. They brushed the sore, reddened bruises from the rigging rope debacle. All at once, a rebellious part of me clashed with my caution.

Careful, he'd told me. He thought I'd nearly strangled because I'd been careless and clumsy. As though I was some fragile thing. As though I hadn't taken on a warped, hideous god-monster in the desert right alongside him.

As though I hadn't earned some *right* to be believed.

Sullen mutiny smoldered in my gut. *Maybe I don't need his permission after all.*

"All right. Take me to Calla."

BRANTWIJN SERRAH

CHAPTER NINE

CALLA—A WILLOWY, very pale Sanraethi, though ferocious and indignant since her liberation—was only too happy to steer me onto a barrel in her bunkroom and help me shed the lingering look of a Vash woman.

When the knife appeared and she set to work shearing and cutting, my confidence wavered again. My heart thumped heavily in my chest, and I had to close my eyes, wondering all over again if it had been the right decision.

Too late now. There's no going back.

Her clever hands worked like swift, determined little birds, parting and weaving, shearing and teasing. When she brought up the polished glass to show me the result, a surge of joy filled me.

"Eye of Akolet!" I whispered, thrilled and daunted all at once. She'd shorn the hair on the left side of my head nearly down to the scalp, and sectioned the rest into a short, wild, regal mane like a lion's. "I really look like one of your clans."

Calla wrinkled her nose. "Sanraethi women don't call on the *snake* god. There's your first lesson, if you really wish to be like us. Though if you ask me, you shouldn't try to imitate a Sanraethi woman. Wearing your hair like us is one thing, but look at you."

She opened her palm before my face as though to frame and display my distinctive features. I prepared myself for her to point out my tattoos, which I needed no help in recognizing. She surprised me, though.

"Sanraethi hair is never so straight and fine as yours, nor quite this color. Some of the northernmost clans might have it, in some families, but even there, I doubt you'd find many. And I've never met any Sanraethi with *gray* eyes."

Rayyan, sitting on the edge of Calla's bunk and watching with eager enthusiasm, twisted his mouth in an uncertain expression, as though he wished to contradict her. Of course, being Southern Vash, he really couldn't.

"It doesn't matter," Calla continued breezily. "If you want to be like a Sanraethi woman, I won't stand in your way. I thought you intended to find your *real* folk, though. I'd expect you to want to adopt *their* ways."

Oh. I put a finger to my lips and watched the woman in the mirror do the same. *I hadn't even thought of that.*

"As soon as we reach land, you must find a serpent and kill it," Calla instructed, moving smoothly past my awkward silence. She drew my hair back from my face and singled out the one smooth, long braid she'd plaited by my right ear. "We'll fashion an ornament from its skull and hang it from the end of this braid, as symbol of your battle against the serpent in the sands."

The braid stood out, though she'd woven no charms or decoration into it yet, explaining to me that such adornments were earned through noble acts and victory.

"Your history with Alaric," she tutted, fluffing up the rest of my hair again. "Not worthy of remembrance. His crusades were evil, and your part in them, an act of shame."

The accusation stung, but I didn't argue. She was right.

"But your battle with the serpent god," she continued. "Let it be the first of many such braids, preserved and decorated with tokens of your redemption."

My heart raced in my chest, half in bright, beautiful glee, and half in dread, unsure whether Bannon would approve of the change, or be annoyed by my vanity.

What I hadn't expected were the looks of outright horror on the faces of the sailors when Rayyan and I reappeared on deck.

The sight of me brought several conversations to an abrupt end. Some furrowed their brows in confusion. Others blanched or turned faintly green. I'd intended to go straight to my Master, eager for his response—hoping desperately it would be one of approval—but I'd hardly made it halfway to the quarterdeck when the stares brought me to a halt.

Eye of Akolet... what is it? What did I do wrong?

My stomach dropped out from under me. The urge to be sick rose in my gut.

Ashe broke apart from a group of deck hands who'd been sharing a mug of beer. The urgent expression on her face only worsened my panic.

"Stay right here," she instructed me, before hurrying down to the lower decks. I traded a worried glance with Rayyan.

"What's wrong?" I demanded. He shook his head, just as baffled as I.

Are they angry I wish to look like one of them? Outraged that the witch *would dare to imitate their customs?*

Moments later, Ashe jogged back up the stairs. In her hands she held three eggshells. She pushed them into my hands.

"Drop them and crush them with your feet. Do it quickly! And take off your boots, your feet must be bare!"

Too surprised to argue, I did as she said. Sliding off my boots, I cast down the shells, and stomped on them.

"More," Ashe commanded. "Crush the pieces as small as you can. The tinier, the better."

"Why am I doing this?" I asked as I obeyed, grating and grinding the thin shells against the boards. All around us, people had begun to move again. Some put their hands to their hearts with sighs of relief, while others shot glances of annoyance at me before returning to their work.

"You never, *ever* cut your hair while at sea," Ashe told me. "It's terrible luck, a great insult to the sea spirits. You crush the eggshells to prevent angry entities from following you and enacting punishment."

I ground the last bit of shell under my heel and inspected the remnants. *Naturally,* I'd make a mistake like this, wouldn't I? First the mob, then the ropes, now an unwitting act of idiocy.

And now if anything unfortunate happens, if anything goes wrong, it will be my fault. Again. Alaric's witch, dooming the voyage home just as she cursed the liberators of his castle.

Tears sprung to my eyes. Ashe pressed her lips together in a sympathetic frown and patted my shoulder.

"Toss the shells overboard," she advised. "The spirits should accept your offering and you will be safe."

She didn't sound certain of it at all.

Rayyan held out his hands. "We didn't know."

Ashe toyed with the ends of her braids and lifted one shoulder in a noncommittal shrug. She turned back toward the sailors she'd been drinking with, tossing one last glance over her shoulder at us as she went.

"We still need to discuss some of the work to be done. Meet me at the mast again in thirty minutes."

I clenched my fists at my side and ground my teeth. Rayyan put his arm around my shoulder.

"It will be all right. It's only superstition. Nothing bad is going to happen."

Stooping, I gathered up the powdery bits of shell and moved to the railing to cast them overboard. "It's already happening, though, isn't it? Those people on the docks... and those ropes *did* move on their own! They looped around me and tried to strangle me, I swear it."

Not just strangle. They meant to pose *me. They were pulling me into position just as the Order would have. Just as Alaric would have.*

Sacred serpent. My hand flew to my throat as I stared out over the water. *Is he... could he still be...*

I jumped as Rayyan took me by the hand.

"Come on." He flashed me an encouraging smile. "We still have to show the Red Bear."

"Rayyan, he'll be furious." I buried my face in my hands. "If I'd spoken with him like I *should* have, certainly he'd have warned me about the superstitions. He'll punish me for sure."

The smile faded. Rayyan dropped my hand, looking puzzled and defeated.

"Well..." He rubbed at the back of his neck. "He'll see it one way or another, won't he?"

With a sigh, I nodded. "You're right. Might as well have it done with. You don't have to come, though. Go join Ashe and the others. I'll meet you when I'm done."

He looked as though he wanted to argue, but I nudged him in the direction of the sailors, and he went. I ran my hand through my hair—*And I really did like the change. It felt so cathartic!* —and set out to find my Master, Schala trotting at my heels.

Torv stood by the arched wooden doorway to the stern, smoking a long-handled pipe. He eyed my hair with a shrewd expression, taking a long draw, and blew out a puff of fragrant, floral-scented smoke.

"Suits you," he grunted, then reached over to push open the door. I tried to muster up a grateful smile but thought it must have come off as more of a grimace, as I passed him.

I found the meeting room by the sound of voices from within. Bannon, Mara, and Arne, discussing the voyage ahead. I knocked at the door, hoping Bannon himself would answer, but of course it was the lieutenant who opened it. She looked me over, her face unreadable.

"Red Bear," she said, stepping aside to admit me. Both men looked up from a table of maps, and I braced myself for their disapproval.

Arne didn't react at all. We hadn't shared more than a perfunctory greeting, and he might not even realize I'd changed my appearance at all. Bannon, on the other hand, stared at me, blinking in surprise.

"Sadira..."

He came to me, arms outstretched. Then, a broad grin broke out on his face and he laughed, a hearty, happy sound.

"Look at you! It's wonderful!"

A wave of relief overtook me as he wrapped me in an enthusiastic embrace. I laid a hand on his chest and met his eyes, hopeful, as he combed his fingers through the short, shaggy new length of my hair.

He touched the single braid. "This should have a token added to it."

"Calla said a serpent's skull." For a moment I almost forgot the others in the room and the business I'd interrupted. "Only there are none on the ship, of course, so I'm to kill one as soon as I'm able, and she'll fashion a token for me then."

"Perfect." He kissed me. "My beautiful kitten."

"You aren't angry at me?"

"Should I be?" He stroked the shorn portion on the left side of my head, sending a shiver of delight down the back of my neck.

"I didn't discuss it with you first."

"Ah."

Mara had returned to the table, and she rolled her eyes. Captain Arne furrowed his brow, drumming his fingers on the maps as he watched our exchange.

Bannon glanced his way before returning his attention to me.

"I suppose you should have at least told me of your intention," he said. "But you're not prisoner to my whims. And you are even more beautiful than ever."

He ran his hand through my hair again, and I leaned my head into his palm, closing my eyes to bask in his touch.

"My fierce desert lioness," he murmured. "Now, I think we both have work to return to, don't we?"

"Yes." I didn't want to work, though. I wanted to drag him back to our cabin and make wild love to him, until I had not an ounce of energy left.

He kissed my brow. "Go on, then. Hop to, back to your duties."

A sweet tingle of anticipation bloomed in my chest. I smiled at him—finding a *real* smile this time—and happily agreed. He saw me out, and even after he'd shut the door to the meeting room I stood in the dim, cool passageway, eyes closed, fingering the end of my braid and glowing inside.

My barbarian. My perfect, adoring barbarian. How I love you.

I'd thought it before. Perhaps I'd even said the word out loud to him. Our arrangement as Master and pet had only been intended to last as long as we were forced together by circumstance in Alaric's castle, prisoners of the savage desert and its cruel customs, pressing in on us both. We were neither of us prisoners anymore, though.

So... how much longer will Bannon find his own satisfaction in these roles?

The beast within me was off its leash. It prowled and purred with its freedom, and perhaps it tested the limits a little more now, pushing the boundaries, seeing if the Master would still—*could* still—contain it. Ultimately, though, I still craved Bannon's touch. His tenderness and affection, yes, but also his savage, salacious domination. As we drew father and farther away from the strange events which brought us together, would *he* still feel such primal passions?

Schala gave a rasping mew at my feet. I crouched to gather her into my arms and buried my face against her fur. I'd be late to meet Ashe and Rayyan again, and it would be one more mark against me in these horrible first few days. Only a few more hours, though, and I'd be back in my barbarian's arms. Alone with him, safe from all this bad luck, and free to express my gratitude in all the ways I wished.

I heaved a sigh of relief. As I stooped to put Schala down, though, the caracal arched her back, and her soothing purr turned into a low, ugly growl. I blinked, and followed her gaze down the passageway, toward the door leading back onto the deck.

Sunlight streamed in the single porthole, illuminating a swirl of golden dust motes and casting a bright circle upon the rich wood. At first, I saw nothing there to set the cat on edge—and then, a movement caught my eye, just the subtlest shifting of darkness behind the ray of light.

A flash of feral eyes, like distant, glowing moons. A figure standing just out of sight.

I took a step forward, wary heat rising at the back of my neck, and opened my mouth to demand they identify themselves.

But the shadowy creature was gone.

CHAPTER TEN

THE MOMENT BANNON arrived in his cabin, I rose to meet him, crossing to him in a single, purposeful stride.

"Sir, I have to tell you—"

He silenced me with a finger to my lips, then he replaced it with his own, cradling my head in his hands as his tongue found mine.

"Later," he murmured as we parted. "Undress."

A shiver traveled through my body. I stepped out of his embrace, taking his hands in mine and meeting his eyes. For a moment, I debated refusing. Insisting he listen first, as I told him about the ropes and the strange, shadowy figure in the passageway, and of the way the doors to the master bedchamber had slammed on me, and everything, *everything* going wrong since I'd left Alaric's castle.

The heat in his gaze stole away the impulse. Putting aside my fears, I obeyed his order, my fingers coming to the cords lacing up my bodice.

He watched me with a handsome and hungry look as I slipped out of my clothing piece by piece, until I stood perfectly naked before him. Then he advanced on me, a patent predator closing in on his prey, forceful and looming in the smallness of the space. His hands closed around my wrists and he bore me down onto the bed, kissing me over and over.

"Ah, my Sadira."

He held me down, pinning my wrists between my breasts with one hand, while the other caressed my cheek. "My beautiful lioness. My goddess of the sands."

"Sir..."

I returned his kisses, full of a surging desire, pressing my body to his. The scents of crisp autumn and fire, and strong, sweet liquor surrounded me, comforting and delicious. His grip on my wrists tightened. I wriggled, giving up a tiny groan as he traveled down my body with his lips.

I gave a soft gasp, surrendering to a lovely quiver when he teased my navel piercing with his tongue. His free hand slid between my thighs.

Bannon entered me with two strong fingers, circling my clitoris with his thumb. I breathed out his name in a gentle sigh, clenching and unclenching my fists.

"Good girl."

Still holding me, he moved to lie between my legs, and lowered his face to my sex. The first wonderful stroke of his tongue brought up a swell of joy from deep inside me, and I pressed to him, needful for more. He teased and feasted upon me, laving the length of my pussy before planting a slow, loving kiss on my clit, and descending again for more. His tongue slipped inside me, making me twist and groan his name, but his grip on my wrists remained tight, keeping me his prisoner.

"Bannon..." I whispered, then fell into a low sound of delight. "Barbarian... *Master*..."

He rose from between my thighs, scrubbing the glistening wetness from his mouth, and moved into place on top of me. His grip on my wrists tightened, squeezing to the point of pain, and I hitched in a short breath. At last, he released my wrists, but not to free me. Instead, he took each of my hands in his and held them down against the bed on either side.

When he kissed my lips, I tasted my own lush desire. Bannon uttered a rumbling growl, nuzzling at my neck and planting more kisses along my ear, my cheek, my jaw, down to my collarbone.

At last, he entered me, and his cock filled me with perfect, urgent need.

"*Oh,* love..." he groaned.

I wrapped my legs around him, and our bodies moved into a gentle rhythm. A wonderful glow of sweet pleasure came to life inside me.

We moved slow, indulging, chasing a thrilling, impassioned climb. Our lips, our hips—his fingers like iron keeping me locked in place. Thighs flexing, abdomens tense, we gasped and sighed each other's names.

"Master..."

"Sadi..."

When Bannon's pace increased. I met him eagerly, embracing the full joy of him moving with me, within me. His thumbs dug into the tender insides of my wrists and he grunted, thrusts deepening. With panting breaths, I urged him on, murmuring, begging, until my orgasm kindled to life and raced toward completion.

"Barbarian!" I rasped in his ear as my nails dug into my palms. "Oh, my love, I'm coming... I'm—"

And as the first surge of climax overtook me, he let go of one wrist to tangle his fingers in my hair, pulling tight, making me turn my face up to his so he could kiss me, tongue storming my mouth. He buried himself inside me and his cock throbbed, hot and hard, flooding me with his seed as I hit a dizzying height, crying out in wordless rapture.

"I love you." I kissed him over and over, as he kept me pinned to the bed. "I love you... oh, I love you...."

He didn't withdraw right away. We lay together for several moments, and the comfortable weight of his body atop me filled me with contentment and peace. He felt like home.

"Thank you," I told him.

He beamed. "Always my pleasure."

We parted at last, and he drew me against his chest. His skin warmed mine. I relaxed in his embrace, full of joy.

"What did you want to tell me?" he mumbled, face buried in my hair.

Oh. Yes.

Now that he'd brought it up, though, the words fled me. Where did I begin? How could I make him understand what I'd seen, without sounding insane or paranoid?

He'll think it is only the lingering fear of Alaric. I'm supposed to be a soldier and a member of his horde now, not a frightened, hysterical woman.

He *had* to know, though. I must make him believe me.

"Earlier, in the stern..."

I searched for the words, clasping his hands in my own. "You should know the crew and soldiers on deck didn't approve of my decision to cut my hair. I didn't know the cutting of hair was a bad omen aboard ships."

"Ah." He freed his hand from mine and stroked his beard. "Yes. I'm familiar with the belief, though I suppose it didn't occur to me, after so many months on land again, far away from sailor's superstitions."

"Ashe made me stamp on eggshells to keep vile spirits from hunting me in revenge. I'm not certain it worked, though. After I left you in the meeting room, I saw... *something* in the passageways."

"What was that?"

I ran my fingers across my lips. "I think... maybe a person? They disappeared right into the shadows, though. As if..."

"As if they weren't real?"

I shifted to peer up at him. Cold gloom stole across the back of my neck. "You think I was mistaken."

His lips twitched into an uncertain grimace. "You've seen much in these last months, Sadira. And you were right about Lord Khan and his dark magic—he was following you after all. But..."

He stroked the close-shaven segment of my hair, sending me into a shiver. His lips touched the crown of my head, and he uttered a soft sigh.

"I had him in my head," he went on. "He had power in him still, but it burned hot and fast. There couldn't have been anything left after the last gasp of that golem he created. Even if we hadn't destroyed it, I doubt Khan could have sustained it much longer. I doubt any part of him survived its destruction."

I lay my head down, furrowing my brow. *But the ropes,* I wanted to say. *I know they tried to strangle me. And the slamming doors at the castle.*

Would he believe any of it, though? Did I, really?

Perhaps it is all in my head. Perhaps I'm simply frightened by all these changes... by the strange path before me.

As he held me, I closed my eyes and listened to the sound of the waves outside the porthole over our heads. The sway of the boat—and the weight of all my questions—made me tired.

"*Something* is going on, though," I murmured. "I know you think I was being clumsy earlier... not watching as I climbed in the shrouds... but..."

"Hm?" He nuzzled his head between my neck and shoulder. "Tell me, Sadi."

The heat of his body swaddled me, though. The slow rocking and the even rhythm of the sea... the beat of his heart... his breath against my skin.

I mumbled something else, but my own words sounded distant and lost. Soon, beautiful sleep pulled me down, and anything else I might have said drifted away like sand in the breeze on a desert night.

A KNOCK AT the cabin door roused me some hours later. I opened my eyes to find night had fallen, a tiny circle of dark, starry sky visible through the porthole. No moon tonight, but a cloud of celestial blue and violet spiraled across the black. I gazed up at it, lost in quiet admiration, until another knock interrupted my thoughts.

Bannon slept on beside me. His arm slid from me as I sat up and managed a sleepy, "Hello?"

No answer. I smoothed down my messy hair and rubbed the back of my neck. A low, gravelly rumble caught my attention, and I wrinkled my nose. *What is that?*

Then I realized.

Schala perched on the end of the bunk, spine arched, the stub of her tail standing straight up. The fur of her ruff bristled, and she growled, flashing green eyes fixed on the door.

I watched her, then followed her gaze, waiting.

Silence. My attention drifted down, to the faint strip of light at the bottom of the door. The lanterns in the corridor cast a dim but steady glow.

If someone's out there, I should see their shadow. There isn't any, though.

I'd just about decided I'd dreamed the sound— and Schala probably only caught scent of a rat—when a furious hail of blows shook the door in its frame.

I gave a start, a short cry escaping me, and I grasped blindly for Bannon's hand. Schala yowled and hissed, bounding down form the bed to stalk back and forth across the floor.

Bannon stirred, squeezing my hand, his voice sleep-muddled and almost inaudible as he mumbled, "Sadi?"

"Did you hear that?" I scooted closer to him. He tried to loop an arm around me and pull me back into place beside him, but my body refused to relax. Trembling, I unwrapped myself from his grip and stood.

Bannon didn't rise. He was asleep again already, and I knew he couldn't have heard what I did. If he had, he'd already be on his feet. Meanwhile, the caracal paced and paced... and the weak crack of light beneath the door slowly faded, going dark before my eyes.

Something is *out there.*

I cast a glance over my shoulder, frowning at Bannon, so eerily unresponsive. *Something... with some kind of power. Something that wants me* alone.

On shaky legs, I crossed the cabin. Our lantern hung on a hook beside the bed, a box of matches stored in a little cubby beneath it. My hands trembled as I lit it. Then I snatched one of my sarongs from the chest at the foot of the bed and wrapped it hastily around my naked body before taking the light, steeling myself.

Another cry escaped me as cold feline paws landed on my shoulder without warning. Schala, jumping up from the floor to settle herself on me, still growling with ugly menace.

"Don't *do* that!" I hissed at her, though I brought up a hand to stroke her all the same. She didn't seem to notice. The growling didn't stop.

Taking a deep breath, I approached the door. Silence, still... but somehow, I *sensed* a dark, grim intelligence waiting for me. As if I could hear—maybe *feel*—its strange, bestial breaths, deep and rhythmic, and the cold, icy beating of its heart.

My hand came down on the doorknob. My heart thundered in my ears.

Now, Sadira. Now or never.

I flung the door open wide.

The passage lay in darkness. The lanterns had been extinguished, leaving only the light in my hand to illuminate the shadowy, narrow corridor. I saw no one, but a frigid cold wafted over me.

After a long, quiet moment, I peeked out, holding up my lantern and checking the passage, first one way, then the other.

Under the archway leading to the cargo holds, a faint shimmer of a figure moved. The light of my lantern reflected in its wide, white eyes, round and bright as moons.

My lantern exploded in a flash of fire, showering me with shards of glass, plunging the hall into freezing   blackness.

Chapter Eleven

Schala gave a sharp feline scream, and before I could stop myself, I screamed with her, throwing the remains of the lantern blindly into the darkness and dodging back into the cabin to slam the door. The cat jumped down from my shoulder as I pressed my back against the wood, praying the creature with those bright moony eyes wouldn't return or start pounding on it again, wouldn't shake and rattle it, trying to get in while I desperately put all my weight in its way.

My face stung. I brought up one hand to probe for damage and found myself mercifully unscathed. A few smarting, shallow scrapes marked my cheeks, but none of the glass had hit my eyes or my lips.

I waited in tense silence, my whole body shaking. Across the cabin, the faint light of the stars cast a glow on Bannon, lying undisturbed on our bed. A horrible certainty touched my heart—he was dead. My scream, the explosion of the lantern, they hadn't woken him because he was dead, not sleeping, and I was alone on this ship. Completely alone.

Except for the thing with those bright, white eyes.

No, Sadira, Stop thinking that way. You can hear him breathing. Bannon is alive, and you are not alone. Whatever you saw—

A creak sounded from the passageway. I held my breath and shut my eyes.

One of the sailors. Or the captain. Bannon may have slept through everything, but I definitely woke someone. Any minute they'll knock, and ask what happened...

No knock. Another soft creak. Somewhere on the other side of the door, a silent, waiting presence lingered.

And it knew I was listening.

I don't know how long I stood there, holding the door closed, waiting for some horrible banging or a ghostly, keening moan. Schala sat on the floor staring up at me, nothing but a feline shadow limned in soft starlight. Nothing came from the other side of the door. My heart thundered in my chest.

After long moments, a creeping, cold touch spread over my back, just between my shoulders. Something like a hand, pressed flat against my skin.

Then, the sense of the *other*—whatever prowling entity had called me from my sleep—was gone.

I LAY AWAKE the rest of the night, tucked in Bannon's arms and curled under the quilts, but seized by a frigid, naked cold. I shivered until dawn, focusing on Bannon's slow breaths in and out to reassure me, and Schala's plush coat under my fingers. As the first gray light eked through the porthole, the sound of sailors and cabin boys stirring from their bunks and making their way to morning duties eased my worry.

I managed to drift down into a doze, until Bannon shifted beside me. He untangled his body from mine and stretched, then gave my shoulder a gentle shake.

"Wake up, pet. We've work to do above deck."

Exhaustion weighed down my whole body. I rolled onto my back to look up into his face, and he bent to kiss me. Then, though, his brow furrowed, and he stroked my cheek.

"What's wrong? You look pale. Is it one of your headaches?"

I hadn't had a migraine since Alaric's last, terrible manifestation crumbled into wasted detritus on the sand. I almost told him so, when all at once an unthinkable transgression occurred to me.

Lie.

Sacred serpent. *Lying* to Master was a cardinal sin. Under Alaric it had meant the harshest punishment, maybe even *days* of punishment, and ruthless, careless denial. Lie to *Bannon?* How could it even cross my mind?

And yet...

"Yes," I found myself saying. "I woke with such pain... my neck is stiff as stone."

Bannon frowned and smoothed back my hair. I closed my eyes and basked in the gentle touch, though a horrible seed of guilt sank into my heart.

"Sir, may I stay in here this morning? You can station me on the night watch instead. I will be fine by then."

"Very well," he agreed. "I'll send Ailsa down to you, too."

"I don't think Ailsa will have anything to help." I rolled onto my side again, pulling the quilt up to my

114

shoulders. "I can endure without troubling her. She'll have her own tasks, won't she?"

"Probably, but she is a healer, and healing comes first." With a final encouraging squeeze of my shoulder, he rose and began to dress. "She can spare the time to see you."

I didn't argue any more, already miserable with the lie. Bannon moved quietly about the tiny room, dressing and readying himself for the day. Then, strangely, he paused.

"What happened to our lantern?"

I didn't answer. He left, and I burrowed into the meager pillows, cradling Schala to my chest.

Despite my remorse, sleep came, and sometime later Ailsa arrived with a steaming mug of herbal tea of chamomile and willow bark. I sipped it obediently until she left, then slept again.

I dreamed of dark corridors and flickers of firelight just ahead of me, around shadowed corners and down ship's passageways running far into the distance, much longer than they should be. I dreamed of my mother calling me, *Seren! Come home, silly face!* Then I dreamed of eyes, poisonous green eyes and flashing blue ones, eyes that weren't human but those of horrible fiends. But only one pair—one pair in the black unknown ahead of me, shone like bright white mirrors in the gloom.

"Sadi?"

Bannon gently shook my shoulder. "Sadi, my kitten. Are you feeling better?"

As the dreams of ancient earth and the creaking sounds of old, abandoned ships sifted away, I propped myself on one arm and rubbed the sleep from my eyes.

"What time is it?" I asked.

"Afternoon. You slept most of the day." His mouth twitched down at the corners and he wrinkled his brow. "Usually that only happens with the worst of your headaches."

I flushed with shame, hoping he wouldn't see as I buried my face against the pillow. Schala wriggled from my arms with a quiet rumble of a growl and bounded down to the cabin floor to groom herself.

"I do think the headache's gone," I told Bannon, sitting up and giving my face a vigorous scrub. "Actually, I feel fine now. Ailsa's willow bark, probably."

"That's great." He rubbed a hand between my shoulders—the same spot where cold fingers had touched me in the darkness. I gave a little jump.

"Something wrong?" he asked.

"Bannon... didn't you hear anything disturbing last night?" I rubbed anxiously at my upper arm. "Someone came pounding at our door, and then in the corridor I saw... some *figure,* some shifting, unearthly figure staring at me. And my lantern burst, but you didn't wake when I screamed—"

He looped an arm around me and gave me a reassuring squeeze. "I have known veterans of war who suffer from grim night terrors. You sound just as they do when they wake."

"It wasn't a night terror." I stood and paced the floor. Pointing at the hook which ought to have held our lantern, I said, "If I'd only been dreaming, what happened to our light? It hung there yesterday, didn't it?"

Bannon scratched at his beard. "Yes... you're right about that, and one of the cabin boys *was* sweeping up a broken one in the corridor this morning. But could you have been walking in your sleep?"

I turned away from him, stung, wrapping my arms around my stomach.

"Sir," I begged. "I need you to believe me."

Bannon rose and came to me, resting his hands on my shoulders.

"Kitten. Whatever is happening, whatever is haunting you, I am here. You are safe."

"Am I, though?" A jolt of petulant anger coursed through me. "When my own Master thinks me mad?"

"I didn't say that."

Turning me around to face him, he took my hand in his. "Come up with me. Into the sun and the fresh air."

Querulous, I almost refused. His touch soothed me, though, even through my frustration. I relaxed and let him lead out into the passageway.

"I didn't dream the thing I saw last night," I insisted as we made our way above deck. "Whether you believe me or not."

He kissed my temple. "Sadira, if something *is* going on, you and I will manage it together."

As we emerged into the open air, I took a deep, calming breath of the cool, sea-salt air. The waves appeared calm today, leaving the rowers below to propel the *Drekakona* northward. The rhythmic sway and bob of the ship on the water apparently left several of the soldiers seasick, and now they lingered in clusters along the siderails with a distinct green cast to their features. At mid-deck, though, others had gathered in a ring, and the sharp sound of wood clashing on wood rose from the center of their gathering.

"A little bit of sparring to pass the time." Bannon led me to them, gesturing to the wide clearing of space they'd left for a pair of fighters. Mara and a man whose name I didn't know practiced their fighting forms with wooden axes and rough, unpainted shields.

We found a place among the spectators. Most cheered Mara on, with a few others hollering for her opponent. Bannon chose neither side, but applauded when Mara swept in low, exploiting an opening the other man left unguarded and thwacking him with the blunted edge of her weapon.

"The horde keep themselves busy wagering coin on the winner," Bannon explained. "It keeps them active while we're at sea and encourages diligence with their skills."

Mara deflected a blow, catching the man's axe with hers and wrenching it aside before striking him with her shield. He fell back, wheeling for balance, but lost it, tumbling through the ring of soldiers. They gave up another round of cheers and clapping, and handfuls of money traded hands.

"Could I try?" I asked as Mara helped her opponent back onto his feet.

The lieutenant eyed me with uncertainty. Bannon sized me up, stroking his beard, and then shrugged.

"I don't see why not."

"Captain," Mara said. "She's not trained with our weapons, nor I with hers."

"I want to learn," I told her. Without waiting for an answer, I crossed to the place the other man's axe had fallen when he lost, and picked it up. "You're obviously one of Bannon's best, Mara, so could you show me?"

The soldiers murmured in interest. A few of them whispered among themselves, probably deciding on betting odds. Out of the corner of my eye, I saw a few more coins being passed back and forth. The gambling didn't interest me, though; I just wanted to get a feel for their weapons, and their bear-like, aggressive style of fighting.

"The khopesh is not entirely different from your axes," I said, testing a few familiar motions with the wooden practice axe. "A hacking weapon. Many of our soldiers fought with one, using a shield, as you do. Alaric and I trained with dual blades, though, and a faster style. Better for striking from the flanks or the back. We were assassins on the battlefield, not duelists."

Mara and a few of the others among the horde wrinkled their noses. "Dirty fighting," the lieutenant spat.

"Maybe so." I flipped the blade in my hand and reached out to the man who'd just lost his bout, beckoning him to give me his shield. "It decided many battles, though, in our favor."

Even Bannon looked displeased.

"Never mind it," I said. As the soldier handed me the shield I dropped back into position. "I learned the one-handed style as well, though many years ago. It would be an honor if you would teach me your methods, Mara, with the Sanraethi blades."

I *did* wish to be taught the barbarian style of fighting, but I had an ulterior motive to my request. No doubt Bannon would show me if I asked him. It must be Mara, though. Bannon's right-hand officer and I were too often at odds, still too distrustful of one another. I needed to bridge the gap between us.

119

Mara didn't seem pleased at all by the prospect, though. She glanced at Bannon, then around the circle of soldiers, as if hoping someone else would wish to take the challenge instead. More whispers made their way through the watchers, and more bets were traded.

I didn't care whether they gambled on me or against me. I didn't even care if I won. I just needed to find a common ground with her.

"All right," she conceded, sliding into the ready posture as well. "I'll be keeping my eye on you for those cheap strikes, though."

Ugh... perhaps I shouldn't have mentioned my previous training.

We circled one another, and I took assessment of her posture. The barbarian shields weren't like those carried by the Vashtarens. Made of thick, hard wood and braced with bands of studded leather and iron, they were heavier and slower to wield, where most shields forged by Alaric's weaponsmiths had been taller, made of hammered metal. The one I held now was little more than a massive wheel sheared from the top of a tree stump and protected only my upper body. I'd have to keep careful watch for blows to my legs.

It didn't surprise me to find the axe heavier and more unwieldy than my khopeshes, even as a mere practice blade. My balance and footwork would have to adapt.

Mara swung in, aiming her blade for my knee. I backed out of the way barely in time—I'd let myself be distracted.

I retaliated with a swooping overhand swing for her side, and she stopped me easily with a shift of her shield. Her wooden axe came down on my bent leg, causing me to falter, and I fell forward to one knee.

"Augh!" I rubbed at the place where she'd cracked me.

"Watch your openings," she barked. "I could have taken your whole lower leg there."

Scowling down at my boots, I resisted a growl, and advanced on her again. I swung my axe overhead, then switched my momentum as I saw hers coming up to deflect, as she had earlier. Instead, I caught hers on the back side of my blade and tried to reverse the deflection on her. The axe didn't twist the way my khopesh would, though, and we wound up in a tug-of-war for control. She won, thrusting my weapon to the side, and coming at me to strike with the same shield bash she'd used before. Even though I'd seen her use the exact move, I couldn't make myself react in time, and she sent me staggering several feet back.

"Come on." She flipped her axe in one hand, jeering at me. "Are you so used to acting the part of the *assassin* you can't face a warrior head-on? You should have seen that coming."

I hadn't fallen out of the circle, so the combat hadn't ended. I regained my balance and faced off with her again, circling.

"You're wasting your time, Vashtaren."

She feinted at me and I dropped back, avoiding any attack of opportunity. "I'm not Vashtaren, Mara. You should be very aware of that by now."

"No? But you *fight* like one."

She lunged in low, aiming for my leg, and I met her, striking away her axe and pressing her for a shot at her vulnerable side. We switched positions, as though we were dancing rather than dueling, and I managed to tap her low on her forearm instead. As we both whirled to face one another, though, she caught me with her axe at the side of my throat.

"There's a reason we won the war," she snarled. "All your 'snake and scorpion' fighters—all your sneaking, backstabbing assassins—couldn't stand up to our ways."

I bit my tongue on an angry retort. "Exactly why I'm hoping to learn."

Pushing her axe back toward her, I dropped into ready position again, preparing for another go. Mara waved me off, though.

"Why bother? You're *not* Sanraethi, girl. You weren't raised in our ways. You're not *born* to be a soldier, like me."

"I *am* a soldier!" I snapped. A rush of heat shot up the back of my neck.

"You? You are a *concubine*."

She darted at me, swinging her axe at my throat. I caught her on my shield and thrust her back with a surge of fury.

Without warning, the *Drekakona* lurched hard to one side, catching us all by surprise. Soldiers in the ring bumped against one another, bracing themselves against each other or against supply crates. I danced a few steps into the pitch, catching myself with a quick shift to my back leg, leaning away.

Mara—carried by the force of my shield crashing on hers—fell backward, out of control, dropping her weapons. A few of the other soldiers reached out to catch her, but she stumbled out of their reach.

Before our very eyes, she hit the siderail and tumbled over it, plunging overboard into the sea.

Brantwijn Serrah

CHAPTER TWELVE

WITHOUT THINKING, I dropped my weapons and sprinted for the siderail after Mara. Firm hands grabbed me by the shoulders, stopping me, and I found Rayyan at my side.

"You can't," he warned me. "Sadira, you don't know how to swim."

I stared back at him, drawing a blank. Rayyan released me, saying no more, and grabbed a length of rope from a heap near the ratlines. It took him only a second to secure it at the rail, and, looping the free end several times around his forearm, he bounded up and over, diving into the water.

The soldiers and Bannon hurried to peer over the side. I did, too, sick with dread. Rayyan was right: I'd never learned to swim. Why would I have? In a desert surrounded by pale sand and white bone? What had I been thinking?

Only of recovering a fellow soldier.

Eye of Akolet, let her be unharmed!

Sailors called back and forth to one another. Two of the smaller deckhands heaved a pile of woven ropes to Torv, standing at the siderail, and Torv unrolled it into a long rope ladder. The ends slipped over a pair of rounded metal posts on the gleaming bannister, and he flung the other end down into the waves.

It took me a long, breathless moment before I located Rayyan, cutting through the waves with strong, purposeful grace. Once I found him, it wasn't hard to also see Mara, treading water several yards away from the ship. As soon as Rayyan reached her, he twined one arm around her.

I let out my breath in a painful groan. *Thank goodness. Oh, thank goodness.*

Despite the strange lurch of the ship, the sea was mellow. Had the swells been higher or more violent, would Rayyan have been able to find the lieutenant at all? With the help of his guideline, he started tugging Mara back toward the ship. The others continued watching, spellbound, but I had to turn away, hugging myself and urging my heart to slow down. Seconds later, Bannon's broad hand rested on my shoulder.

"Are you all right?"

I swiped away the first hints of tears on my lashes and swallowed back the lump in my throat before I faced him.

"Yes, my barbarian. I'm all right. Will she be?"

"I think so." He glanced over his shoulder, where Torv reached over to help Mara back up over the rail.

"I didn't mean to knock her overboard," I told Bannon.

"Sadira, that's not what happened. We were all here, we know it was the lean of the ship."

He gave me a reassuring pat and stepped away, joining the group now surrounding the rope ladder. He would have to check on Mara, of course, in case she'd been injured. I wandered away from the activity, drifting toward the stern deck, out of sight of the others.

An accident. The lean of the ship. But the waves are so still today. How often does a person get thrown *overboard on a calm sea when I'm* not *here?*

I touched the place where my collar used to be. The familiar feeling that had haunted me all during the siege of Alaric's castle returned. For weeks I'd suspected he'd somehow turned me into a living curse meant to carry his revenge out on his enemies. As it turned out, he'd bound the magic into my collar, knowing I wouldn't know how to part with it. His spell had broken when the collar was destroyed.

Or had it?

My fingers moved up to the scar along my jawline, left by the knife I'd used to slice through the leather. I climbed up to the stern deck and slid to my knees against the base of the ship's grand, upward-sloping tail. I crossed my arms atop my knees and rested my head on them.

After a moment, a short chirruping sound made me look up. Schala had appeared, and as I raised my head, she bounded up onto me, climbing to my shoulder and butting my cheek with her head.

"Why do these awful things keep following me?" I asked, as if she could understand me or provide an answer. "It's dark magic. It must be. Ghosts and black dogs and hanging ropes? Will it follow me all the way to Sanraeth?"

"Sadira."

Bannon climbed the steps up to join me. He rested his hands on his hips, gazing down at me, expression unreadable. Presently he gave a sigh and sat down beside me.

"I know that look on your face." He lifted a hand and scratched Schala's ears. The caracal gave a quiet, uncertain grumble, but she didn't shrink away from his touch. "You can't blame yourself for every spot of bad luck one of us encounters."

Bad luck. I ran a hand through my hair and remembered what Ashe had said. *You never, ever cut your hair while at sea. It's terrible luck, a great insult to the sea spirits.*

I seemed to keep crossing malevolent spirits somehow. In Alaric's case, he'd made sure he'd remain connected to me, even after death. The creature now haunting me, gallows keeper in the ratlines and shadow in the corridor... what had I done to call it upon me?

It isn't because I cut my hair, or any sailor's superstition. These things began before I even boarded the ship. So, is it really an angry sea spirit? Or has it followed me all the way from Vash?

I thought I knew the answer, and I didn't like it.

Will I ever escape the Ruined Sands, and Akolet's poison grasp?

"Sadi?"

I'd been ignoring Bannon. First lying, now ignoring.

"Sir," I told him. "I am... not myself. And I am not the slave you deserve, right now."

"I know." He traced a hand down my cheek. "But I'm not surprised. Everything you knew is changing. There is a big world beyond the confines Alaric kept you to. You once said you craved subjugation because you needed to be held down, or else fall to pieces. I see now what you meant."

"Yes." I brushed my fingers over my lips. "Yes... that's exactly how I feel. I don't know what to do with all this... *chaos* inside me."

"I have an idea," he said. "You wanted to learn my people's weapons and fighting style, and so you shall. It will require daily regiment and physical engagement. Will that satisfy the chaos?"

"Sir, no," I protested. "Not with Mara."

"Not with Mara," he agreed. "I'm not blind. You two get along about as well as two female wolverines."

"What is a wolverine?"

"An ill-tempered and very *un*friendly animal. No, Sadi, *I* will train you in the ways of a Sanraethi soldier. Are you willing to let me?"

"That would please me very much," I said. "But as it comes to assuaging my restless mind... I prefer other methods."

I hadn't realized how much I feared he might be losing interest in our arrangement, as we traveled farther away from the dark circumstances which had brought us so violently together. Bannon tilted my face to his, though, claiming my mouth with a kiss, and gave my upper arm a fierce squeeze.

"Oh, I had no intention of neglecting you in *that* regard," he rumbled. "For one thing, I won't have you sulking and worrying over things like sailor's superstition. So, you'll be getting a good paddling tonight, for sure."

His playful tone made me smile. A small relief cooled the heat of my anxiety.

"Now get up," he instructed, and I did, rising with him. He took me by the shoulders and looked me in the eyes, face somber.

"No more sulking."

His tone was not playful, not gentle or encouraging, not compassionate. He *commanded* me, and with that simple, succinct instruction he lifted the weight of the worry from my heart. I might not have any more answers about the troubling events, but at his direction, I didn't need any. He freed me from the burden of responsibility for these mysteries, and from the bottom of my heart, I gratefully obeyed.

"Very good," he told me, as though he read my mind. My expression must have told him all he needed to know. His kissed the top of my head. "Your training begins tomorrow. You'll start by serving shifts at the oars. I will inform the master of the rowers."

I twined my fingers with his and gave his hand a tiny squeeze. "Yes, Sir. Thank you."

"As for tonight, you'll be in the cabin by the time first watch is called. If I hear the page calling for watch and you are not on your knees before me, bare-bottomed and ready for your spanking, I'll double your punishment and there will be no play for the night. Understand?"

An impish thrill flickered in my chest. "Yes, Sir. I will be there as you say."

He kissed my brow. "Very good, kitten. I shall see you then."

I MADE IT a point to return to the cabin well before my barbarian and waited for him exactly as he'd instructed. I even went a step further, excited by a flutter of inspiration. He'd instructed me to leave my bottom bare, but he'd said nothing about other attire.

I located a black-and-red corset among my meager clothing, a well-crafted and enticing piece I'd always found daring and desirous, and a pair of fine black leather boots to match. Before assuming my kneeling position, I selected the riding crop from the small collection of toys we'd brought, and as I settled onto my knees, I held it out before me in both hands like an offering.

Bannon arrived not long after, shutting the cabin door behind him.

"Very good!" he exclaimed. "What initiative. You truly know your art, my kitten."

Joy lit up inside me. "I am eager to please you, Sir."

He ordered me to rise and bend over, spreading my legs and placing my hands one over another on the footboard of the bed. The first red-hot slap of leather on my buttocks jolted me with rapturous delight. All the dread and regrets of the day sifted away as my Master delivered my absolution.

Afterward, as I slipped into the blissful gratification of surrender, Bannon put me on my knees and gave me his cock to worship. He stroked my hair and crooned sweet words as I obliged him, and we took our time in a flirtatious dance of indulgence and denial. A careful game of cock teasing, drawing out our play long past midnight and culminating in his final, forceful, overwhelming climax. He plunged his wet cock in my mouth, thrusting deep until I struggled to manage him without gagging. As he came, I swallowed, overjoyed to bring him to such a finish.

"Show me," he demanded, and I opened my mouth to let him see I'd gladly taken it all.

At last, I crawled into his arms, and he lifted me into bed, covering me with the quilts and sliding in beside me. He kissed my shoulder, my neck, my earlobe, whispering, "Good girl. Such a good girl. My beautiful and obedient harlot."

I slept easily, and no terrible dreams—no horrid sounds in the night—troubled me at all.

When I rose the next morning, my rear end still stung from our excessive, attentive round of hard spanking, and my thighs were fatigued from kneeling to serve my Master's desires. Wonderful. I always loved play so rough I still felt it for days afterward.

I dressed to report to the rower's galley and looked myself over in the small, round mirror on our cabin wall.

Why rowing? I wondered for the first time. Bannon had already risen and gone to join the morning watch, but he'd arranged for me to work at the oars for the entire morning shift—a deeply demanding physical exercise. How would it aid me in learning to fight like a Sanraethi, though?

Schala bounded straight from the floor to my shoulder, leaning into me with a heavy, vibrating purr. The sudden weight made me stumble—she might be a kitten, but caracals are not simple housecats. Still, I scratched her chin and clucked my tongue at her, pleased by her company. She'd wormed her way into my heart.

I left the room and turned down the passage which would lead me to the rower's gallery. It was accessible by our deck and the one below us, and the entrance wasn't far. Any minute I'd hear the first rumble of the drum they used to measure time, as it called the first shift to their stations.

My next turn, though, led me to an unfamiliar passageway. I stared, confused, throwing a glance back the way I'd come. Had I missed an intersection?

The narrow hall behind me looked completely unfamiliar. The lantern I'd passed just a moment ago... had it been on the left, on the inner wall? Now it hung to the side of a porthole peering out into gray morning fog.

Was the porthole even there?

I turned a slow circle. How could it be possible? I'd gone less than a dozen yards.

Was I mistaken about the direction in the first place? I thought for certain there was an entrance to the gallery on this deck. Didn't Ashe show us?

It had to be nearby. I pressed onward and took the next corner moving toward the center of the boat, listening for the sound of the drum.

Silence. I didn't even hear the voices of sailors, or the thud of boots from the open deck overhead.

I took two more turns seeking an exit, a stairwell, even a simple door to an inner cabin. By now I should have reached some sort of open cargo or staging area or run into deckhands busy with their morning tasks. The *Drekakona* was not a labyrinth.

I couldn't make sense of any of it.

And I was lost.

CHAPTER THIRTEEN

FOCUS, SADIRA.

I paused to lean against the wall, closing my eyes and rubbing at my temples. *Is this another dream? More tunnels to explore, looking for that dying light?*

No. The smell of wood and resin, and the cool, flat, metallic scent of the early morning sea, shrouded in fog, grounded me in stark reality. The corridors were not dark, though they weren't precisely bright, either. Still, though, no beating glow beckoned me.

As though to drive the point home, Schala shifted on my shoulder, briefly gripping me with her claws before bounding down to the floor. I winced and rubbed at the place where it stung.

Come on, think.

A fearful cold came over me, and I fought the urge to shiver, forcing myself to remain calm. My stomach did a nervous flip, and goosebumps ran up my arms.

Schala wound around my ankles, purring harder. I let out a low sigh and resumed walking, and she bounded into step beside me. We wandered blindly for several moments more, until I wondered if we were even still on the *Drekakona* at all.

"Let's... try to go back," I said to the cat, as though she could understand me.

I turned on my heel—and found myself faced with a passage entirely different from the one I'd just passed through.

Wait. Did someone just slip around that corner?

Adrenaline shot through my veins. I scooped Schala up in my arms and strode quickly for the intersection of corridors where I'd just caught a glimpse of a person. When we turned the corner, the last flicker of a shadow disappeared ahead of us, around another bend.

Any last thought of reporting to the rower's gallery fled my mind. I picked up my pace, hurrying after the unseen figure, while Schala trembled, tense in my arms.

The next turn took us to a row of compartments I recognized: supply closets and cargo holds on the rear orlop.

The orlop? But I was on the middle deck! How could I have come down two whole—

Freezing in place, I caught my breath. Straight ahead of me, waiting before one of the closed doors, stood a woman.

Me?

Tall and blonde; almost regal in a Vashtaren ceremonial bodice and long, black sarong. Unmistakable, though, were the scrolling tattoos and brands and scars, a dark history on rose-honey skin.

My breath caught in my throat, and my heart nearly stopped. The figure wavered and shimmered, a smoky, ghostly shape aglow with faint silvery light. She—I—hovered before one of the doors, hand upon its brass doorknob.

The image lasted only an instant. As I let out the breath nearly bursting in my lungs, she disappeared, shivering from existence like pipe smoke snatched by the breeze.

The door...

Schala whined and struggled in my grip. I loosened my hold on her, and she slipped smoothly up to my shoulder. I approached the door, expecting the caracal to start growling or making her low, throaty complaints, but she remained silent.

The door had no marks on it. Nothing to denote any significant secrets. I lay my palm flat upon it and felt nothing strange; only smooth, old wood.

It will be locked, I told myself. My hand fell to the knob anyway, though, and when I tried it, it turned smoothly.

The door swung open.

At once, a sweet, pleasant scent greeted me, mingled with an understated whiff of dust. Medium-sized crates stood in stacks around the small, crowded room. A clean beam of morning sunlight poured in from a single porthole across from me.

Wasn't it still dark, though? Wasn't the sea still covered in fog?

I took a step into the room, searching for the source of the sweet smell. Something about it struck me with a vague familiarity. I couldn't place it, but it called up a warmth and excitement within me. An old, childlike delight.

The door swung quietly back on its hinges as I moved further in, searching for the source of the aroma. Atop one of the stacks, a crate stood with its lid askew.

"That's not right..." I lifted a hand and scratched Schala's chin. "Even if somebody had reason to pry it open, they wouldn't leave it like that. Whatever's inside could be raided by rats, or spill, or..."

Shrouds of thin muslin packing had been left unfolded and opened, revealing the contents inside. Round, red fruits the size of pomegranates, with a tantalizing, glossy skin; smaller, berry-like clusters, their color dark and shining like blood; round, mottled nuts, vaguely heart-shaped.

The sight of them, like sweet and precious jewels, made my mouth water. I plucked up one of the fruit clusters and turned it over in my hand, examining the three plump berries. I plucked one from its thin stem and popped it into my mouth. Rich, tart juice filled my mouth, and a shiver of pleasure ran through my whole body.

Cherries. The word came into my mind from somewhere deep in its hidden corners and forgotten shadows. *These are cherries.* Real *cherries. These are—* were—*Seren's favorite.*

I spit the cherry pit into my palm and then ate the other two. A soft moan of delight escaped me. I sat down on another stack of crates as I selected a fresh batch of cherries to nibble on.

And these are apples.

I selected one of the bigger fruits and sank my teeth into it. The apple was fresh and bursting with a refreshing, cool taste.

Schala uttered a throaty, curious mew, butting her head against my ankle before bounding up on the crate beside me. She sniffed at the fruits and pawed at the muslin packing but seemed to find nothing of interest.

As I finished the apple, wiping the juice from my lips, a flash of light drew my attention. I hadn't noticed it before, but atop one of the stacks of crates, an ornate mirror sat propped against the wall.

Alaric's mirror. The one I'd chosen to keep and wrapped in furs to protect.

What's it doing here?

I rose again, climbing up on a shorter stack to get a closer look. I recognized the small spots of tarnish along the edges of the glass, and one chipped corner. No mistaking it: this *was* Alaric's—*my*—mirror. Someone had unpacked it without permission and left it in this cargo hold, loose and unanchored. One good lurch of the ship and it could slide from its place and shatter to pieces.

What's sailor's superstition on that, *I wonder?*

I wanted to scowl and be angry. I *should* have been angry. I only had a few possessions to call my own, and I hadn't allowed anyone to remove them from their places, only to leave them in other careless, unprotected spots.

The emotions evaporated before they could come to a boil, however. I leaned closer, narrowing my eyes. My own reflection peered back at me, but I had the distinct impression there were other eyes on me. Cold, bright eyes.

You crush the eggshells to prevent angry entities from following you.

I touched the mirror. My reflection did the same.

The cargo hold had grown chilly around me. Had the porthole been open when I came in? The morning fog appeared to have seeped in around me, sending goosebumps up my arms.

My reflection wore a sharp, wicked smile. I brought my fingers to my lips, wondering if I wore the same expression.

My reflection's hand didn't move.

My heart skipped. I tried to pull away from the mirror, when all at once, gravity seemed to tilt. The room rolled; I thrust my hands out, overtaken by the sensation of falling forward, tumbling into the glass as everything turned upside down.

The reflection wasn't me anymore. Shocking, electric-blue eyes like storm lightning swallowed me. Hands pale as milk reached out for me, and icy fingers dug into my upper arms.

I ducked my head, and fell into a dark, burgeoning world of shadow.

Fog surrounded me. Black, rolling clouds, like thick smoke. It didn't smell like smoke, though: when I inhaled, the scents of crisp water and lush river plants rushed in on me. Cedar and something sharp, almost acrid. Tree sap?

No more hands on me. I still felt the sting of their strength, digging into my skin, though. And somehow, I knew I wasn't alone in this unfamiliar darkness. Somewhere in these swirling clouds, something reptilian—something *huge* and primal—lurked.

It's... female. Like... like the monitor lizards of the Ruined Sands. The females crouched to defend a clutch of eggs.

Thoughts bloomed in my mind unbidden, random, and alien. This had happened to me before: strange thoughts, strange words, finding their ways into my mind.

Somewhere in the miasma, a bird called. Hoofbeats thudded through grass, and as the images took shape in my brain I *stood* in that grass, a field of waving green stalks as high as my waist. I hardly had time to take it in when a trio of racing creatures, like antelopes, rushed past me. I caught the breeze off their flanks and the blunt, wild aroma of their hides.

A different world materialized before me. A still, dark blue lake on my left; a line of unfamiliar trees ahead. The tall grass of the field spread in all other directions, dotted with white clusters of flowers like bells. When the gentle wind sifted through them, they even tinkled and chimed in a soft, barely audible melody.

Here is your wood. Here are your people.

"What?" I glanced back and forth, turned in a circle, but I was alone.

Dae Caedan. Dae Catori.

Here, where the dragon sleeps.

My people. I waded through the sea of grasses, searching the shifting light and shadow of the trees before me. The scents of apples and cherries wafted toward me on the wind—and walnuts, yes, the round brown nuts were *walnuts*—and I paused, closing my eyes, inhaling with a soft sound of pleasure.

"Seren!"

My eyes flew open. '*Madrēn?*"

A hopeful thrill fluttered to life in my chest. I moved faster, picking up speed into a jog as I reached the edge of the wood. Clean sunlight and cool spots of shade danced around me.

Ahead, though... The skin prickled at the back of my neck. *The light. I know it... the blue light.*

Soon I was running, and the trees flew past. The daylight dimmed as the forest grew thicker and thicker around me. And yes—*there* was the light, glowing and pulsing, beating like a heart. And my mother—

But my thoughts started to scatter. The wild aroma of the trees and fallen leaves and deep, cool soil called me instead; the cry of rooks and the low, sweet hoot of an owl. There was a light ahead, but it was the light of a flickering bonfire, bright orange and wickedly beautiful, calling to me like home.

I came to a stop as the trees gave way to a clearing bathed in that feral orange glow: a pair of torches set before a stone altar, amid the tumbled fragments of ivory columns and the broken segments of a frieze. A fallen temple.

A woman kneeled before the shrine, naked except for a headdress and cloak seemingly made of the skin of one of the horned animals I'd seen before. As I watched, she sat upright and lifted her arms skyward, chanting in a language I did not recognize. Except—

Dae Catori, madrēn en tal...

Dae Catori. Those words, over and over. When I heard them, I closed my eyes and drew in a long, deep breath. They came to me like oxygen, new and replenishing, filling my lungs and heart and mind.

Here are your people.

When I opened my eyes again, I no longer looked upon the woman at the altar. I *was* the woman, bowing and supplicating myself, murmuring words I did not know. Spread before me, white chalk lines formed a geometric figure of seven lines and seven points, forming a star. Its prominent point, larger than the others, aimed directly at me. Small bones and stones and feathers had been arranged—*by these hands, her hands,* my *hands*—around the figure in some sequence. In the center, the familiar skull of a cobra grinned.

Thoughts of Akolet and Alaric, and the hideous seven-headed golem raised from the dead upon the Ruined Sands, filled my mind with terror. The eye, pulsing within the monster where a heart should be, rolling and wheeling to find me.

Me.

These hands. *My* hands.

While I balked at the symbols and implications, the woman repeated her genuflection, bowing low, chanting the ancient words, opening her arms to the sky overhead. Her skin was not like my skin; no dark tattoos or neat white scars. Even as I looked, though, pale, unblemished arms turned warm and tan, and patterns in some kind of deep, indigo ink like henna traveled upward, ringing wrists to elbows. Now I was a different woman, before the same altar, offering up the same words in a new, melodious voice.

Dae Caedan. Dae Catori.

The serpent skull smiled up at me, seeming to laugh and laugh.

Seasons passed—I changed. The moon and sun rose and set, and the hands outspread before me shifted: old hands; young hands; scarred; thin; bloodied; white; brown. Some painted, some inked; adorned with rings of bone or wood or woven leather. The tokens arranged in the seven-sided ritual space changed in shape and size, new collections replacing those of times passed.

All except the skull.

A serpent. Akolet, the sacred serpent. Lord of barren lands, poisoned people. Holy deity of the Ruined Sands.

These hands. My hands

A sharp pain struck my ankle, jolting me from the vision.

"Schala?"

The caracal kitten had sunk her juvenile fangs into my heel, tugging at me, her lambent green eyes beseeching.

"But... you are..."

The spell broke. A groan escaped me as the strange scene dimmed, and in a slow, dizzy spiral I tried to find myself again in the darkness.

I'm falling to pieces... I'm losing control. I feel mad. I feel...

Alone.

My knees struck the wood of the crate beneath me. I crouched on it, gripping the side of another crate, resting my brow against it. Schala butted her head against my hip and let out an unhappy miaow.

"What was that?" I whispered. "Who..."

Here are your people.

Serpent worshippers? Followers of Akolet?

I closed my eyes and shook my head. "No. I refuse to believe it. I refuse!"

I pounded a fist on the crate. Then, overcome, I struck it again, uttering a frustrated growl through my teeth, and again, wishing for the first time ever that Alaric were still alive, so I could punch him right in his smug face.

A scrape and a rattle caught my attention. I looked up just in time to see the mirror totter and tilt—then it was swinging down at me, and I ducked just in time to avoid it cracking over my head. It struck my back and tumbled, shattering on the floor.

"Eye of Akolet..."

Carefully I crawled down from the pile of crates, avoiding the glass. Schala followed me, and I pulled her down into my arms before she could bound onto the floor.

"More ill omens," I muttered at her, scratching her between the ears. "More bad luck. I don't think those eggshells worked at all."

When I stepped out into the passageway, I found the familiar corridors of the orlop awaiting me. I trudged my way to the ladder leading up to the middle deck, avoiding the rower's gallery, where the steady beat of the drum and the high-spirited chant of the rowers was well underway.

Should I tell Bannon? Or will he only think I've been sleepwalking, or that I've become hysterical?

I hated the thoughts, even as I indulged them. As I returned to our cabin, greeted by morning sunlight streaming in through the porthole, burning away the morning fog, I put Schala down and let out an irritated huff. I'd no doubt be missed from my morning work assignment, but I couldn't find the strength to care. Not after what I'd just been through. Not after what I'd just *seen*.

Not serpent worshippers. Please, let it not be true, let me not *be the child of more serpent worshippers!*

I sat on the bed, leaning elbows on knees, and propping my chin in my hands.

As the thin mattress sunk under my weight, something tumbled from the meager pillows and rested against my thigh. I picked it up—

A bolt of terror shot through my chest, and my throat tightened.

The skull of a desert cobra.

CHAPTER FOURTEEN

BY THE TIME I'd found Bannon and led him down to the orlop, the cargo hold with the apples and cherries had disappeared.

"It was here!" I paced the exterior passage, searching for the door. None of the storage spaces *had* doors, though. All of them, open archways, their cargo secured by ropes and nets. No doors, and no box of ripe red fruits and walnuts... no shattered mirror.

Bannon peered into each hold, searching for the room I'd described, but I didn't need him to confirm what I'd already seen for myself. The things I'd seen were not there.

I hadn't shown him the serpent's skull. I'd hidden it away in a canvas sack in our cabin, sick at the sight of it. Maybe when I looked into the sack again, the horrible token would also be gone, just a figment of a bad dream.

I sank to my knees, exhausted with the wild swing from confidence and conviction to crumbling doubt. My heart raced. I thought it might beat hard enough to break my ribs.

"The cherries..."

I spread my hands out before me. "Look, my barbarian... the stains are still on my fingers."

Bannon crouched, taking my hands in his. I closed my eyes, sure he would tell me he saw nothing. I even wished he would, and wished he'd become angry, and assign me punishment. Whip me, flog me, bind me and command me to kneel all night in bound contrition. I couldn't stand the restless, untethered imbalance inside me. I needed him to ground me again.

"Strange," he murmured, touching the dark blots of cherry juice on my fingertips. "But there could be no cherries nor apples in our cargo hold. Where would we have taken them on? They aren't native to the desert continent."

I met his gaze. "Alaric's mirror. Someone left Alaric's mirror there, too, unsecured. Why would they do that, Sir? It was certain to shatter, and it did."

Bannon rose, and with one firm hand guided me to my feet as well.

"Come," he said, and I followed.

He took me back to our cabin, and as I watched, he opened the trunk set at the foot of the bed. In it lay my furs, packed as I remembered. Even before Bannon unwrapped them, a sour, nasty anxiety pooled in my gut.

Alaric's mirror lay in my Master's lap, as it had been, swaddled in the safety of the thick blankets. It gleamed, intact, nearly perfect except for the chip at one corner.

I FLINCHED IN suspense as Ailsa let out a wild, fearless cry, raising her shield to block the axe her father lobbed at her head. The harsh *tock* of wood cracking against wood echoed across the deck of the *Drekakona*, as the medicine woman deflected the weapon, following the move with a lunge and swing of her own axe, bringing it up in a powerful arc to strike Bannon hard in the flank.

I'd already mentally calculated counter maneuvers and dodging tactics, when Bannon caught Ailsa's axe with the palm of his hands, avoiding the whack on the ribs.

"There," he said. "See the opening I've left her. A deadly mistake to make. The Sanraethi battle axe demands a strong swing and powerful momentum. Unfortunately, it can leave your entire body vulnerable if your opponent survives to strike back."

Ailsa dropped back, firming her grip on the weapon—only a blunted, wooden toy made for practice—and beat it against her shield twice in a gesture I'd seen other Sanraethi soldiers use, a sort of salute to their leader. The sailors had given us space on the mid-deck for our exercises, allowing me, Ailsa, Bannon, and Rayyan to review the first lessons in Sanraethi axe combat.

"Come, Sadira." Bannon reached out a hand to me. I obeyed, and Rayyan retrieved the wooden axe Bannon had thrown, returning it to him. Bannon put it in my hand, pointing out the position of my grip.

"Hold it here, and you'll have the greatest control. Too high, and you sacrifice reach and force. Too low, and you'll find no precision."

As I tested the weight and heft of the weapon, Bannon selected a shield—also a simple, undecorated piece meant only for training—and put it in my other hand.

"All right, now, you'll lunge and swing at her, slowly, and you'll see how she moves to block."

Our training with Bannon had begun at the noonday bell. After the maddening events of the morning, I'd barely had the stomach to finish a single bowl of fish stew in the galley before joining my Master at the mid-deck for instruction. Rayyan wore a deep expression of interest, but for the second day, a mixture of exhaustion and chagrin curdled in my gut, making it difficult to concentrate.

Normally physical training calmed me, though, centering me in the moment, grounding me in my own body. Similar, sometimes, to being bound with rope or disciplined with tests of endurance, like kneeling. If I hadn't felt so tired, perhaps I'd have enjoyed it more.

Bannon guided me through the motions, hands on my wrists. I closed my eyes for a moment, inhaling a deep breath as I appreciated the firm, broad frame of his body around me.

"Strike like this..."

He stepped forward with me and aimed the blow at Ailsa's left hip. We did it slowly, giving her ample time to step back, and she rebounded to touch her axe against my exposed upper flank.

"So, what can you do to cover yourself from such a counterstrike?"

Rayyan screwed up his face in thought. I considered the position of my body and Ailsa's, and frowned.

"If I were using my khopeshes, I'd follow up the first swing by pushing forward and slashing with both swords across her own exposed side when she advances at me."

147

"If you can switch motion quickly enough, you can do something similar here. But it's got to be fast."

He demonstrated, leading me, demonstrating a smooth switch from the downward arc to the forward press and parry.

"But what if she guards with her shield and then bashes you with it?"

After we'd stepped out the movement in careful practice, he left me and Ailsa to drill while he paired off with Rayyan.

Ailsa, shrewd and practical even at nineteen, kept her feelings about me mostly to herself. She'd never shunned me like the other barbarians, accepted my aid in times of need, and had even gone out of her way to tend to my injuries and illness. Her duties as healer took precedence over her personal feelings, and in that sense, we'd been able to work together without incident. At the same time, I had no reason to think she *liked* me, either. As we worked through our combat forms, alternating attacker and defender, her expression remained stolid, and she said little.

Better than trying to learn from Mara, at least.

As she lifted her shield to easily deflect an overhead blow, Ailsa gestured to me with a tilt of her chin. "You didn't make it to your shift at the oars this morning. If you think you're going to pull off swings like that, you really need to build up your shoulder muscles."

My grim worry stirred back to life with unsettling ease. "I... got lost in the passageways."

She arched an eyebrow. "Pretty hard to lose your way from the officer's cabins to the gallery. The stairway is practically right outside your door."

Gritting my teeth, I grumbled, "I know."

"Sadira was waylaid," Bannon put in as he and Rayyan took a pause. Ailsa and I relaxed our stances as well, setting down our shields. Ailsa was right: my arms burned from the strain, even from the simple wooden training axe.

The expression on Ailsa's face immediately made me worry she'd taken her father's statement to mean something salacious. "I was on my way to the gallery," I said quickly. "But then I... I fell into some kind of vision. The corridors all looked different, and somehow I found my way to one of the cargo holds."

Bannon's lips pressed into a fine, thoughtful line, but he said nothing. The disappearing cargo hold with the impossible cherries and apples troubled him, I knew. He'd seen the evidence—or at least *some* evidence—and couldn't be any surer about the mystery than me.

"Hm." Ailsa flipped her axe and caught it in a well-practiced motion. "You are sure this vision wasn't simply a dream? Perhaps you were sleepwalking."

"*No.*" I took up my shield again, ready to resume our drills. "Something led me to the hold. Something on this ship has been *haunting* me for days."

"Ah." She regained her own ready stance. "Do you know what?"

"No."

We played out the forms again, and she led me through a second sequence with a wide, wheeling spin.

"One of the sailors' *evil spirits,* I suppose," I said. "Ashe warned me about them after I sheared my hair."

"Yes, bad omens." She gave a dismissive wave of her axe. "After what happened in Vashtaren, and with your former king, I daresay the reason behind your bad dream is far more mundane."

I scowled at her. "You think I'm mad."

"I think you've endured a great deal of harrowing experience at the hands of a madman," she amended, gesturing for me to adjust my stance as I moved toward her. "And the echoes of that experience are the things that haunt you, not some silly, angry spirit dreamt up by an imaginative sailor."

Rayyan executed an admirable block as Bannon swept toward him with a powerful underhand strike. "Respectfully, Lady Ailsa, *you* of all people ought to trust Sadira when she speaks of dark magic and hauntings. You were right there with us when the black magician's revenant soul crawled back from the grave."

"Right," I agreed. "*Both* of you saw the monster. You saw the horrible eye at its center, like a festering mutant heart."

"Yes, we did." Ailsa ducked my next swing but missed my swift follow-up; triumphantly, I tapped the edge of my wooden axe at the inside of her knee, and she gave a little start. It pleased me to see the spark of approval in her eyes.

"Very good," she complimented me. "Let's reverse roles now. I'll advance—you defend."

I nodded and adjusted my form.

"Lord Khan possessed a dark power we never expected," Bannon admitted. "In Sanraeth, magic is thought of as only tricks and illusions, the workings of a festival entertainer. Divination and true enchantment are rare to find, and usually manifest only among the miracle workers of the church. Khan drew his wicked ability from an evil source, and yes, he tormented the whole castle for his vengeance. But I *saw* his mind, in the end. He *burned*. Whatever power he had left, that last, horrible monster devoured it."

"Perhaps, then, there are *other* dark spirits at work," Rayyan proposed, before I could say anything. I shut my mouth, biting my tongue against my own retort: the hateful sense of spite in the slamming of the doors back in the castle; the determination in the rigging ropes to twist me into my former master's beloved rope suspensions; the horrible, demanding force of the creature assailing our cabin door in the night.

Bannon might be certain Alaric's soul was gone for good, but I wasn't. Even if the black magician himself had passed into oblivion, the entity now haunting me felt somehow, *intimately* connected to him.

"But you have no enemies here," Ailsa assured me as she tested my defense with an aggressive push one way, then the other. She lowered her voice and added, "Don't let yourselves be swayed too much by sailor's lore. We are no longer prisoners in the poisoned world of the serpent Akolet. The Goddess Sherida shines upon us, seer of *all*. There are no wild spirits or angry demons out to wreak vengeance on you, Sadira."

"Then the cherries?" I asked. "The apples? What about the—"

I caught myself before I said *serpent's skull*. I still didn't want to admit its appearance to any of them. Not even myself, really.

151

Ailsa dropped her fighting stance, raising her shoulders in a shrug.

"You have lived an entire life on your knees. It may be some time before you no longer feel like a slave."

I relaxed my stance as well, setting down my shield and bringing a hand up to my neck. Her eyes followed the gesture, and I knew she was thinking of the leather collar just like I was.

No longer feel like a slave? She means no longer a submissive pet. No longer the beast in need of taming.

She thought me mad because of the cuffs and chains I chose to bear. Because of my love of pain... and my desire to be controlled.

I couldn't look her in the face. I couldn't look at Bannon, who must also see what his daughter, the shrewd healer, saw. Shed of my collar, released from my prison, here I stood, meeting my freedom with outlandish fantasy and paranoia. Visions of dark shadows leading me through a maze below decks? Mirrors toppling and shattering before me when all the while they lay safely in their crates, unpacked and unharmed?

"The stains from the cherries..." I mumbled.

Bannon rested a hand on my shoulder. "Perhaps they came from the resins or paints the deck crew have been using. You might have brushed up against something freshly coated with a dark treatment, and not known so."

I covered my face with my hands. "I'm not *mad!* I swear I have not just *imagined* these things!"

Ailsa came nearer, giving my bicep a gentle squeeze. "You would not be the first refugee from Lord Khan's kingdom to suffer such trauma, Sadira.

I've spoken with many like you, plagued with nightmares, and violent fits of anger or sorrow. Especially those who served in the harem. You have *no enemies* on this ship."

"I'm not *mad*," I repeated. "I'm not."

Am   I?

CHAPTER FIFTEEN

THE HAMMOCK OF ropes around me shifted and bobbed, alerting me to the approach of another climber. I'd been lying back in a shroud of ratlines above the foredeck, hanging off the forward archery tower. In the quiet dark of evening, this spot remained quiet and mostly undisturbed—which was exactly the reason I'd chosen to hide away there.

Bannon had found me, though. He hauled himself up toward my hammock from the middle story of the archery tower. He didn't move as easily among the ropes as I did, but he moved with a sure, strong confidence I'd recognize anywhere.

"Found the stargazing spot, have you?" He pulled himself up alongside my comfortable pocket of rigging ropes and rolled over to drop into place beside me. He must have already known about this calm resting place.

"It is quite a good vantage point." I shifted positions to give him more room and gestured at the speckled night sky above. "Clear and free of sails, ropes, spars..."

"I've always liked it myself," he agreed with a smile. Stretching an arm around me, he kissed my temple. "I might have guessed my kitten would find it and fit herself right into it. Ah, see? The heaven star is out tonight."

He pointed at a brilliant, shimmering star in the eastern sky. It shone pure and bright as a diamond catching the sun, and a faint corona of violet and pink and blue tinted the edges of its light.

"That's amazing!" I brought a hand to my mouth. "I've never seen such a gorgeous star before."

"Here at sea, it seems like the sky is always changing, and yet always constant and true, as it guides ships to shore."

I twined my fingers in the web of ratlines suspending us. The gentle sea breeze brought the scent of fresh salt and brine, and as it sifted through my hair it sent a gentle tingle across my scalp.

"Are you angry with me, Sadira?"

I gave a start, causing the ropes to shake. "Angry? No, Sir—"

"You have sworn always to be truthful with me. If you choose to break your oath, I suppose I can't stop you. But if I find out later you haven't been honest, I'll have to punish you severely. I want no lies between us."

My stomach rolled. His hand found mine and gave it a tight squeeze.

"Sadira. Please. Tell me if you are angry."

Why not demand it? I shouted inside my head. *Why not seize me by the wrists and hold me down,* wring *the truth out of me? You are my* Master!

I slipped my hand from his and rolled onto my side, facing away from him.

"*You* should believe me," I told him. "And what Ailsa said today while we trained... she thinks I can't be trusted to know my own mind, because I remain a submissive by choice. I told you, Bannon, I *won't* have you—have anyone—assume I am damaged. I *told* you—"

"You told me you feared you would fall to pieces," he interjected. "You crave subjugation because you need someone to implement control. Now you're finding ghosts in the ship's lower decks and stumbling upon mysterious lost cargo holds. Is there no chance Ailsa is right, and these are all nightmares brought on from Khan's torture?"

"No!" I snapped. "I am *not* insane!"

"Not insane. Distressed."

"I am not distressed, either!"

"Sadira." His voice dropped to a low, serious note. "Think of what happened when I bound you in the forge."

As if he'd burned me, my whole body tightened, and I clenched my fists around the ropes.

Bannon slid closer and wrapped his arms around me.

"Why won't you believe me?" I sighed.

"Ah, my kitten." He sighed. "I only want you to find peace. Peace with what happened to you... peace with whatever is troubling you now. I don't disbelieve you. I know that these things are real, in some way. But I don't think you're being haunted by anything but your own past horrors. You are so convinced it is dark magic, you miss the simple, mundane possibilities. Sleepwalking. Night terrors. Stains on your fingers left by paint or oils freshly applied to the wood by the crew."

I squeezed my eyes shut. "Please don't think I am broken, Bannon. I can't stand it."

He said nothing, but he gave me a long and tender squeeze, and kissed the top of my head. That was almost worse.

I lay in his arms for a long time, fighting the whirling storm of emotion within. Flashing anger like lightning; lonely yellow sorrow, so in need of touch and security. *This is what it is like,* I wanted to tell him. *This is the chaos within me that needs to be tempered. Needs to be constrained. Needs direction.*

I am a beast. Perhaps that is not so bad. Perhaps a beast is not a monster, after all. But a beast left loose to rampage really is *mad. It needs a strong hand to make it docile and give it peace.*

I stared out into the eastern sky, and the faintly violet halo of light surrounding what he called the heaven star.

Somewhere on the deck, voices called back and forth. I shifted to peek over my shoulder at Bannon, frowning.

"Do you smell—"

His eyes widened in alarm. "*Smoke!*"

We rolled over in our hammock to search the ship below. Horror hit me right in the stomach: clouds of smoke rose from the gangways down into the lower levels near the stern. Sailors sounded the alarm back and forth, and in teams they seized water barrels to pass along a brigade line.

"It's on our side of the ship!" I grabbed the ratlines to pull myself up. "Schala's in our cabin!"

Bannon braced himself in the ropes as they swayed under my movement, then followed me down to the bow. I moved faster, though, panic blooming in my chest—I couldn't shake the terrible image from my mind of the helpless caracal, cowering alone and afraid as fire devoured the wooden ship around her.

My feet hit the deck and I raced for the stern. Behind me, Bannon called out, but his words were lost in my frantic haste. One of the sailors in the brigade line called out to me, throwing a leather waterskin to me, and I caught it and slung it over my shoulder without stopping.

Fire response was something Ashe and the crew drilled into us almost daily. Of all the dangers at sea, flames might be the worst. If they spread too far, they could cripple a ship at sea, even a ship as big and as well-equipped as the *Drekakona*.

I reached the stairway and plunged into the dim interior. The smoke hovered in the air above me, acrid and somehow verdant, weedy, as though at its heart burned rich green creepers and vines rather than treated cedar and oak.

Down here the shouts came louder, and bodies plunged through the corridors at disastrous speed. The haze made it nearly impossible to see anyone. I managed to duck out of the way of a pair of cabin boys thanks only to the thump of their bare feet on the boards before they barreled out of the din.

Why don't I see any firelight? Are the flames below? Where is the galley from here?

The galley was on the second deck, but on the opposite side of the ship. The fire had broken out somewhere nearby, though, I was sure. The thickest smoke was stuck *here*.

There is *light. But...*

Blue light.

Blue fire, flickering somewhere ahead. Not dying this time. Growing. Feeding. Destroying the Dragon Maiden from within.

A crack and snap from the beams overhead gave me a split-second's warning. I jumped back a step just as they collapsed before me. Azure sparks and a cloud of ash flew up around me, making me cough. I uncorked the waterskin and sprayed about half on the glittering sapphire flames, reducing them just enough to make a strong leap over them.

Schala. Don't be afraid. I'm coming.

More and more flame surrounded me as I dashed for our cabin. The fire must have sparked from somewhere in the officer's cabins or the crew's barracks below.

Why blue, though? Someone's pipe, full of exotic flowers?

I didn't think so.

At last, I came to our door. Propping the water skin on my hip, ready to pour, I lifted one foot and kicked at the dark wood. It swung open easily, and I stormed into the room.

The head of the bed had caught fire, and the exterior wall had picked up the sapphire sheen thin flames. My eyes fell on the trunk at the foot of the bed, containing the only things I'd brought with me from Vashtaren. Those possessions weren't the reason I'd dashed down here, though; whirling in place, I searched for my caracal.

"Schala!"

I heard her low, miserable cry, but she was nowhere to be seen. I coughed harder, dizzy from the smoke.

"*Scha—*"

A pair of strong arms looped around my middle and pulled me from the room. I struggled against them until Bannon's rough voice in my ear commanded me, "No, kitten! You'll burn!"

"But the cat!" I rasped, even as I relaxed. "She's helpless, we can't abandon her to—"

"*Not* at the cost of *your* life!" he shouted.

Real rage flared in me. "She *needs* me!"

I wrenched from his grip and plunged past the growing blue flames climbing the doorjamb. His fingers nearly closed around my wrist, but a knot in one of the planks burst suddenly, sending up scorching cinders between us. Before he could follow me, the lintel gave way, crashing down across the doorway and blocking him.

I lifted my arm up to cover my nose and mouth as I searched the room once more. Where *was* she?

The fire snarled and snapped. It danced along the walls in undulating waves, and as I turned in place it seemed to me like serpent's coils. Rolling and winding, surrounding me, as I had always imagined Alaric's vile god surrounding me, closing in on me. It didn't frighten me, though. No... it infuriated me. In the flickering, shimmering flames I could almost make out its angular, snakish head and bright, blazing eyes, as if it would leap out to strike me.

"Come on, then!" I challenged. "Whatever you are, clinging to me like shed skin, come on out and get me! I'm *not* afraid of you!"

To my shock, the flames shifted. My hammering heart nearly came to a stop as what I had vaguely imagined as the head of a great viper *moved*. The amalgamation of blue flames swelled, and it wasn't a winding asp clinging and weaving around the room—

but the shrouded, moony-eyed silhouette following me from the shadows. Its shining eyes, white as the heaven star, turned to me like beacons, and staring into them I felt all the strength run out of me.

I fell to my knees, empty of all strength, but my anger remained.

"*Leave me,* monster!" I screamed. "I will not be your prisoner! I will *never* be anyone's prisoner *again!*"

The shape vanished, leaving only the flicker and dance of wild azure flames. Before I could duck aside, a rolling wave of fire came rushing at me.

"Get *down!*"

Bannon shoved me flat on my stomach. The heat of the fire stung my back but left me untouched. My barbarian let out a strangled cry above me, and as I rolled to look up and see him, my mouth dropped open.

"No, *no,* Bannon..."

His upraised arm had taken most of the burn, but blisters rose along the left side of his brow, down to his ear. He scowled at me, and before I could resist, he seized me around the waist, hoisting me over his shoulder and hauling me into the corridor.

"I *told* you to stay out!" he snapped, setting me down. The passageway's interior wall had been soaked down and he pinned me against it, giving me nowhere to run. I stared up at his scorched, reddened skin, lifting my fingers to it without quite daring to touch.

"Bannon... oh, my barbarian..."

Behind us, the brigade line had reached our cabin and flung heavy buckets of water over the burning entrance. A heartrending moan of a caracal reached my ears, and pain shot through my heart.

"Schala?"

161

I peered past my poor, injured barbarian, terrified of what might have become of the little creature, whom I'd left alone in the room. Had I allowed them both to be hurt? Would they both now bear the scars of my choices?

The brigade line had made it into our cabin now, and I'd lost sight of the man in the lead. The splash of water and hiss of steam filled the room, and bubbling black clouds melted into gray, thinning tendrils of smoke.

Schala's unhappy miaow sounded overhead. I looked up to find her—blessedly unharmed—moving swiftly along a beam above us. The fur along her back spiked up in fear, and her brilliant green eyes were wide with animal panic. Seeing her safe brought a rush of tears to my eyes, and I reached out my arms for her. She dropped down into them with a sad groan.

I buried my face in her fur, crying. "I'm sorry, Bannon... I couldn't leave her. I couldn't let her be caught in that, not alone."

Bannon let out a low, angry snort. When I looked again into his face, and the ugly burn there, my tears turned into sobs. I leaned into his chest, cradling Schala between us.

"Please forgive me. I just..."

To my relief, he lowered his arms, wrapping both of us in an embrace.

"And how do you think I'd have managed, if you'd been hurt?" he muttered. Anger still seethed in him, lacing his dark tone, but he kept his voice calm and even. "Did you not think of what it would mean to me, to lose you?"

I wiped away tears and didn't answer. I hadn't. The life of an innocent caracal had seemed to me as priceless as any wealth or valuables I could have taken from my former master's great treasuries. Schala had never done wrong by anyone, had never betrayed anyone or misled them. She was a pure and irreplaceable soul, and I could never leave her to such a horrible fate as burning alive. Me, though?

I would not have burned. I know it. I am fast, and I am smart. The strange intelligence behind those flames—that monstrous creature—I could fight it.

I could... stop it.

"I was all right," I tried to assure him.

"No." As he crushed me to him, his fingers dug into my back. His voice was hoarse, thick. "Sadi, don't you know how it would *break* me to lose you?"

A terrible pain rose in my chest. A fist tightening around my heart; a spike of guilt sinking deep into my lungs.

"I'm sorry," I said again. The hazy remnants of the smoke choked me, and I fell into a rough coughing fit.

The smells of wet, scorched wood and muddy ash surrounded us. Up and down the corridor, sailors called all clear. The last of the fire had been extinguished.

But the damage was done. The *Drekakona* could not sail on.

CHAPTER SIXTEEN

THE FIRE LEFT portions of the *Drekakona's* outer hull broken and exposed on the starboard side, and several quarters on the middle deck and second deck were uninhabitable until repairs could be made. Torv and Arne assessed the worst of the damage and determined even a few of the internal support beams would have to be replaced.

We could limp along—carefully—with the strength of the rowers, but only until we found a safe place to make port. Foul weather or choppy seas could be devastating now, and it might be weeks before we could take to the wide-open sea again. Of course, Torv assured us, it could have been far worse.

"Could've sunk us outright," he told a group of us over a breakfast of pork and eggs the next morning. "Could've taken the whole stern up in a conflagration or caught the sails. As far as shipboard blazes go, I'll be glad to lose a few officer's cabins and a storage hold of rice and hay, rather than half the ship."

None of the crew had been lost, either, though there'd been more than a few burns. Ailsa and the ship's surgeon had spent the whole night with members of the brigade line, managing salves, painkillers, and careful bandaging. When Ailsa missed the breakfast bell, I volunteered to take a tray of food to the physician's quarters for her. The sailors and soldiers there had started digging into their supplies of wine and mead for comfort. Flasks were passed back and forth while Ailsa packed away the remaining contents of her medicine stores.

"All in all, Torv is right," she told me. "Fires onboard can be true disasters. We're damn lucky."

Bannon's burns would heal, she promised. As I handed over her food, she slipped a familiar tin of salve into my hand, she added, "I'm sure you can tend to them just as easily as I."

Her gesture of trust overwhelmed me. I left the surgeon's quarters speechless, cradling the medicine in both hands, a mixture of guilt and pride teeming in my chest. Bannon wouldn't be burned at all if I hadn't defied him. Ailsa didn't know that, though, and she'd given me responsibility over his care.

Though the trunk containing our belongings emerged intact, the fire had left our cabin uninhabitable, one of the most seriously damaged and exposed to the open air. Bannon and I had been moved to a temporary lodging in one of the crew's quarters, normally shared among four of Arne's sailors. The sailors cleared out and found other arrangements, perhaps unwilling to intrude on the Red Bear and his concubine.

I thought for certain Bannon would banish me from his bed. I'd defied him in a spectacular manner, and worse, he'd been injured because of it. Surely, I'd be assigned a place among the regular crew, forbidden from his intimate company for days. Maybe weeks.

Maybe for good.

As punishment he assigned me three days of celibacy. Three days forbidden to serve him, even to touch him. Denied physical connection.

He might as well have cast me out, I sulked as the command was handed down. *I hate celibacy.*

"You must understand what it would mean to me, if I lost you," he explained, extinguishing my resentment on the spot. "You might have left me forever when you ran into that fire. Left me without the smell of your hair. The touch of your skin. The taste of your mouth. I need for you to experience that grief in some small way. I want your skin to feel the absence of mine. I need you to know my pain."

He gave me low, menial tasks: cleaning away the ash and debris from the fire; scrubbing the filthy, soot-stained corners and cracks on hands and knees; hauling materials for the shipwrights as they cleared away the wreckage and prepared the area for repair. No one was to help me. He refused to allow even Schala to accompany me during my work times, confining the cat to the bunkroom or the lower cargo holds, where she could do her own job of catching vermin.

In the last hours of my second day of punishment, though, as I scratched and plucked at a charred, stinking mess of a burnt resin cask, Bannon surprised me. He cornered me in the supply hold and pinned me up against a cluster of barrels, greedily seizing my clothing and tearing it from me.

"See how you rule me?" he rasped between harsh kisses, fingers digging into the soft curves of my buttocks as he lifted me from my feet. "I can't even abide by my own rules. I can't stand the thought of not touching you, not holding you, Sadira. Don't you ever, *ever* leave me like that again!"

We made rough love, clumsy and desperate and beautiful. And I apologized, over and over, tears streaming down my face as we found our climax together.

THREE DAYS AFTER the fire, we made port in a sandy bay surrounded by chalky white hills. A crowded village of squat, square domiciles and red clay roofs climbed rocky embankments, and tall palm trees swayed in the winds, heavy with a reddish fruit I didn't recognize.

"It's not one of our normal supply ports," Ashe confided to me and Ravyan as we helped prepare the rigging lines and the anchors. "Captain might be familiar, and probably some of the old salts like Torv, but I've never been here myself."

I stood on the bow gazing at the unfamiliar landscape. Lush green flora spilled over the tops of the craggy rocks, dotted with vibrant blooms in violet and pink. Children played along the white, sandy beach, beautiful young figures with olive skin and curly mops of dark hair. Along a stony reef, older folks caught enormous red crabs and stuffed them into baskets, and glorious, pale pink sea birds wheeled and cried overhead.

"Is Sanraeth like this?" I asked Bannon as he approached behind me. I recognized the tread of his footsteps, and his wonderful, reassuring scent.

"Nothing like this." He rested a hand on my hip. "Sanraeth is all grand blue peaks capped with snow, and fresh, green forests for miles around. We'll sail upon it through an icy fjord, and pass through the gate of Boga, a grand old ancient sculpture taller than Lord Khan's castle by half. A pair of godly statues flanks the passage through two giant boulders rising up from the waters."

Snow? Fjord? I didn't know those words. I didn't interrupt, though, and leaned my head against his chest as he spoke. The ban on touching now lifted, I basked in his warmth.

"Come, then." He backed away from the ship's rail and took me by the hand. "Let's find out what awaits us in port. Since we're here, we should find lodgings off the ship, and spend our time out of the way of the shipwrights."

I followed. Before we descended the gangplank to the dock, Schala bounded up to sit on my shoulder, and I stroked her silvery head.

The crab fishers approached us the instant we disembarked, offering us the fresh catch in exchange for gold. The price was good, and the crabs smelled fine and briny in the cool beach air, but Bannon gave them a polite dismissal, letting them know the ship's cook would no doubt come looking for good crab in short time. As we ascended to the path from the sandy shore up toward the city, some of the children came racing up to see us, wide-eyed and excited.

My skin prickled. They'd come to stare at *me* and my tattoos. One of the boys reached out to touch a twining red design on my arm, making me flinch away.

"Stop it!" I snapped. The boy laughed as though I'd shown him some wonderful trick, though, and he and his friends ran away, calling out in a different language, wheeling like the sea birds above.

Bannon kept his mouth shut, but I caught the quirk of amusement tugging at his lips.

"It isn't funny. People gawking at me and laying hands on me without permission."

"You're right," he conceded. "I apologize, kitten."

I couldn't escape the stares, though, just as I'd expected. When we came to the first few buildings marking the edge of town, people looked up from their chores in the dooryards, each face filling with confusion or curiosity when they fell on me. I put my shoulders back and held my head high, unwilling to let anyone see me upset by it, but inside, uncharitable thoughts stewed like a brooding storm.

The worst part was I didn't feel the shame or disdain other people seemed to when they beheld the marks on me. I'd had no choice in bearing Alaric's strange artwork, but I'd grown accustomed to it. Even, in some ways, proud. What did it mean that these fierce and primal sigils, which turned so many decent people away, held a personal, secret beauty to me?

Just another sign of the monster Alaric made me. The dark beast, reveling in dark mementos.

The marketplace was better, with most people too interested in their shopping to take notice of Bannon or me. Some of the crew had arrived ahead of us, and I saw Ashe and three of her mates huddled around a fruit stand selecting bright, swollen melons and handfuls of the reddish things from the palms.

"Dates," the vendor told us as we approached and I picked up one of the fruits, examining it with a quirk of my brow.

"You'll like them, Sadira," Ashe assured me. "They're quite sweet."

Bannon passed the vendor a coin as I brought the date to my mouth and took a bite. The meat was softer, chewier than I'd expected, but as Ashe promised, deliciously sweet. As I nibbled away at it, Schala reached out one curious paw to bat the pit.

"I love seeing you smile like that." Bannon stroked my hair as I finished the fruit. Returning his attention to the vendor, he drew a sack of coin from the satchel at his side to purchase more of the fruits, along with some of the melons and a flask of some local liquor.

"Is there an inn here?" he asked as the vendor handed over the purchases. "Our ship will be in port for a fortnight, I expect, and I'm eager to spend the time on shore instead of in cramped bunks."

"You'll find the rooms at the inn aren't much bigger," the fruit vendor said. He pointed down the crowded narrow, cobbled street. "Down at the end, under the sign of a ram. They rent out rooms by the day and serve some excellent food as well."

Bannon flipped him another coin. "My thanks."

The inn under the sign of the ram looked like an old building, its white clay walls showing respectable cracks of age. An old man in an apron, with long, curly hair nearly the same color as Schala's fur, stood outside sweeping the stoop.

While Bannon conferred with the old man, I drifted across to a shop door flanked by vivid ferns. *Probably an apothecary,* I mused as I fingered a bright, coral-pink bloom standing up from the wide green fans of an unfamiliar plant. The flower smelled strong and sweet, almost as saccharine as the date, and a pair of bees bobbed about its fellows, pausing to crawl across firm, bright petals.

"I saw flowers like these in Vashtaren sometimes," I told Bannon as he joined me, evidently finished with his conversation. I touched another one of the blooms as the bees abandoned it. "Only these are so much more fragrant."

"There's that smile again." He crooked a finger under my chin and touched his thumb to my lips. "You look happier than you have in days, my kitten. I thought that child with his grabby hands would have you in a prickly mood all morning."

I frowned. "I suppose not. At least there've been no others trying to snatch at me or throwing rocks and rotten eggs.'

In truth, I thought it was the distance from the *Drekakona* improving my mood, and the promise of spending our time in port onshore instead of below decks. Each new day on the ship seemed to bring me more trouble, and more reasons for Bannon and the others to think I might be out of my mind. I still hadn't told him about the serpent's skull, or the impossible vision I'd seen in the flames—*blue* flames, like the blue light in my dreams.

The sailors muttered about the unusual color of the flames, and the source of the fire remained a mystery to all. Arne had finally decided some exotic treasure from the war, one of the foreign spices or oils, had combusted under bad storage conditions.

I doubted it was so simple.

"What will we do while we're here?" I asked, hoping against hope for nothing but sunshine, good food, and lots of decadent, loving sex. He grinned at me, as though he could read my mind.

"Staying on land gives us an excellent opportunity to continue your training with the axe and shield.

Tomorrow, I think, we'll find a place where we can practice freely, and start you out with a real weapon instead of the wooden ones. It would please me, too, if you would teach my daughter the use of your sickle swords."

"I've never taught someone to fight before."

"Consider it a trade for what she will teach you."

Not a carefree retreat, but I could be happy with time spent in training. Bannon took my arm and turned me away from the fragrant flowers, toward the inn and the scent of cooking food.

Long, dry fingers seized my wrist from behind, jerking me back. We spun to find a short, white-faced woman in the door to the flower shop, staring daggers at me. Schala hissed, putting up her back, claws pricking my shoulder.

Though the blood had drained from the woman's face, high, bright spots of color rode her cheeks, and she clenched her teeth so hard I thought she must be causing herself terrible pain. She wore a simple green shawl which had dropped loose from one shoulder, and in her free hand she gripped a short-handled knife with a waving, curvy blade.

"*Traitor!*" she shrieked, raising the knife over her head. I tried to jerk away but she held onto me like iron, screaming as she attacked.

Switching my balance, I sidestepped, avoiding her forward rush. Schala bounded down to the street and swiped at the woman's ankles, uttering a wild yowl. The woman swung again, and I ducked, thrusting my palm forward in a flat strike up into her ribs, catching her unaware and stunning her—she released my wrist. Bannon grabbed the hand with the knife and twisted it behind her back until she dropped it.

"*Traitor!*" she repeated, jabbing a finger at me. "*Apostate!* The loyal people of the serpent will see you punished for your betrayal! Akolet will have his vengeance, you unfaithful *whore!*"

Chapter Seventeen

My mouth dropped open. Schala yowled again and lunged to bite the woman's leg but caught a swift kick to the ribs.

Without thinking I swept in and grabbed the woman by the throat, squeezing hard. "Don't you *dare* touch my cat!"

She gurgled a weak reply, and I tightened my grip. At last she relaxed, ceasing her resistance.

"*Good,*" I spat as I released her. Others on the street had stopped their business and stared at us, pricking my every instinct, making me wary. Another attack could come from any side, at any moment. I stooped to seize the knife she'd dropped.

"What are you here for?" Bannon growled. The woman gave a simpering cry as he ratcheted her arm back a little further, putting on pressure. "Who sent you after Sadira?"

"After who?"

Her voice, harsh and high and shrill only seconds ago, flattened into a quavering, fearful confusion. The wild look in her expression brought a knowing dismay to my gut.

"She doesn't know." I took a step back, scooping Schala into my arms. Immediately the caracal climbed up onto my shoulder and uttered a growl at the woman. "Like the men in Alaric's castle who lost their senses. The Vash boy and Jarl. She doesn't know what she did."

Bannon narrowed his eyes. "Are you sure? I see no stigmata on her."

"I'm sure," I muttered, overcome by cold grief. It really *was* happening again, wasn't it?

The woman showed none of the signs of possession, as Bannon said. When Alaric's foul spirit inhabited his temporary hosts before, he left them marked with a horrible, crimson affliction around their eyes, turning them a vibrant, swollen red, and making their tears stream down like blood. This would-be assassin looked blanched, and she trembled with violent fear, but she showed no horrible mark of Alaric's dark possession.

Still, she stared at us both, looking from me, up to Bannon, then to me again.

"I didn't mean to... I just... I saw you there, looking at the firebird flowers and then—"

I turned away in disgust, unable to listen to more. Bannon released the woman and moved to my side, resting his hands on my shaking arms.

"Hush, now, hush, kitten." He tilted my face up to his, searching my eyes, and pulled me into an embrace. "It's all right, love. He's not here."

"Is *this* only the result of an anxious mind?" I pushed away from him, burning with frantic, riotous alarm. "Did I imagine it, Bannon?"

"Sadira—"

"You should have believed me!"

His face fell, and his shoulders slumped. Rubbing the back of his neck, he glanced back and forth, considering the woman who'd attacked me, the old man with the broom outside the inn, the handful of shoppers, all now staring at us. Before he could say anything, I whirled away, storming down the cobblestones.

"Sadira!"

Jogging to catch up, he fell into step beside me. "Sadi, I don't know what to say."

"You could apologize," I suggested, surprising myself with the fierce defiance in my tone. I hadn't spoken to Bannon so boldly since our first uncertain days together, when neither of us could decide what to do about the other.

He took me by the arm and spun me to face him. Jolted by the motion, Schala bounded down to the ground.

"You are right, Sadira. You *were* right. I apologize for failing to hear you."

"Good." I started walking again.

"Where are you going?"

"Away!" I told him. "It's too... too *tight* here. Too many corners and avenues, too many doorways where some other surprise can jump out at me with one of these."

I held up the knife. I'd forgotten I still held it clutched in one fist. I hadn't even wondered why the shop woman would have such a thing or where she might have gotten it. The curvy blade certainly wouldn't be any good for cutting flowers or slicing herbs, or anything botanical. I handed it to Bannon, who slipped it into his satchel.

Once he'd stowed the knife, Bannon took my hand in both his own.

"What do you need, Sadi? How can I help quell the turmoil?"

I stared at him, unsure of the answer myself. Schala wound around my calves, giving me a gentle butt of her head and striking up a loud, rumbling purr. She, too, seemed to sense the rising panic and agitation inside.

Tie me up? Lash me until all this terrible energy burns away? Strap me to bed and fuck me into a stupor?

I dug my fingers into my hair. "I just want to get away from here!"

"All right."

He took my wrists in gentle hands and guided them back to my sides. Touching my temple, he murmured, "Look at me, kitten. Just look at me now. If you trust me, I have an idea."

A mean urge almost made me demand to know how I *could* trust him, when he'd dismissed my fears so easily before. I managed to keep my mouth shut, though, and merely nodded my assent.

He led me down the village's main street, back to the beach path. Down by the water, the children looked up, eager perhaps for another chance to jabber and grin over my appearance, but after a quick search in the opposite direction, Bannon steered me away from them. Instead of heading for the *Drekakona,* he took us to where the sandy shore gave way to a hilly rise of speckled gray rocks.

We made our way up to a smooth rise of bright, low scrub and mossy greenery, where Bannon paused again, looking back and forth. Just ahead, a lush stand of trees seemed to mark the beginning of a tropical forest.

Glancing over my shoulder, I saw the children give up their interest in us and return to their other activities. Once we reached the edge of the trees, we'd be out of sight of the beach and the road into the city, though close enough still to hear the vendors crying back and forth and the birds calling overhead.

What does my barbarian have in mind?

Bannon led me to the shady shelter of wide, fat trunks and large, waxy leaves. I reached out to inspect one of the spotted, jade-colored fronds, when his first command cut me off.

"Strip."

"What?" I spun to face him, frowning. "Here? We're not even out of earshot of the people on the beach."

He returned my gaze with a serious, unwavering expression. "I know. We're going to play a little game, and you get to be the bunny. Bunnies don't wear leggings or bodices or boots. So, *strip.*"

The tone in his voice brought a quick shiver to my spine. Underneath my simple jerkin, my nipples tingled and stiffened. Strip, here? Where it would be so easy for someone to come upon us? What if traders or lumber workers moved through these woods?

Keeping my eyes on Bannon's, I slowly stooped to obey. Schala hopped down from my shoulder as I slipped off my boots, then my belt and leggings. Bannon observed me, intent, as though he felt no need at all to watch our surroundings or worry about interruption.

After all, I realized, beginning to understand this exercise. *I may be the bunny, but* he *is the bear. What fear does a bear have of whatever lies in the woods?*

I shed my jerkin and the simple breast band underneath, and at last my simple underthings. I folded them into a pile and stood to hold them out, uncertain what he'd want me to do with them.

He tipped his head toward one of the trees nearby, whose roots arched up from the soil in one place to create a sort of crawl space. I hid my clothing there, crawling on hands and knees in rich, sweet-smelling soil, and called Schala into the hiding spot with them. When she'd settled on top of the clothing, I crept back out and climbed to my feet, utterly naked before my Master. My studded nipples gave a little throb against their hard metal barbells, flush under his scrutiny, and the first warm stir of wicked arousal bloomed in my belly.

Bannon sauntered in a circle around me. "Still agitated, little bunny?"

"Yes," I admitted. "Though your idea of distraction is proving effective, with you baring my body to the world."

"Aren't you used to nakedness by now?"

"Not like this."

He resumed his place in front of me and rubbed at his chin. A spark of something hungry and dangerous lit up his eyes, and a grin spread across his face.

"Okay now, pet. Run."

Again, I stared. Run? Run where?

When I didn't move, he lunged at me, turning me around and striking me on the behind. The hot flash of his palm on my ass shocked me into a quick stutter-step forward.

"Go on and run," he repeated. "Run fast and hide, because the Red Bear of Sanraeth is going to hunt you down, and if he catches you..."

A flare of wild exhilaration overtook me. Instinct blazed to life, and all at once I knew *exactly* how to play this game my Master had in mind.

I lunged into a sprint and ran.

My heart flew into a fast, ferocious beat, and all the hectic, ugly energy in my limbs and stomach and head went to work, speeding me on. The shady breeze, faint with the distant scent of the ocean, teased and tickled my naked skin as I ran, making me vibrantly aware again how easy it would be for me to chance upon some local on a stroll through their familiar forest. Despite the events of the morning— or maybe in part, because of them—wild, breathless laughter bubbled up inside me.

Still agitated? Yes. And my Master knew when fear and agitation overwhelmed me, it took action, strain, stimulation, release to purge them from my head and my heart. The pure, primal joy of burning energy and pounding blood in my veins.

Today, a race between predator and prey.

I ducked between enormous bushes and huge, fragrant flowers the color of bright, ripe pomegranates. Behind me, Bannon's voice carried through the trees.

"You won't evade me long, kitten! I've tracked prey for miles across snowy mountains and valleys! I'll have your ass before the hour's out!"

I spotted a cluster of boulders beside a squat tree and darted behind them. Two of them formed a shadowy passage just above the ground, and I crawled into it, lying on my belly to watch the direction from which I'd come.

The soil's too soft and springy here. I must have left obvious footprints and he'll find me for su—

A hand closed around my ankle and dragged me from between the rocks with perfect ease. I whipped onto my back and Bannon descended on me, straddling my hips, and pinning my wrists over my head. My heart hammered in my chest as he drew his big hunting knife from his belt.

My thoughts immediately flashed back to our conversation in the torture chamber, and I was not afraid. Beneath the thrill of the chase, trust ran steady.

Bannon flipped the blade to show me the blunt side before he lowered it to my chest and drew it across my skin. The firm, cold pressure of metal on my flesh sent up a hot, dangerous desire. So near to drawing hot, crimson blood, and yet no danger at all. I rolled back my head with a moan.

"That's one," Bannon whispered. "I think I'm going to finally claim your ass when I win this hunt, Sadira. Be ready."

Sweet, lustful heat ran through my body. Bannon released me and rose, helping me to my feet.

"Find a better hiding spot this time," he warned with a grin, and slapped my behind again.

I hopped into action, throwing a glance over my shoulder at him, returning his smile. The coiled tension and fear had gone, burned away by a liberating joy. He might catch me out, he might even threaten me with the thrill of pain, but underneath the wild struggle, I knew all I had to do was speak the word, and the game would end.

But I don't want it to end. Is this what I've been missing? This purge of all my uncertainty and doubt, the exorcism of ugly fears... a return to the most primal, most invigorating contest of wills. A clash of strength. His inevitable domination.

Yes. I had needed this. Needed to return to the simple, beautiful beast inside, and the hunter who would take her.

I moved in a zigzagging pattern this time, trying to obscure my tracks where I could find solid ground, stony spots peeking up from the soft, cool dirt. In a moment of inspiration, I selected one of the low, squat trees and scaled its smooth trunk, climbing along through interlacing boughs.

"Too easy, kitten."

Bannon had caught up again and spotted me under the leaves. I laughed and tried to climb higher, but he snatched me down easily and backed me against the trunk. The knife appeared, and he drew the blunt edge down the side of one breast, making me shiver and arch against the tree.

"Two." He leaned in to kiss me. "Next time I catch you, I'm going to put you on your hands and knees, and the weapon I draw will most definitely *not* be harmless."

He sheathed the knife and raised his fingers to my chest, running them down my body. His hand slipped between my thighs and he found my clitoris, leisurely rolling it under his fingertips, teasing me into another soft, yearning moan.

"I'll wring a sweet, wet climax from you first," he promised, making it almost a threat. "So then you'll be even tighter when I thrust my cock in you. So tight, Sadira... you'll be feeling it for *days.*"

182

I let out another senseless laugh, simultaneously giddy and menaced by his tone. "How do you know I won't turn the tables on you? One good, swift kick, and *you'll* be the one feeling it for days."

"You can try." His grin widened, showing me his teeth, and I snapped my own at him in reply. "You should know, you only make me harder when you fight me."

He seized my hand and brought it to his crotch. The shape of his cock strained against the leather of his breeches, unmistakably ready. I gave it a vicious squeeze, but that only seemed to rile him up more, as he gave a sharp bark of laughter.

"Go on, then," he said, letting me go. "Last chance. Run, run, little bunny... don't let the big, bad bear catch you in his jaws again."

I flew from him this time, digging deep to pull ahead. By now my body was filthy with smudges of dirt and green stains from the moss; my forearms and the balls of my bare feet stung from scraping stone and rough tree bark, and my buttocks smarted from his spankings. I'd outrun him this time for sure—he'd have to *earn* the prize he felt so sure of, and maybe if I got the upper hand, I'd take something sweet from him instead. Thoughts of pinning *him* to the ground, straddling him and taking *my* pleasure as I liked, thrummed through my mind, and filled my belly with delicious, flagrant lust.

He'd chased me deep into the forest now, and nearly all the sunlight had been choked out by the canopy of leaves above. In the last bright fingers of it, I spied a wall of rock and a round, dark cave. I made a sharp turn for it, and coming closer I found it wasn't a cave, but a tunnel. The sound of splashing water and the golden glow of open sun beckoned me from the other side.

I came through to find a mossy rise, overlooking a pool of the bluest water I'd ever seen. A waterfall poured into it from atop a shelf of glittering white stone, covered in an emerald blanket of smooth, soft grass and coils of fern. Honeysuckle and bougainvillea perfumed the air, and directly across from me, perched atop the falls, a brightly colored peacock stared down in comical, offended surprise.

"It's gorgeous..."

I moved up the smooth rise above the basin, caught in wonder. The breeze sifted through the leaves, making the sunlight dance. A sense of perfect calm, of welcome, filled me.

"It is," agreed Bannon's voice behind me. His warm, heavy hand came down on my shoulder. "And that's three."

CHAPTER EIGHTEEN

I WHIPPED ON my heel with a shriek and a laugh, twisting free of Bannon's grip to run farther ahead up the rise. He sprinted after me with a spirited shout, and before I made it to the rocky shelves of the waterfall he dove for my legs, taking us both to the ground. We rolled in the plush, cool moss, batting and wrestling with one another, each fighting to be on top.

"You lost, Sadi! Now be a good girl and present that bottom!"

"What if I'm not so good today?" I taunted. I shifted my hip, seizing the momentum, and pushed myself into a sitting position atop him. As he'd done so many times with me, I seized his wrists and pinned them over his head. He struggled and squirmed, until I ground my naked sex against the stiff shape of his cock.

"*Unh...*" He arched his neck and closed his eyes. "Willful little bunny, are you?"

"I'm not your *bunny*. I'm a *she-cat,* remember? Your kitten, with teeth and claws!"

"Keep this up, and you'll have a prettily pinkened and smarting ass before I have my way with you."

He struggled beneath my grip. I bent to kiss him, making it a vicious tease, nipping his lower lip and making him shout.

I gave a triumphant cackle, but my victory proved short-lived. He planted his heels on the ground and swung his hips up against me with full force, disrupting my balance. As I struggled to keep my position, he threw us into another roll, and we bounced down the green slope until we nearly fell over the edge, into the pond below.

"All right, fun's over!" Bannon held me down and thrust one hand between my thighs. His broad, beautiful grin and the humorous sparkle in his eyes brought a giddy peal of laughter bubbling up in my chest. My struggles grew weak and unfocused, and as he slid two fingers into my wet, warm sheath, I surrendered to a soft groan.

"Let's have you come, then." He leaned over me, a hair's breadth from brushing his skin against mine, his voice a salacious rumble. "I'm going to drive you to such climax, Sadira, you'll be *drowning* in it. I'm going to make you come until it's too much to bear."

I writhed under his touch and rocked my hips to him with a groan. He bent close to kiss me, his lips still salty with a hint of blood, as his thumb circled my jeweled clitoris.

"And then," he whispered. "Then, when you're exhausted from orgasms, when your legs are weak and your throat is sore, when you just can't take anymore... I'll only just be getting started."

"Think you can hold me down that long?" I challenged. "Maybe I'll take the upper hand when you least suspect and have my way with *you*."

"Not a chance."

He withdrew his fingers and swung one leg over me, straddling me and pinning my arms with his knees. While I wriggled and muttered empty threats, he dove into his satchel and pulled out a length of smooth, velvety rope.

My mouth dropped open. "That's rope from the torture chamber! You had this planned all along!"

"I admit I've been keen to tie you down and wanted to be prepared." He slipped the rope from its neat loops and wound it around my wrists. "I thought you'd appreciate something softer and less coarse than the ship's rigging lines. You're not opposed, I take it?"

Slinky velvet slithered into place with titillating ease. Bannon tugged the ropes tight, testing the give to be sure he wouldn't leave me with any loss of feeling, and then continued winding satiny lengths across my torso, under and between my breasts, looping around my shoulders. He wove a skillful pattern like a star across my chest and bound my arms in simple restraint behind my back.

The tingle of the rope abrading my skin and the familiar delight of the harness he spun around me filled me with joy as I twisted and struggled. Bannon knew much about immobilizing prey or prisoners; once my arms and chest were bound, he spread my legs and tied them in a bent position, calves to thighs, in a manner our special book called a *frog tie*.

"Think you can get the upper hand now?" he taunted me.

I smirked. "Just don't let your guard down."

"Give up. The fight is over. You *lost*."

He crawled down my body, sliding between my legs and seizing the soft curves of my ass in his hands.

"And now, as promised..."

He descended on my pussy like a man plunging into a decadent feast. I strained against the ropes, rolling my head back with a moan, helpless beneath him. His tongue tickled and explored me, flicking the jewel of my piercing, teasing my clitoris with swift, lavish strokes.

I clenched my fists and growled, but already my body responded to him. Pleasure bloomed like a wide, luscious red flower as my barbarian stroked and kissed me, coaxing the sweet rush of frantic, needful bliss. All tension and pain, all worry, melted from me like dew under the sun, seeping away into the damp moss beneath us, and I pressed myself to him, yearning for more.

True to his word, he stroked me to a bright, shimmering pinnacle, and before I knew it, I climbed toward hot climax. He plunged two fingers into me just as my body reached its peak, and I cried out in joy, rocking to his touch. As the trembling faded, though, he continued—moving fingers in and out of my tight entrance, he leaned in again to renew his attentions on my clit, flicking and strumming it with his tongue.

I writhed, a desperate groan escaping through clenched teeth, dancing on an edge between sweet, sensual enchantment and hard, glittering intensity. My second orgasm hit, like a high note in a song, like a flash of heat lightning, and I gave a stammering moan.

"*Oh...* oh, Bannon—*please*—"

"Please what?" he taunted me, looking up from between my legs. "Are you already spent, Sadira? Had enough? My sweet slut, I thought you were a glutton for pleasure like this. Wasn't it you who said you could come for me, for *days?*"

I tugged at the ropes, twisting back and forth, as my thighs and pussy shuddered and convulsed. When he returned his mouth to my clit, I let out a quavering, pleading cry, but he ignored it. Tears of overwhelming emotion streamed down my face.

As he toyed with me, tormenting my sensitive, overstimulated sex, I twitched and tried to pull away, bucked my hips to escape his touch, rolled and mewled and begged. He took it all as encouragement, and wrung another wet climax from me, and another, until every nerve thrummed with high, humming, gilded pain. My nipples throbbed and my thighs quivered at every touch.

"*Please,*" I gasped, close to sinking into a low, exhausted trance. "Please..."

Bannon rose to crawl over my body and took my chin in his hand, forcing me to meet his gaze. His mouth came down on mine, and through the haze of emotions, I returned his kiss with a deep gratitude. My own wet, bittersweet taste lingered on his lips.

"Think you're ready, pet?" he murmured as we parted. "Ready to yield that pert, tight ass to me? Or do you still have strength to resist?"

He brushed a thumb across the wet tear tracks on my cheek. I had no words. I could only offer a gentle sigh of surrender and a single, soft nod of my head. Bannon kissed me again, all at once slow and loving, the game of predator and prey forgotten. He moved his way down my body with warm caresses and tender kisses, cupping my breasts as he nuzzled them, brushing the swell of my abdomen with his cheek.

The lavish attention to my pussy and all my fierce, forced orgasms had left me dripping wet. Bannon pressed a gentle thumb against the tight resistance of my rear entrance, and I moaned, aching.

"Shh, now." He flashed me a smile as he coaxed and massaged me, readying me for the next part. A shiver traveled down my body, through my breasts and belly, straight to my loins.

He unclasped his belt, releasing his beautiful, rigid cock, then slid his hands under my buttocks, lifting me up and moving himself into position. When his great, rigid shaft slid into me, a sharp, sparkling pain made me gasp, tightening from head to toe, and then let out a long, lusty exhale.

"*Oh*... Sir..."

"There's my good girl," Bannon soothed. He moved slowly, claiming me in inches, until the pain eased away into transgressive pleasure.

"That's right," he breathed, beginning a steady rhythm. A groan escaped him, and he rolled his head back. "*Fuck,* Sadi... Goddess, I knew your ass would be sweet..."

I answered him with a wordless cry, meeting his motions and urging him on. My body trembled in a place between bliss and torment, and my skin burned under his lustful, beastly conquest.

"I love you," I whispered. "Oh, I love you."

"My good girl... yes... oh, yes, kitten..."

His pace grew steadily fiercer, and I arched against the mossy ground. He descended to a series of quiet, rough, primitive grunts as he thrust into me, his cock like hot, barbarian iron inside me. It defied my body's every resistant reflex, forceful and demanding, and every motion threatened to break me under his desire.

"Oh, *fuck,* Sadi—*oh,* yes—*Sadi*—"

"Sir!" I cried out for him. His thumbs dug into my hips and he thrust harder, faster. At last, he plunged in to the hilt, and his cock gave a huge, heavy throb. I relinquished a hoarse, stuttering cry, each pulse of his orgasm beating within my sore, exhausted body. Delicious, primally possessive pain.

He withdrew, leaving me with one final, unexpected sting of discomfort, and leaned down to capture my chin again for a kiss. Every part of me ached in beautiful ways, used for his pleasure, and purged of the ugly energy it had carried before.

Bannon spent long moments unwrapping the ropes from my limbs and helping me stretch and flex my joints again. Once each velvet length was unwound and all were returned to his satchel, he set it aside, and stretched out next to me in the moss. Unbound, I lay with my head against his chest, taking stock of each sore twinge and delighted tingle still echoing through my body.

"Beautiful girl," he murmured in my ear, stroking my arm. "Beautiful, magnificent, wonderful girl."

I didn't have the words to tell him how well he'd managed my panic and my fears with his game of predator and prey. The spiraling chaos inside me seemed put to rest. At least, for the time being. The *Drekakona,* the stalking figure in the corridors, the monstrous creature in the fire, the woman with the knife... all now so far away, and out of my hands. Time would bring them back, I knew. For now, though, he'd relieved me of their burden, and released me to simple pleasure again.

Good girl, he called me. Not *witch.* Not *traitor.* Not *serpent worshipper.* Simply his good girl, desired and beloved.

"Heh." He traced a thumb down my cheek. "You're filthy, you know. Covered in dirt and grass stains, twigs and bits of leaf in your hair..."

"Somebody set me to run through the woods naked," I murmured. "Blame him."

He chuckled and sat up, stripping off his loose cotton shirt. "We'll have to get you clean before we venture back to the village. Fancy a swim?"

I tilted my head to gaze down at the pool below. Beautiful and cold and clear, its surface a swirl of blues and whites under the rush of the waterfall.

It did look enticing. I glanced back at Bannon, though, as he kicked off his boots and slipped out of his jeans. "I can't swim."

"You can't?"

His smile widened. Sliding his arms beneath me, he scooped me up and lifted me in his arms as he stood. "All the more reason, then, to throw you in."

"No!" I shrieked, but I was giggling even as I beat at his chest in protest. He carried me in big, overdramatic gestures to the edge of our mossy overlook, and, tightening his grip on me, leapt out into space.

We plunged down and made great splash, icy water rushing in all around us. The drowsiness of our post-coital bliss evaporated as the raw cold shocked me awake, and I tightened my grip around Bannon's neck, kicking my feet. An instant later, we broke the surface, and Bannon gave me a gentle, reassuring squeeze.

"Nothing to it!" He kissed my nose. "Now, I'm going to let you go—"

"Don't!" I shook my head and buried my face against his shoulder. "Bannon, really!"

"It's all right, kitten, I'm going to show you."

Sliding his hands under my arms to keep me above water, he shifted to float in front of me, facing me. "Just kick your feet, and I'll guide you to the shallow end."

Fighting a nervous smile, I did as he asked. We moved together toward the shore, Bannon murmuring encouragement all the way.

"Don't you know cats hate water?' I teased him softly.

"*My* she-cat is too fierce to be afraid of anything. All right now, the water's not very deep here. Just trust me."

At his coaxing, I eased myself down until my feet touched soft, wet sand, slipping and squishing between my toes with a sensual, soothing ease. Not at all like the coarse, gritty sand of Vashtaren.

"See, my lovely?" Bannon guided me a few steps forward, as though we were dancers before a court, motions smooth and sure. The water came up to my chest, invigorating in its crisp, cold purity, and before long my Master had let me go entirely, leaving me to stand on my own.

"Not so bad, is it?"

"No," I admitted, sure a hint of pink chagrin must be lighting up my cheeks. "You were right, Sir."

"Let's get you clean," he suggested. "And once you're free of all those marks and scuffs, we'll teach you to swim."

"Is it so easy, then?" I turned toward the waterfall, to run my fingers through its smooth, silvery curtain before ducking my head in. "Think you'll have me diving overboard to save drowning crewmates after a single afternoon?"

"Maybe not quite so simple." He winked and joined me, leaning his head back in the falls to rinse his thick, red mane. "But we're stuck in port for the time being. We'll have plenty of time to teach you all you need to know."

"And..."

I brushed my fingers over his bicep. "Is that... all we'll do?"

"If you mean, will I be tying you up and having my way with you again while we're here, the answer is of course." Bannon flashed me a leer. "Are you so eager to get back to it?"

"Always," I said with a smile. "But Sir, I meant will we discuss what has been happening to me? Will you listen to me now when I tell you something is not right aboard that ship?"

His face turned serious, and he dropped his hands to his sides. Confusion and indecision clashed in his expression. Even after what he'd seen today, he must still doubt the strange episodes plaguing me.

A shadow of grief darkened my sky. I sidestepped away from him, bowing my head, and clasping my hands to my chest. "I see."

Bannon reached out, taking hold of my forearm and drawing me back to face him.

"Hey, now, Sadi. Don't lose faith in me so easily. I don't know what is haunting you, or how it's come to do so, but we *will* find out."

194

He ran his fingers through my short, wet hair. "You seem to think because I don't understand, I don't aim to help you. I have *never* said I would not help you."

"How can you, if you think it's only madness?" I bristled. "If you think my visions only so many figments of the imagination? Think me crazy!"

"I *do not* think you are crazy."

He cupped my chin in his hands and looked me straight in the eyes. The intensity in his, like burning autumn fires, silenced my questions and reminded me again he had claimed me. Taken ownership of me, and all my worries too.

"You are sharp and reflective, Sadira. Like a strong, well-honed blade. I have no doubt about the soundness of your mind."

He let the words hang between us for a beat, gazing at me with solemn earnest. Then he softened, though, turning sad, and brushed his thumbs over my cheeks.

"But you have also endured a true nightmare. Your night in the dungeons. The golem in the sands."

He looked pained as he added, "Me. Me under the influence of your truest enemy. I know how it's affected you, Sadira. I know why we slept so many nights together without indulging in our desires, as we did so freely before. I know why you panicked when I put my hand to your throat. I have never wished to harm you, and yet Alaric Khan turned me into a source of fear."

"Bannon, I—"

"Quiet." He put a finger to my lips. "I know the aftermath of horror. I endured night terrors for weeks after my imprisonment under the giants. I saw the loss of my companions. I felt the beatings, over and over, and the scars they inflicted on me. And I hear you now, in your sleep, facing down demons in your dreams, as I did. Ailsa could be dead wrong about your fears. At the same time, though, *you* need to acknowledge you have yet much healing to do, before you can leave Alaric's madness behind for good."

He released me, and I bowed my head, wrapping my arms around my belly. "I told you I won't have you assume me damaged. My nature, my... *desires...* will not be reduced to scars and trauma. I am who I am, and whether Alaric tormented me, I will always, intrinsically be this way. I couldn't stand to have my *Master* see me as some wounded, perverted victim."

"That isn't how I see you, and never will be."

He came to me in the water, wrapping his arms around me, resting his chin on my head.

"You are my delightfully twisted, beautifully sweet slut." He gave me a gentle squeeze, and I heard the smile in his voice. "And you need a strong partner to keep you well-fucked, and well-cared-for. If Alaric Khan's hate has left you in pain, your Master will tend to your wounds. And then he shall continue to be your Master, and bind you when you need it, and indulge your need for pain. He will care for you as hard as he fucks you. Just as I promised."

I closed my eyes, wanting so badly to find solace in his words. Doubt and trouble danced through my mind, and I couldn't seem to find steady ground.

"We will discover the truth behind your encounters," he vowed. "But you must at least consider they may be no more than echoes and night terrors. One of your headaches, fooling your senses."

I shook my head. "Bannon, it's *not*. I haven't even had such a headache for months."

He paused. Moving to hold me at arm's length, he leveled me with a curious gaze. "Haven't you?"

"No. Not since I cast away my collar, and Alaric's last curse."

His brow furrowed. "But Sadi... not more than a week ago, you told me your head was in agony again. I told the crew you were sick and couldn't work. You remained in our cabin most of the day, remember?"

At first, I didn't. Then, cold, fleeting fear hit my stomach like an arrow.

He must have read the guilt on my face. Withdrawing from our embrace, he took a step back. He studied me for a long, heavy beat, and then, he looked away.

"So." His tone frightened me, low and stiff. "You lied."

CHAPTER NINETEEN

THERE WAS NO punishment this time. I don't think Bannon had the heart to punish me, not after we'd both just spent days struggling through the last measure of discipline. Something in his eyes said he blamed himself for this, and that look cut more deeply than anything else could have.

We walked back toward the town in silence, the pleasant playfulness of our afternoon ruined. After our dip in the pond, the clear golden sunshine seemed not hot enough, and—still naked—I shivered as we picked our way through the trees to find my stashed clothes.

Schala prowled out from the hiding place with a happy trill. I stooped to stroke her, then crouched to retrieve my belongings, but Bannon stopped me with a hand.

"You'll only get dirty again, right after your rinse. I'll get them."

He sounds so unlike himself. So miserable and upset. Oh, my barbarian, I've been so unfair to you...

I'd apologized, of course, and explained myself. I made no excuses. I didn't plead or try to justify my choice. I'd known what a trespass it was to lie, even as

I'd done it, and I knew my Master had every right to exact serious punishment.

But he didn't.

Maybe he's simply thinking up an appropriate sentence.

He rose from the tangle of roots, offering me my folded clothing.

"Thank you, Sir," I whispered. He nodded and leaned against the tree to let me dress.

"I deserve whatever you decide for me," I prompted, pulling my leggings on and wrapping the breast band around my chest. "Please. You know I am not too soft to stand a demanding retribution."

"I know," he mumbled. "But there won't be any. I'm not going to punish you for lying."

Not being punished was almost worse. I knew how to deal with punishment—not how to deal with this silence hanging between us, the doubt and uncertainty. If he decided to spank me, whip me, ground me to one of the ship's bunks by myself, I could tolerate it because I knew once the penance was complete, the transgressions were past. I would be his *good girl* again, purged of my sins and forgiven. Those were the rules in our game.

Without it, how could I know when I'd earned back his trust? When would he forgive me?

What if he doesn't forgive me at all?

I rubbed at the anxious pain my chest, closing my eyes on the tears threatening to fall.

Bannon climbed the ridge a bit further and stood gazing out at the beach and the cove. I stayed where I was, watching him.

"I think staying in town is a mistake after all." He rubbed at his beard, pivoting to scan the scrubby field instead.

"Why is that?"

"I don't like the idea of staying anywhere near a stranger who tried to stab you. Whatever else may be going on, it's possible Khan has loyalists even here, or the serpent worshippers have stretched their coils out farther than we imagined. If the Order of Akolet has spies in the city, I don't want you within their grasp."

I moved to his side. "So, what will we do? Return to the ship after all?"

He shook his head. "Not while Arne and his shipwrights are at work. The fewer restless souls to manage, the better. I think we must make camp, here, in the clearing. The horde, too. Not enough room in that inn for us all, anyway. We'll stick together, in case there really *are* enemies lying in wait here."

I fiddled with the end of my single braid. *Ashe did mention this isn't one of the usual ports. How far is the reach of the seven-headed serpent?*

We hadn't sailed far from the Ruined Sands, true, but could there really be devotees of that great viper here as well? I'd believed the woman at the flower shop to be possessed. Perhaps she could just as easily have been a skilled spy, or an assassin deployed by the Order.

And of course, I would be an easy target to identify. The moment I stepped through the city gates, anyone who saw me would know. If there are *adherents to the serpent's way, they certainly know me.*

I hugged myself, running my hands along the tattoos on my arms. Even if they didn't know my name, even if they didn't know my history, the sigils and lines on my skin would betray me.

What had she called me?

Apostate.

The afternoon had grown colder all around me. Overhead, the clear blue sky from earlier now gathered thick, rolling clouds. A chill slipped down my arms and I gave a shiver.

Oh, Bannon... won't you hold me? Don't you see how frightened I am?

I couldn't blame him for his detachment. I'd angered him. No... I'd *hurt* him.

"Come." He started off down the path toward the beach. "Let's find Mara. She'll have the soldiers striking camp before the sun sets."

Pausing, he tilted his head up to the sky. "The sooner the better. Looks like rain."

THE STORM BREWED quickly, shutting out the sun and filling the air with a frigid bite less than two hours after we'd departed our warm, cozy spot by the pool. Along with Mara and the others, we went to work raising hasty tents in the field, and barely managed half the camp before the rain broke loose. No gradual progression of mere sprinkles to light rain, either. One moment, the rumble of a thundercrack sounded overhead, and the next, sheets of ran beat down on us, soaking us in seconds.

Everyone scrambled under shelter, crowding in the finished tents, and building quick, small fires for warmth. Bannon erected ours in a matter of moments. Vents overhead let the smoke escape, leaving us sheltered and comfortable as the storm beat down on the canvas over our heads.

I sat, legs crossed, staring up at the pale roof of the tent, Schala sprawled in my lap. The rain sounded like drums and made the tent rattle with a pleasant sound. Oddly, I found a deep sense of calm and relief in the downpour. A soothing rhythm of nature, unlike anything the violent and scorching storms in the Ruined Sands.

"Was it raining the night he took me from my home?" I wondered aloud.

Across from me, Bannon sharpened his axe. At my question, he paused, giving me a thoughtful look.

Of course, he wouldn't know. I hadn't asked *him,* really, and I think he knew it. I listened to the rain drum on for several seconds, closing my eyes and trying to remember.

"I hadn't thought of that night in almost twenty-five years," I told him. "Not until recently. I'm sorry... I'm sure I forgot to tell you, after all that happened. I didn't mean to keep it from you."

He set his axe aside and leaned forward, resting his elbows on his knees. He looked tired and troubled, and I wondered if he wrestled with doubt as I did. A living thing like a weasel, gnawing and chewing at the corners of his mind, and so difficult to lay hands on and evict. The sting of catching me in a real lie, an intentional lie, must still be fresh, even though the lie itself had been so small. So trivial.

It was my failure to trust that was the *real* issue, and the thing that truly wounded him. I wanted desperately for him to believe there'd been no other deliberate deception, no other lapses in my faith, and I had not withheld these revelations on purpose.

Perhaps Ailsa was right, at least in some way. Leaving the Ruined Sands, embarking on a quest which might unravel the dark shroud around my past, frightened me. In my fright, I'd acted out against the master I'd vowed to trust and obey. I'd *never* have dared such spoiled and selfish behavior with Alaric. But only because Alaric would hurt me, deeply, personally, if I did. Bannon would never resort to real torment like that.

Bannon deserved better.

"I had a dream," I began. "A dream... or a memory, maybe. It was the night Alaric stole me from my home. I remember the clash of his war drums. Smoke, and fire. People wailing in despair."

In silence, Bannon rose from his spot and came to sit by me. Our shoulders brushed. He slid his hand into mine, loosely twining our fingers. Schala opened sleepy eyes to watch him, but made no noise, only stretching her paws out and then curling up tighter in my lap.

"I was lying in the bottom of a boat. Just a... just a simple boat. A fisher's canoe, maybe. There were others with me. Other children."

I blinked my eyes open and looked into the fire, brows furrowing. "You know, I never knew anyone like me in Vash, though. No one who looked like me or had these gray eyes. What happened to the other children they stole? They wouldn't have—"

He said nothing, but scooted closer, switching hands and stretching one arm around my shoulder. The question hung like lead in my chest. No, it wasn't likely Alaric or his raiders would have killed all the children besides me. More likely, the others had been sold into slavery, bartered to ally tribes and warlords as human livestock.

Even if they hadn't died by Alaric's own hand, though, the savage Vashtaren desert swallowed them up. No children like me, for twenty-five years. Not in war councils, not in ceremonial gatherings. No servants among the nomad tribes with gray eyes. For whatever reason, the shivering bodies next to me in the bottom of that canoe were all long gone.

"Why?"

This time I did ask Bannon, turning to meet his eyes. "*You* saw his mind, barbarian. Why did he cast aside all from my home except for me? Why would I be the only slave he kept when he must have carried away dozens? Why would I *never* have seen anyone like me in all these years?"

"I don't know." Bannon broke our gaze, looking instead at the floor. "I know only that his father sent him out to find you and bring you back for the Order sorcerers to kill. I know Alaric's search lasted years. He must have wanted you isolated from them. Truly cut off from all your own tribe."

I chewed my lip and toyed with the end of my braid.

"What else do you remember?" he asked.

"My mother's voice. A man's voice, calling with hers. Not my father, I think... my grandfather. I heard them crying out for me—no, that's not right. They called out for a child named Seren. I suppose, before Alaric made me his desert rose, that's who I was."

"Anything else?"

I closed my eyes again, letting the sound of the rain soothe me. "No. When I dream, though, I hear her voice again. My mother. She calls out to me from somewhere deep in the earth, where a light beats like a heart. Blue light, like the fire on the ship. Then, when I found the cargo hold with the cherries, I saw... someplace, some wood far away in my mind. I saw..."

The altar. The offering arranged in a seven-pointed star. Like the seven heads of Akolet.

The serpent's skull.

These hands, her hands, my *hands.*

I shuddered, wrapping my arms around myself. "Serpent worshippers, Bannon. What if my people are serpent worshippers, like Alaric? Like the Order? I couldn't stand it. To be descended from such... such..."

We both fell quiet again for several more minutes. He lifted his arm from me, and shifted, breaking the contact of our bodies. He rested his chin in his hands, staring into the fire.

I touched his arm. "I am sorry I lied to you. Truly I am. It was unforgivable to deceive my Master so."

"Am I your Master?"

The question didn't surprise me as much as it should have. I think we'd both recognized the straining connection between us. I dropped my hand to my side, bowing my head.

"I don't know what lies ahead of me," I whispered. I touched my naked throat, longing for the familiar feel of leather beneath my fingertips. "Everything is so unfamiliar."

"When I asked you to come with me, Sadira, I asked you to trust me. What have I done to lose that trust?"

His wounded tone cut through me like a knife. The fire crackled and danced. The rain drummed. I had no answer. Only Alaric's whispered promise, echoing in my mind.

As long as you live... you will belong to me.

"I'm afraid, Bannon. I'm so afraid. I suspected Alaric's sorcerers of dark magic, I even believed he might have arranged one final, terrible curse before he died, to avenge himself. To hear his voice, though...

to see his *eyes,* looking at me through... through your face..."

"I fought him," he said in a strained voice. "You must believe me, Sadi, I *fought* him every step of the way. I tried to wrest back control and protect you!"

"I do believe you. But now, all I see are spirits and shadows, I wake in the night to violent sounds only I can hear. And the fire, the fire was *blue,* just like the light in my dreams. I'm afraid, and I don't..."

My voice cracked. "I don't know what's *wrong* with me."

With a curious rumble of a meow, Schala lifted her head from my knee and looked up at me. As though she understood my ache, she climbed to her feet and pressed herself to my stomach, starting up a loud purr. I buried my face in my hands.

"Is this what it will be like for me, forever?"

Bannon picked up a long stick and stirred at the fire. His mouth quirked into a frown, and thoughtful lines crossed his brow.

"Were we in my home country, I know where I would take you," he told me. "To the temple of Sherida, where her soothsayers and disciples might have answers for you that I do not. There is a shrine on the *Drekakona,* where the sailors may make their daily devotions.... but I'm afraid we have no priests or sisters among us who can attempt to divine the truth around you."

I wrinkled my nose. "Your goddess Sherida."

"Aye." He stroked his beard. "Ailsa is more devoted, religiously, than I. But even she isn't trained in the ways of the holy sisterhood to interpret your dreams or call upon the goddess's powers to heal you."

"Heal me?"

"*If,*" he amended, "there is anything to heal. Or, if there are some manner of dark spirits clinging to you still."

I lifted Schala to my shoulder and hugged my knees to my chest. I tried not to let my skepticism show on my face. I didn't like the idea of Sherida's priests any more than Akolet's.

"So then, what do we do, as long as your goddess and her disciples are still so far away?"

"I wish I could tell you. I'm no spiritualist. I don't know anything about spirits or ghosts or curses. I will do anything I can to protect you. I just don't know what I'm protecting you from."

I heaved a sigh and stood, walking to the tent flap to gaze out into the gray, sheeting rain.

"Tomorrow," Bannon continued behind me. "We'll go back into the city. You'll buy some parchment, or a book. A journal. You'll begin writing down these visions and any other strange experiences you may have, from now until we can visit a temple to the goddess and seek the aid of their seers."

"Yes, Sir," I murmured, out of habit more than anything.

"I'm sorry," he said. "Until you give me an enemy to fight, I don't know what else to do."

An enemy to fight.

Our last enemy had been an unnatural monster, a construct from the black, dark place beyond death. Now, I saw vague figures in the shadows, and white, glowing eyes in waves of blue flames. How could I point them out to Bannon and say, *there is the enemy. There is my fear and my pain. Slay it for me.*

And slave or no, did I really expect my Master to slay my demons *for* me?

I am a soldier, too, damnit.

The rain drummed on. We said nothing. Somewhere between us, our bond lay cracked and damaged, and more than anything I wished I could see it, touch it with my own hands, *fix* it.

That must be how he feels about my strange visions and evening visitors.

Far in the distance, the shape of the *Drekakona* rose above the beach. Her sails reefed, her rigging swaying and blowing in the stormy wind. She looked like a ghost herself at this distance—a gray shape in a gray world, almost transparent. If I stood at her side and put out my hand to touch her hull, would I even meet the familiar, firm resistance of hard wood?

Another sigh escaped me. The world seemed to melt like spun sugar under the storm.

A single light shone from the ship. Somewhere on the middle deck, near the stern. In my heart, I knew where it came from. It shone from the officer's cabin belonging to Bannon and me.

A blue light. Beating softly in the storm, like a heart.

CHAPTER TWENTY

THE RAIN LASTED long into the next day. Bannon took me into the city, as promised, and this time the streets were nearly empty of people. Streams and runnels and whole rivers of rainwater flowed along the cobblestoned intersections, leaving some areas too flooded to explore. The people we did see huddled in their doorways, cloaked heavily against the cold and wet, watching us with mildly curious expressions.

They weren't unfriendly. Some even waved and wished us a good day. Only the weather kept them from coming out and socializing with the gusto they had the previous day, and it stopped many of the merchants from rolling out their carts of wares and setting up sales

I liked the cool and the quiet. Vash had never been like this. We weren't accustomed to rain, of course, as it had *never* rained over the Ruined Sands. I loved how it covered the world like a soft blanket, the gray clouds keeping everything close and quiet, driving people together to seek warmth and comfort.

Well. Not everyone.

Bannon walked beside me without touching me. No hand around my waist. No fingers twining with mine. A chaos of fear and sorrow raged in my chest, senseless without his reassurance, but I walked with him in silence. I couldn't bear to be the one who invited more talk about painful disappointments, when neither of us would have any more answers than before.

It took us some time to find a supply shop carrying journals, and when we did, the store owner seemed in a crabby mood, much worse than anyone had been the day before, as if the weather itself had somehow personally wronged him. He was stingy with the purchase, and stingier still when we asked for writing implements. As we left, I couldn't help but think his foul mood had worsened ours as well. Bannon took on a grim and unapproachable mien as we walked back to our camp.

He assigned me to remain in our tent for the day, recording the details we'd discussed. He wanted to be away from me, I thought. He still hurt, and now felt uncertain as to our association. No sense of Master or slave between us now. We might have been anyone, two people thrown together on a voyage with no real connection, besides that I needed his instruction in a world I didn't know.

He left me to my work, going to his, erecting the remaining areas of camp. I spent the morning writing, in sullen distraction, alone except for Schala, who'd caught herself a fat rodent of some kind and crouched at the back of the tent snacking on it.

I hardly knew where to begin. I paced the tent in circles, pausing only to stoop and scratch at Schala's ears, wondering where it all started.

Was it when she came to me on the docks in Olyb? Or in the marketplace there? What about before then, when the doors in Alaric's castle slammed shut on me, barring me from my previous life altogether?

Probably there, I decided, and sat to write once more. Yet still, it nagged at me, incorrect somehow. Incomplete.

My hand came up to where my collar used to be. I stood and paced some more.

What about the cargo hold full of cherries and apples? The mirror that drew me into some foreign time and place? Was it real? Or only a delusion?

I thought of the woman, then women, whose bodies and hands I'd seen. I'd been them, hadn't I? Hadn't that been the point of the vision?

My gaze wandered wistfully to the tent entrance and the gray morning beyond. To the woods where yesterday I'd run free, like a creature of the wilderness myself.

Also like my vision. Running through the forest toward... something. Toward the temple. The shrine to—

I poked my head out into the rain. Bannon led a team of soldiers raising another tent on the other side of the clearing. Mara stood beside him, bellowing orders.

At the sight of her, a streak of red, bubbling anger hit my chest.

"*Mara,*" I grumbled. At the tone in my voice, Schala looked up from her breakfast, uttering a curious chirrup. Jumping to her feet, she came to my side, butting against my ankles and winding around my legs with a purr.

"Why is *she* always ready to come to his side whenever things are worst?" I snapped. Letting the

211

tent flap fall shut, I picked up my cat and stroked her, circling again. "Probably jumped at the chance to get close to him the second she sensed he and I were at odds. Can't *wait* for an opportunity to say evil things about me and remind him all about my vile past."

Be sensible, Sadira. Of course, she's doing no such thing. She's his lieutenant. She's only doing her job instructing his soldiers.

"Horse shit!"

I kicked at a basket of breads and cheese, my foul temper worsening as I watched them tumble out over the floor. All at once, I *hated* Mara to the very core. I loathed her smug, polished professionalism and her cold, insufferable stares. "That tight, frigid, mean bitch!"

And as soon as the words escaped me, my mind plunged into unwelcome images, visions of Mara's transformation into a sultry woman of desire in *my* Master's arms. Of Bannon's warm, dusky skin against hers, all her stiff unpleasantness cast aside as she revealed her true intentions at last.

"Damnit!"

I dropped Schala and tore at my hair.

I'd *never* been jealous before, not of anyone. I'd feared dismissal, certainly, if Alaric paid particular attention to another consort or spoke about how much more pleasing the other ladies of the harem could be. He'd never been exclusive, of course. In fact, he'd bade me watch him with other partners many times. Not only women. I'd watched him fuck men and be fucked by them, had seen him claim androgyne slaves and slaves expressing both masculine and feminine roles at his command.

And did any of them ever upset me? No. I feared Alaric, *not them. Because he wished me to. He wanted me to be afraid, to worry he would replace me and cast me aside.*

Bannon would never do that.

So why did the sight of Mara at his side make me downright furious?

"*Ugh!*" I screamed, desperate for something to break or someone to fight. *I ought to write this down,* I realized as my eyes fell on the journal again. But no. Bannon could read it. I would die of shame if he knew the ugly, petty thoughts about him and Mara running through my head.

I swallowed the bile in my throat and returned to my pacing.

As our days in port continued—along with the rain—Bannon brought us together again to hone our skills with the axe, as promised. He called Rayyan and Ailsa and me to practice every morning and brought along some of the younger soldiers to break us into sparring teams. We continued the use of the wooden weapons at first, but soon he asked us to wield true blades, and showed us how to throw them.

When Bannon threw his axe, he could stick it deep into one of the thick, short trees all the way up to the eye. The trunks we used for targets bore dozens of deep, ugly scars after his demonstrations, and sap oozed from the deadly-looking wounds.

I didn't have the strength to launch nearly so great an attack, and Ailsa, despite her own familiarity as a shield maiden, couldn't manage the same impressive destruction as her towering father. Rayyan, on the other hand, had built up a noticeable sheath of muscles in his arms and chest. When *he* threw the battle axe, it flew with beautiful grace and *thunked* home with an audible, appreciable sound, as though splitting a man's skull like a gourd.

"It's all the rowing," he confided to me, showing off his newly defined biceps. After missing my initial shift at the oars, of course, I'd missed the chance to build my own strength in the same way. Once the ship set sail again, I vowed I would elect for double shifts in the gallery to make up for it.

Each day, after the sun reached its apex and began descending to the west, Bannon dismissed the rest of the soldiers and kept just Rayyan, Ailsa, and me. "That's enough time with the axes for today," he'd say. "Sadira, retrieve your khopeshes, and let's have you show us your style of two-handed swordplay."

Ailsa had her own first set of wooden blades to meet mine, but after a few quick demonstrations it became clear I must use wood as well, or else leave her defending with only a pair of sliced-up sticks.

I despised using the wooden khopeshes. Something Mara appeared to pick up on when she came to observe us, studying my movements with shrewd eyes and rubbing her chin. Worse, she strolled to Bannon's side to exchange critiques, pointing, shaking her head, speaking in a murmur too low for me to hear.

My ugly jealousies returned along with her. I seethed under her observance, my mind treating me to all the unpleasant, negative remarks she must be whispering in *my* Master's ear as Ailsa and I sparred.

I am tired of this! Let her try me again now. Let me at her with my own weapons, on even ground.

As I wrapped up my quick match with Ailsa, I bowed to her in customary respect. Before she could take up a defensive position again for a new round, though, I pointed my weapon at Mara.

"Care for another round, Lieutenant? Perhaps you'd like to try and learn the way of the black magician's blades, now that we have the time?"

Mara's expression soured. Bannon's turned puzzled; his lips tucked into an uncertain grimace as he considered the merits of my challenge.

"Certainly, the Red Bear's best soldier isn't afraid to try her hand at the khopeshes?" I prodded. "These wooden toys are really no substitute, though. Maybe you'd like to bear your own axe against me for now, and pay mind to my technique when I pry it from your grip?"

The lieutenant narrowed her eyes. "I have no interest in learning an assassin's blade. Your desert style is a dirty and dishonorable art. Those weapons are cheater's weapons."

"Do you think so?" I jeered. "Or are you simply intimidated? Of course, you must know that a fighter with two khopeshes is at a disadvantage coming at a Sanraethi shield maiden head-on. My style is not meant for direct combat and yet, I'm willing to pit my skills against yours. Are you so afraid I would stab you in the back?"

"That is *exactly* what I'm afraid of," she grumbled. "As there is no ship's railing handy to cast me overboard this time."

More anger flared. Accusing me of throwing her off the ship *on purpose?*

"That's ridiculous!" I held up my blades at the ready. "Get in here and let me see you *really* fight!"

She ground her teeth, eyes flashing. "I said—"

"Ah." I straightened. "So, I see even the Sanraethi hordes may harbor soldiers with no spines."

That tripped her anger. Mara's face turned a sharp, brick red as she snapped, "All right! Somebody bring me my axe so I can show this serpent-worshiping whore the folly of challenging a Sanraethi blade!"

I seethed but refused to contradict her. Giving her any response meant giving her the opportunity to discard it like trash in the street, and I didn't need to give her a psychological upper hand like that. I was no serpent-worshipper, no matter what my visions indicated, and she should be clear on the matter by now. Telling her so wouldn't make a difference. I was going to lay her out flat on her back and *make* her see.

One of her squires brought her axe and shield. I crouched into a ready position, scowling. Behind Mara, Bannon looked on with disapproval, but I ignored him for the time being. I was going up against an opponent with the advantage in close melee, and I knew it. I'd have to be faster and cleverer than Mara because I *wasn't* going to let her win.

"Get on with it!" I taunted her, clashing my khopeshes. She entered the circle we'd marked with stones, and rain streaked down her blade and shield, making them somehow stand out, bold and solid against the gray landscape.

"Let's see you fight, desert rat!" she hissed, thumping her weapon against her shield. "Do you think you can win without resorting to the cheap tactics Lord Khan was known for?"

"Maybe I can and maybe I can't." We slowly began to circle on another, while the other soldiers closed in. "What you need to understand, Mara, is it doesn't matter, if I kill you."

CHAPTER TWENTY-ONE

MARA'S FACE TWISTED up with sharp fury and alarm. I lunged in, swinging with both blades while she was distracted, and she raised her shield to meet me. I'd known she would—one of the biggest disadvantages of two-handed khopesh fighting was a shield blocking both strikes—so I dropped back in a feint and lunged in again from the side.

One of the *advantages* of two-handed khopesh fighting against an axe and shield was the speed I could abuse. Mara had a weighty, wooden obstacle in one hand which did wonders to protect her when in the right position. On the other hand, I could pry at the shield with one of my sickle-swords, and she would have to contend with me trying to drag her off-balance.

I could out-maneuver her, but she could outlast me, if I didn't take her down quickly. If I could keep myself squarely behind her shield, prompting her to try and bash me with it, I could feint back and possibly dart to one side, attacking her vulnerable flanks.

Cheap tactics. That would be her undoing. If she insisted on fighting to uphold some semblance of *honor* instead of fighting to win, I'd come out on top.

Why so eager to prove it to her?

I ducked to the right as Mara tried to sweep me with her axe, forcing her to open up from behind the shield. She backed up a step, and I knew already she wasn't used to an opponent darting in so close, so quickly. I had to keep the pressure on her; if I gave her the opportunity to create a strong field of defense, to push me out of the dangerous zone, she'd have all the advantage.

Why the need to defend *Alaric's ways?*

For once, I didn't care if my associations with Alaric Khan made me look bad. Mara wanted me to feel inferior. She wanted me to doubt the training and customs of my upbringing. Not *everything* I'd learned was tainted by Alaric's madness. I fought *well.* I was *strong.*

I wouldn't allow her to make me seem small in front of my Master.

I brought one khopesh crashing down against her shield, and she pushed back, attempting the shield bash I'd hoped she would. I took the thrust, lunging back with it—I didn't yet want her to realize how I could turn it against her. Let her grow confident in it and frustrated with my defense.

Let her throw all her strength into it.

Her axe came swinging down from above. I slipped out of the way and brought my khopesh down on top of it, catching the axe head under the hook of the blade, giving it a twist and a yank to pull it from her grasp. It put us in a tug-of-war, until I flipped my blade free and sent Mara wheeling back, carried by her own momentum.

This was the trick. I needed to wear her down using her own strength. The harder she came at me, the more I could pull her off-balance and into a disadvantageous misstep.

I put myself in a bad spot, allowing her another opportunity to strike me with the shield. She'd have to push me back if she wanted any chance at all to hit me with her axe—this time, though, she seemed to catch on, and dropped away, trying to put distance between us.

Oh no, Mara, that won't do.

I took a flying leap, raising both swords overhead, in a calculated gambit. She shifted her weight onto her back leg, tilting shield up, raising her axe to strike back as soon as she'd deflected. As I struck her shield, though, I met her force and rolled off, letting her push me aside.

She realized the mistake just as I swept in low and caught her ankle with the curve of my sword. I yanked, and she slid in the mud, fighting not to fall. It took a wide, wheeling maneuver for her to rebalance and come at me with a swing of her axe, and already I'd rolled to the side again, keeping even with her profile.

"Filthy sand rat!" she screeched, swinging her shield. The others cried out in protest, too, but I intended them to see exactly this.

"You can't win by playing fair, Mara," I taunted. "This isn't an honor match. It's a *grudge* match. And I'm more than willing to get dirty."

The blade came down again. I rolled again. Mud flew up between us, and I couldn't help it—I let out a raucous, wicked laugh. Sneaking out with one khopesh I hooked her belt and pulled her to me, raising the other to deflect her axe. It was a bad step, on my part; this time when she bashed me, both my weapons were extended, and she caught me full in the face with a ringing crash. Blood spurted from my nose and stars exploded across my field of vision. I released my holds and reclaimed my khopeshes, laughing still.

"Nice," I said, wiping blood from my mouth. "But you know me, Mara... I *like* pain. So come on, sweetie. Hit me *harder.*"

Disgust filled her face. She lunged and I stepped into it, catching her axe and spinning to twist it from her grip with my sword. As it clattered to the mud I stepped in and threw myself against her shield, pressing her back, keeping her from the weapon.

"Hit me again. Come on, Mara. Make me *feel* it."

She sneered, gripping her shield now with both hands. I pushed harder, sweeping and slashing with both khopeshes against the wooden barrier, forcing her nearly to the edge of the ring. She knew I would soon force her out of bounds, and I saw the desperate flash in her eyes. Her balance shifted; I readied myself for the final step.

With a roar, Mara shoved the shield at my face, attempting one massive, bone-shattering shield bash to knock me off my feet and away from her. She wanted room to move, to reclaim her axe. She didn't know, though, that I was done with this fight. As she lunged into the strike, I dropped into a backwards roll, leaving her no resistance at all.

Her swing carried her several steps forward. With nothing to leverage on, she was left open and exposed, and off-balance.

Rolling back onto my feet, I sprung forward, thrusting both khopeshes straight at her gut.

I missed on purpose.

Mara stood stunned, staring at me, the blades of my swords hovering in the air to either side of her. It was obvious, had I meant to, they would have gone straight through her belly.

"Congratulations," I told her with a grin, blood streaking down my chin. "Your honorable warrior's tactics have just left you with your bowels strewn all over *my* battlefield. You lose."

Her face *burned.* With a furious grunt she hit me in the face again with her shield, knocking me onto my back. I let her, and I lay in the rain laughing, tasting more blood, reasonably certain she'd broken my nose out of spite. Still, I laughed, giddily satisfied.

The other soldiers seemed uncertain how to feel about our tussle. They glanced back and forth among one another, trading uneasy grimaces, and little by little melting away to go back to other duties. Mara straightened and spat at me before handing axe and shield to one of the other Sanraethi and storming away.

Rayyan crouched by my side, silent, checking my injuries but offering no congratulations. Ailsa, too, came to examine me, but seemed reasonably certain I'd be all right without extensive medical attention.

"That was a cheap win," Bannon muttered. I looked up to see him standing over me, arms crossed over his chest, wearing a grim look of displeasure.

"Whether it was cheap or not is not the point," I told him. The pain, loud as it was in my head, felt right, and it comforted me. "The point was winning. And it helps to know how angry it made her to lose."

"Seems very petty of you." He offered his hand, and I took it, letting him help me up.

"I needed the release."

He arched an eyebrow. "Did you?"

I wiped more blood from my mouth and lifted my face into the rain, letting it wash away the last of it.

"When it comes to Mara," I told him, "it's a matter of pride. Perhaps the lion cannot see the significance of the lionesses circling, or the way they swipe and clash with one another. Perhaps it is beyond your notice. That's fine. Just remember, if it ever comes down to a *real* fight between us, Mara will have to learn to fight just as dirty, or she'll end up dead."

Bannon's expression darkened. Somewhere inside, I knew I'd done myself no favors with him. In the Sands, such a victory would cement my standing with my mate. It would prove my strength and desirability. If I'd humiliated one of Alaric's favorite officers in such a way, he'd have had me back to his rooms already with a raging erection and wild need to possess every part of me.

We weren't in Vashtaren anymore, though. The Sanraethi held different views. If anything, my show of force against Bannon's trusted lieutenant would only push Bannon further away.

Pleasure in my victory turned to sour regret in my gut.

I FOUND LITTLE to ease my frustrations as the days passed by. I wrote in the journal and watched my Master from across what seemed like a vast gulch; a chasm of things unspoken. We shared a bedroll, but a stifling and silent one. Schala slept in the crook of my arm, purring through the night, as though she thought it could heal me.

I dreamed of my mother again, calling me from somewhere always out of reach. I never reached her—never found the shining light at the heart of the maze in my mind. Always, the creeping, slithering sounds of snakes surrounded me, and their coils ensnared my limbs to hold me back.

The light—the Light—is dying.

Sometimes the vague figure from the *Drekakona* stalked me through my visions instead, skirting the edges of my sight, twisting and changing the pathways around me until all the light faded away, lost behind me as I blindly felt my way through an empty darkness. I called out for my mother, for Rayyan, for Bannon, *anyone* to come and find me, but the only one to answer me was the being with the white, shining eyes.

During the day, work on the *Drekakona* progressed at a good speed. The rain continued for half a week, but it did little to interfere with the interior repairs. We would have to hope it faded before construction began on the ship exterior. Time on shore grew tedious, as we were only allowed to enter the city at certain times in the day. Besides continuing athletic exercise and practice with new weapons, we did little in the camp, and I spent a great deal of time inside, writing in my journal or, quite often, fretting over things I didn't wish to record.

Bannon remained cool with me. Throwing myself in the path of a fire was far more easily forgiven than the betrayal of his trust, and in his frustration over the lie and my ugly clash with Mara, he seemed to see more of Alaric's slave in me, losing sight of his own devoted kitten. I sat with him by the fire at night, comforted by his nearness, even as I felt him slowly drifting away.

I'm so lost.

Again.

Far from everything I knew, I couldn't find my footing after all.

I should have stayed home, where I understood the world around me. I should have made a new life in a place where I knew the rules.

Most mornings I rose before Bannon and lay in the pre-dawn light, staring up at the roof of the tent. Sometimes the rain fell heavily, soothing me with its sure presence all around. Other times, it drizzled, soft and somehow kind, like a companion with a willing ear.

Today, though, it seemed to have stopped. I listened to the silence in its place: the soft, steady breaths of Bannon beside me, and the tinier, nearly inaudible sighs of Schala, curled up on my belly. Outside the tent, no sound at all rose from the field or the soldiers around us. No early footsteps of the morning watch. No quiet conversations from a few tents over, or the sound of spoons stirring a breakfast pot. No crickets; no birds.

Have I reached the hour before even nature awakes?

Stroking Schala, I closed my eyes, thinking it best I simply go back to sleep. Then, though, something outside *did* make a noise.

The soft, careful sound of a footstep in the grass.

My eyes flew open. From her place on my stomach, Schala had also come awake, lifting her head and pricking her ears in the direction of the sound. A dread certainty filled my stomach.

It isn't one of the soldiers. It isn't anyone.

Something lingered outside, yes. The thing with the bright, moony eyes. The figure moving among the shadows on the ship.

I held my breath and listened for more. The world around me seemed to wait with me in perfect silence. Until...

Schala climbed to her feet, stretching briefly before hopping to the floor and heading for the tent entrance.

"*No!*" I whispered, reaching for her, but she'd already moved out of my reach. The sense of strange intelligence loomed, and in my head, I pictured a hungry, waiting ghost in the field, silver in the damp mists, salivating for prey. I scrambled to my feet to snatch the caracal back to me before she caught its notice.

The little gray bob of Schala's tail disappeared through the tent flap just as I grabbed for her, and the icy chill of gray morning cut in like a knife slicing at my naked flesh. I gritted my teeth, bracing myself for the cold, and thrust the flap aside.

The clearing I stepped into wasn't the field of short grasses and rocky sand above the beach. There was no beach at all, and no city, and no huddled Sanraethi tents. Schala stood only a few steps ahead of me, peering over her shoulder to meet my eyes, and before me stretched a shimmering field of lush, dewy grass, deep sapphire blue in the darkness.

Anxious suspicion squeezed my heart. I refused to look around me or take in more of my changed surroundings. I made a grab for Schala, determined to reclaim her and duck back into my tent with Bannon, safe from this unwelcome vision. The caracal, though, slipped through my fingers again and trotted several feet away.

I don't want to look. I don't want to look!

I didn't have to, though. I sensed it all around me: the hovering, hungry attention of a predator. The thump in my chest quickened to a light, frantic pitch. *Run! Run, run, kitten, because the* big cats *are hunting tonight!*

"Schala!"

I'd almost lost sight of her in the thick, rich blades of grass. Only her little stub tail and the tufts of her pointy ears gave her away as she wandered ahead. "Just where do you think you're *going?*"

Run, elathae. *Run fast and hide, because we are going to hunt you down, and if we catch you...*

I straightened. Something like fear gilded by excitement shot through my body, making me stand tall as I searched the empty field around me.

Run, elathae.

Familiar words. A familiar thrill from... somewhere. I stood naked in an open landscape, limbs tight and coiled for action. The smell of deep rain carried to me on the breeze, and somewhere, *somewhere* a hunter—*my* hunter—lurked, ready to chase me down.

It is like my vision of the shrine. Part of an ancient past. These hands, her hands, my hands...

My night. My chase. I know this game.

So, I took off at a sprint.

Wet grass flew by beneath me. The cloudy cold raised the hair along my arms and the back of my neck, cutting like a blade as I breathed it in and yet fueling me with brisk, hectic energy. I ran as the deer, as the rabbit, as the fox—prey animals, all, scurrying from the predator, but I had no fear. I knew the hunter. The hunter who named me, who forged my strength and tempered my wild, primal power.

I am her. Her, and me. Beauty... and beast.

I ran for the trees which swallowed me up almost before I knew they were there. The scents of sweet pine and stoic oak, of aspen and alder and apple tree and cherry. Their leaves whispered to me as I raced beneath their shelter, and from deep within the tangle of their many branches came the soothing cries of night birds and the fluttering wings of bats. My bare feet thundered against cold, wet earth, sinking into soil, slipping on fallen leaves, and yet each step carried me, sure and true, like a ship cutting across the sea.

That's one, kitten.

"Take me," I breathed, surrendering to race with joy. Somewhere ahead was the shelter I sought, and I knew my course would guide me there, as sure as I knew what would happen when my hunter ran me down.

That's two.

White stone. Granite? Marble? Tumbled columns and eroded figures carved along an old, broken, fallen frieze. Steps half-hidden in the grass and moss; creeping morning glories closed tight until the sun called them open again, winding up old stone bones of a fallen shrine. *This* was where my body led. This place, where my hunter would find me, because that had been the purpose all along.

To be found. To be captured.

Already I felt his breath at my neck. Hot hands grasping for my ankles. The trees seemed to close in, as they always did just before I emerged on the old temple, and *there*—

Before I could leap up onto the altar stone, the hunter closed his grip upon my waist. I struggled and wriggled in his grasp, throwing all my strength against him, and still he held me. Blood roared in my ears; I snarled and bit at him, and he seized my jaw in one big, rough hand. My naked body responded, a flash of heat lighting up my belly, breasts, and thighs.

It's gorgeous.

It is, kitten. And that's three.

He bore me down onto the white stone altar. His mouth found mine, his breath like the breath of my own lungs. He smelled of blood and sweat, of steel and leather and fire. One hand still gripped my jaw while the other seized my thigh, fingers digging into soft flesh.

He is not the Red Bear. I am not his she-cat. Yet we are, and always have been. Hunter, lover, prey.

Just as I watched the hands before me change over years, just as I saw the shrine and the serpent skull. So, we have been born into this ancient rite.

"*Yield* to me."

"I never yield," I replied in breathless defiance. "Take what you want if you can. Subdue the beast or go from this place, unworthy. But I will never yield."

Bind me and hold me down... for a I fear I will break into pieces.

He forced his way between my thighs, and I raked at his face with my nails, drawing blood. Strong fingers closed around my wrist, squeezing, lifting it over my head to bend me back until I lay completely beneath him on the stone. He kissed me again, and our bodies seemed as one, every heartbeat, every rush of heat, every electric touch shared between us.

When his tongue met mine, he stole away a taste of my primal, raging power, and when his hand fell to my breast, caressing it, he imbued my heart with a measure of calm, cool peace.

"Take it from me," I whispered as our lips parted. "Take this fire from my blood... take this wild madness. Soothe my spirit and make my soul still and calm once more."

He bound my wrists in a length of silk he produced from within his sleeve. Wedging himself between my thighs, he released his cock from his trews and guided it into my entrance. The cry that ripped through my body was part pleasure, part wail, part feral screech, as he grasped me by the hips and thrust into me, claiming me in a hot, yearning rush of power.

I raged beneath him, despite my utter joy. The beast within cried out to fight, struggled to shove him away, even as I welcomed him deeper, moaning his name, raising my legs to wrap them around him and draw him tighter against me.

Bind me down on hands and knees. Give me no choice but to submit to you.

When he kissed me again, I bit his lip, drawing blood, and he seized me by the throat to hold me back down. No panic this time—no fear of distant masters or vengeful ghosts. I laughed, and he slapped my breasts before giving three hard, mean thrusts so deep I thought he might break me. While I twisted against the silk around my wrists, a sweet, salacious heat ran through my loins.

"Let me go," I snarled. But those weren't the words to bring this play to an end. Again, he slapped my breasts and my body jumped. I arched to take him deeper into me, welcoming him to my very core, twisting beneath his grip and writhing to feel his iron inside me.

Hold me down... make *me yield... give me no choice but to give you all of me...*

For I fear I will fly to pieces...

"Now, little monster," he rumbled. "Now, *come* for me."

The burning steel in his voice, like a blade fresh from the blacksmith's forge, called the response from me, wringing a swell of pleasure from my whole body. Yet still, I resisted, biting down on my tongue, squeezing my thighs hard around him, desperate to deny his power. Why? Simply for the thrill. The pride. To make him fight—make him *fuck*—even harder.

"I said, *come!*" he demanded, pressing his body to mine, clasping my chin in his hand to make me look into his eyes. Deep and endless eyes, warrior's eyes, hunter's eyes.

My Red Bear. Not the Red Bear.

Without fear, he kissed me again, and I tasted the blood on his lips. His free hand slid beneath my buttocks and held me to him, giving me no room to wriggle or twist away.

At last, I could resist no longer. I broke our kiss with a high, aching cry of pleasure, tightening around him, thrusting in time to ride his wonderful cock as I came. It swept over me like water over a breaking dam, all pain and tension giving way to overwhelming desire. My nails dug against the stone—my toes curled, and I begged him to complete the act, meeting me with his own climax and filling me with his seed.

Instead, he withdrew, pulling me roughly up from the altar before turning me around and pushing me down on my belly. He pried apart my legs and plunged this time into my tight, resisting rear entrance, invading me with a sharp, piercing pain. All at once it felt as though my whole body broke beneath his; with each thrust my strength waned and he took over, pushing me down, claiming me completely.

The strain and struggle burned down and dwindled. The fight in me evaporated, and all that remained was deep, delicious pleasure spiked with pain. Sweet and scorching and shining.

"*Yield*," he demanded again, and this time I did. I arched to meet his thrusts, moaning, whispering desperate encouragement as he fucked.

"I love you," I whispered. "I love you... I love you."

As he reached his peak, he thrust in me to the very hilt and I cried out. I thought I might pass out from the dizzying pain and whirling delight. But he withdrew in a swift motion, leaving my body empty and bereft, until the heat of his seed jetted across my buttocks and lower back.

"*Mine,*" he growled as he leaned over me again, clasping one possessive hand around my throat. "*Mine. Mine.*"

"Yes," I groaned, joyfully exhausted, beautifully used. "Yours... forever yours."

Then came darkness. Somewhere distant, a ringing chant. A pulsing blue light. As though awakening, I remembered the caracal kitten, and the tent I'd left behind. A man, asleep in a bedroll. A boat—a mission.

This is not real. This is...

An echo.

"*Elathae,*" my hunter whispered in my ear. "Little monster. My wicked, wild, wanton witch."

Witch. Always *witch.*

The cat. The man in the tent. The boat. The—

Light. Blue light. It is dying.

I must reach.. that...light!

CHAPTER TWENTY-TWO

I WOKE TO find myself lying in the mossy scrub of a shady wood. The verdant, wet scent of dewy leaves hung heavy in the air around me.

I lifted my head, puzzled. For a moment, I couldn't remember my name, or where I'd come from, or what I was doing here in this strange, dark, damp place, in the middle of the night.

Only the thinnest veil of morning light had begun to outline the shapes and shadows around me, defining low, thick trees and wide, wafting fronds and ferns. I rose from my supine position, giving a sudden start when something tugged at my wrists. Like a tight, unyielding rope, it held me, and I pulled at it with a surge of panic, until just like that, it seemed to evaporate. The bond broke; my wrists were free, as though nothing had really held them at all.

I sat up and rubbed at one temple. The dream began to fizzle and sift away. I recognized the place, at last: it was not far from the path where Bannon had chased me several days ago. The cold night air raised gooseflesh along my naked skin, and streaks of soil and moss covered me.

Naked?

Glancing back and forth, I found myself alone. How had I come to be here?

"I... was following the cat..."

Schala. Yes. I'd risen from our tent to chase her when she'd slipped out into the night, because—

Because there was something waiting out here. Something waiting... for me.

Bracing myself on a nearby tree limb, I climbed to my feet. "Schala?"

Nothing. No familiar chirrup. No purring, no head butting my ankles.

How long had I been lying here? My body *ached.* Back and hips, even my neck.

My breasts, too. My thighs, and my—

I swallowed hard. Gingerly, I touched the deliciously sore, throbbing place between my legs. Yes, my body stung all over with the satisfying bruises of rough sex It had only been a vision, though, hadn't it? A dream, fleeting and meaningless.

A clenching pain seized my heart. My hands shook. A vision, yes. One of fierce, primal play and domination.

"No semen, though," I reassured myself. In the vision, the hunter had marked flesh in a clear display of ownership and power. *My* flesh bore only the stains of dirt and moss.

Can I find my way back to camp? Naked, in the dark?

If I didn't, would the others find me?

"Bannon..."

I touched my fingers to my lips. If he woke without me beside him, he'd be furious, I was sure. Frightened, maybe, worried, maybe, but *furious,* underneath. The cool, quietly widening rift between us would only get bigger, if he thought I'd run away from him to go traipsing about alone in the night, in unfamiliar woods.

But... did I?

Furrowing my brow, I tried to remember how I'd come to be here. I didn't recall entering the woods. Only following Schala out of the tent flap, and then—

"Sleepwalking." The sound of my own voice in the pre-dawn quiet calmed me, grounding me. "Just like Bannon and Ailsa suspected... I was sleepwalking after all."

A nervous, queasy feeling in my gut begged to differ, but I had no time to stand here alone, shivering and naked, to think it through. I had to return to camp as quickly and quietly as I could and hope not to cross anyone else's path on the way. There was just no way to explain this.

I searched for my own footprints, but they were difficult to discern in the dark. Once I did settle on a pattern in the soil I thought *must* be my own, I peered closer, and a shiver slipped through my heart like a needle.

Another set of tracks appeared beside mine.

Yield, whispered a faraway voice in the back of my mind.

"Never mind!" I hissed at myself, stamping my foot in the dewy moss. I had to get back to camp, hopefully before Bannon caught me missing. I could tell him about this—I *would* tell him—but first I needed to be back, and safe, before he had a chance to become angry.

I took off at a trot, nervous in the darkness. At least the rain had stopped, leaving only a partly cloudy sky overhead. It lightened by fractional degrees, still barely enough, as I stumbled my way back.

"*Ow!*"

A tree root caught my ankle, and I tumbled forward. Brambles scraped my arms, and I struck my head on a hard scuff of stone just off the path. "Damnit!"

"Who's there?"

I glanced up, searching for the owner of the familiar voice. "Olsen? It's me, soldier. Sadira!"

His footsteps scuffed along the path, and I had only enough time to remember my nakedness before he appeared, the light of his torch illuminating the patch of ground just to the left of me. I scooted quickly behind one of the thick ferns before he could shift his lantern my way.

"What are you doing out here, this hour?" Olsen grumbled.

We hadn't exactly become fast friends since our clashes back at the castle. I'd once believed him a brazen predator, and while that rather distasteful aspect of his character appeared to have dissipated along with Alaric's looming curse, Olsen still didn't care much for me, nor I for him.

"Well, what do you think?" I grumbled, peering at him over the top of the ferns. "It's my menses if you must know. Care to be of help?"

He lifted his lantern higher, illuminating his face, drawn tight in revulsion. *Oh, please. Didn't Bannon tell me you were married?*

"Well, if you can't be of use yourself, send me Ailsa," I told him, trying to hide the left side of my face, where blood now dripped from the cut the rock had given me. Olsen's grimace hardened, and he gave me a nod before turning back toward the camp.

Thank goodness. I sighed with relief and hoped Ailsa wouldn't be long. Several moments later, though, it was Rayyan returned with Olsen, carrying a fold of cloth.

"There she is," Olsen grumped, waving a hand toward me. Rayyan nodded and thanked him, effectively dismissing him, before coming to join me behind the bush.

"It's my time, too," he confided to me, measuring out a length of cloth. "Olsen said you needed some—sacred serpent, Sadira, where are your clothes?"

I brushed aside the fabric he offered. "I don't need it, I just had to get Olsen to keep his distance. Can you go to the tent I share with Bannon and bring me something to wear? Or even a blanket to cover me while I slip back in there?"

"Not if this is some game or punishment your master has assigned you," he replied with a serious expression. Rayyan knew the ways of sensual slavery, even if he no longer followed them himself.

"It's not!" I insisted. "I... I think I must have been sleepwalking. I woke up deep in the wood, off the path, and... and I tripped on my way back, and now I'm bleeding. Ry, can you please just help me get back to my tent?"

"Of course. Here, stand behind me."

Rayyan stood shorter than me, but he'd put on weight and muscle since his harem days. He offered me his hand and pulled me to my feet, then led the way back toward camp with his lantern held high and ahead of us, obscuring the view.

"Sleepwalking, are you?"

"I think." I wiped the tacky blood from the side of my face. "I don't know. I thought I was awake, and Schala ran off into the field—"

A field of tall, thick grass. Not this scrubby, rocky heath.

"Speaking of the cat, she's been stalking all over the camp tonight." Rayya swung the lantern back and forth as we came to the edge of the wood, but none of the other guards appeared near enough to see us. "Making those unhappy sounds she makes when she wants your attention. You know, the grumbling and the moaning?"

So, Schala didn't know where I went? She didn't follow me? Couldn't *follow me by scent?*

We approached the tent I shared with Bannon, and as though she'd been waiting for just that moment, Schala bounded up from the ground just beside the entrance and came trotting to me. She chirped and purred, winding in circles around my legs until I crouched to pick her up.

"Sadira?"

The tent flap opened, and Bannon emerged, bleary-eyed. Before he could notice the strangeness of the situation, I gave Rayyan a quick peck on the cheek in thanks and darted into the tent. I grabbed Bannon's hand and pulled him in after me.

"What's going on?" he rumbled. Then, in a sharper tone, "Why are you naked?"

"Please, I'll explain." I drew him down beside our firepit, letting Schala drop onto the rumpled fabric of the bedroll. As I searched for the flint to strike the fire, I sensed Bannon's eyes roaming over me.

"You're bleeding." He touched the scrape on my head, making me pause. I lifted my hand to touch his.

"I fell," I said. All at once, I lost my sense of direction and purpose. I fell against him, resting my head on his chest, a deep, childlike loss welling up within me.

"I didn't mean to go," I whispered as he held me. "I woke in the woods. I had... such a strange dream. I can't seem to recall everything, only that there... there was *someone* with me. Someone called me there, and I thought... I thought..."

The Red Bear. Not the Red Bear. I am not his she-cat. Yet we are, and always have been. Hunter, lover, prey.

To my relief, he brought up a hand to stroke my hair, and curled his strong arms tighter around me. We'd been at odds for many days now, and I'd feared he might no longer share the need for this closeness, as he discovered more and more of the beast I really was inside.

Little monster.

I closed my eyes and crawled into his lap.

"Are you very hurt?" he asked.

I shook my head. "A few bruises, I think. The scrape bled badly, but it isn't very deep."

He sighed. "My troublesome kitten. Can't turn my back on you for a minute, it seems."

"I'm sorry." I took one of his hands in mine, twining fingers, giving him a squeeze. "Bannon... I am sorry to have been so difficult during this voyage. To have caused you such trouble, and... I'm so sorry I lied."

He gave a tired, quiet grumble, but said no more. I closed my eyes and soaked in his familiar warmth, silently vowing I would make it up to him. I would make everything right again.

OUR LAST FEW days in port were sunny and warm again, and trade in the city resumed in a bright, lively celebration. With the final repairs on the *Drekakona* coming to completion, Ashe and other sailors began coming ashore more often to purchase fresh supplies and stock up on a few luxuries, like the plump, juicy dates and the bigger, round, yellow papayas. Several mornings in a row, the ship's cook emerged to join the crab fishers on the rocks, grinning madly as he captured fresh crustaceans in his traps.

I helped Rayyan and Ashe haul supply crates back on board the ship. Perhaps I was more eager than most to get back on the sea, ever since my unexplained nightly sojourn and the heavy set of tracks—not Bannon's—I'd found by my side in the deep woods. No recurrence of my dreams, yet, and no new instances of sleepwalking, but I wanted to be gone from these shores and the strange visions they induced.

"Strange indeed," Ailsa murmured as we dropped off boxes of fresh linens and some medicinal herbs for her teas. "Before we came into port you seemed certain it was the *ship* being haunted. Now you long to return to it."

I knew Bannon's daughter as a fair and practical woman, rarely swayed by the swell of emotions in those around her when facts spoke their own truth. It wasn't like her to inject that hint of superiority and smugness into her tone, and though it was subtle, it jabbed at me.

"I don't know *what* is at hand," I said, leaning against the pile of crates we'd just delivered while Ashe and Rayyan retreated to fetch the next load. All the strangeness and uncertainty around me had left me exhausted to the bone. "I'm not asking for these circumstances to keep haunting me, Ailsa."

"Of course you're not."

The practical healing woman returned as she neatened the cabinets and cubbies of her sick bay and cast a quick glance over her shoulder at the single soldier—a woman who seemed to be suffering from an overdose of sun—lying in one of the bunks. Satisfied her patient seemed to be resting quietly and comfortably, Ailsa touched my arm.

"Come with me."

"We're due to leave port within the hour. I have other loads of cargo to—"

"It won't take long."

With a huff of surrender, I followed. It seemed less draining than arguing.

She led me through the middle deck, to the center of the vessel, which I'd heard Torv refer to as the waist. I'd only come to this part of the ship once, when Ashe guided Rayyan and me through the decks, showing us the work we'd be asked to do. At the very center of the middle deck stood the shrine to Sherida, and this was where Ailsa led me now.

Though I'd learned something of the Sanraethi spiritual path and their goddess, the great seer, I hadn't made any real effort to visit the shrine or delve into their practices. I'd met at least one creature of so-called *divinity*. I had little appetite for more.

"Why bring me here?" I asked Ailsa.

"I thought it might soothe you." She touched the altar, tilting her face up toward a holy sigil hung upon the wall behind it. "A place of prayer and meditation to welcome you, when your fears plague you."

I tried to hide a snort. Shrines and ritual spaces were hardly places of comfort for me.

"Sherida, seer of all,' she said, as though I needed to be told. The reverence in her voice put me on edge. I'd only ever heard such tones from the sorcerers of Akolet, immersed in their worship, calling out in ecstasy to the seven-headed serpent. The hairs rose on the back of my neck as I examined the holy sigil of Sherida, and I found myself grimacing.

"You must forgive me," I told Ailsa in a low tone. "I am not much interested in matters of worship. It reminds me too much of the men who would have fed me to their holy snake god."

"Our goddess is nothing like your snake," she assured me. "Sherida is a goddess of light and wisdom."

"So they said of Akolet."

I didn't wish for her to see me bristle. I had no quarrel with her faith or her goddess. It only reeked to me of the same intent, the same embrace of forces I had never been built to understand.

"It is through Sherida's wisdom I have learned to heal." Ailsa came to my side, crossing her arms over her chest. "I am not overtly sentimental. You know that by now. But I do know many of your fellow harem slaves have begun to find peace, and heal their scars, here in this shrine. Meditation on the seer's ways brings serenity to their souls."

"You know I am not like them."

"I know you think you can't be," she corrected. "Can't lay down the things that were done to you."

I stepped away from her, out of the shrine and back into the corridors. I didn't know if she would follow me, but she did, falling into step beside me.

"I know you are a proud medicine woman, and your clan reveres your skill," I said, terse. "But you seek to treat a malady I do not have. Sherida will do no better soothing my mind than Akolet did destroying it."

"I watched your fight with Mara," she pointed out. "The way the pain... *charged* you. It isn't normal."

"You've never before known a warrior thrilled by the heat and sting of battle?" I challenged. She hesitated, grimacing.

"It's not the same."

"Ailsa." I stopped before the ladder back to the main weather deck, turning to look her in the eyes. "*Understand* me. As much as it discomfits you, as much as you wish you could fit it into your ordered understanding, I am not mad."

"No," she said. "Not mad—"

"And my *reputation,* infamous as it may be, is not the whole truth of me. What you think you know thanks to nasty rumor and curious speculation is *not* who I am. I have told your father and I will tell you, too, and anybody else who needs to hear it: I *am not* broken. Alaric may have left me with scars, but underneath those scars, you will not find some innocent, victimized child. I am not ashamed of who I am, Ailsa, and I won't allow you, nor Mara, nor Bannon to *make* me ashamed."

She frowned and crossed her arms again. I thought she must want to say something more, but either she anticipated an unpleasant retort or something I'd said had finally gotten through. She rubbed her chin, eyeing me, but remained silent.

"There are more loads of supplies to carry," I told her again, before seizing the first rung of the ladder to climb up to the open weather deck.

I'd only just emerged into the sunlight when a pair of leather boots appeared right in front of me. I looked up and found Lieutenant Mara, looking back down at me, her dark, olive-green eyes intent.

"Supplies are loaded," she told me. Something in her expression made me feel certain I was about to be kicked in the face.

"Head back down. You and I have something to settle."

CHAPTER TWENTY-THREE

BRISTLING AT MARA'S tone, nevertheless I followed her as she guided me down to the third deck, and toward the rower's gallery. I had no rank of my own, of course, and no place to deny her orders, but so far Bannon had been wise enough *not* to leave her in charge of me. With him occupied elsewhere, probably with Captain Arne, there was no one to step between us now.

"Rowers are to report to their places before the next bell," she told me as we strode through the gallery, past the mostly empty benches and a few hands already waiting for their next instructions.

"Ah," I said. "So, the Red Bear wishes for me to join their team today?"

"Aye," she confirmed. Choosing a bench, she gestured for me to sit. I did, watching her carefully, even as Schala jumped up into my lap.

To my astonishment, Mara took the seat beside me.

"You and me," she said. "They'll call down to start the drum probably in the next half hour. You haven't done a shift at the oars yet, have you?"

"No." I seethed, certain Bannon hadn't been the one to set this assignment.

"Then you'll begin on the inner position. It will take time and practice before you can manage this side of the oar."

She belittled me in every word, and I knew it. I closed my eyes, nodding, and straightened my shoulders. We might be tasked with rowing together, but I didn't have to speak with her. I stroked Schala instead, and scratched her ears, grounding myself in the soft texture of her fur.

The caracal gave a sly miaow, green eyes slitted as she peered at Mara. Her back legs grew tense, claws pricking my thigh.

"Call off your fam—"

Mara cleared her throat, glancing askance. "Your cat. I'm not here to fight with you."

"Hush, Schala," I murmured to the cat. She settled into place again, tail twitching, eyes still locked on the lieutenant.

"How did you train her like that?" Mara tilted her head to one side, arching one dark eyebrow. "I've only ever seen working hounds take direction, and certainly no cat I've ever known will listen to a damn word anybody says."

I shrugged. "I didn't train her. She simply follows my lead. At least most of the time."

"Hm."

I had the distinct impression I'd only made Mara more convinced the caracal was some sort of familiar, rather than a simple feline companion. I let out a low sigh, my anger simmering, and I gave Schala an indulgent scratch behind the ear. I wished I had fresh bits of crab or chicken to offer her as reward for distrusting Mara just as much as I did.

"There's no use pretending we can get along," the lieutenant said. She'd turned her face away from me, maybe thinking if she met my eyes, I'd put some sort of wicked hex on her. "But if we both wish to continue serving the Red Bear, I think it's imperative we find some sort of common ground."

"Why are you so keen on serving Bannon, instead of some other warlord?" I jibed. "Surely there are other Sanraethi worth fighting for. If you disagree with your captain accepting me into his horde, surely he'd understand if you swear your axe in service to another."

"There are enough noble Sanraethi soldiers to fight the stars in the sky," she retorted with pride. "And enough loyal warlords in service to Rhode, I could have my pick of great blades to follow into battle. I will not, though. My axe—and my life—belong to Bannon."

She lifted one hand and ran her fingers along her temple, over a fine starburst of scars I'd never noticed before. Her tightly coiled braids began right above it, making it easy to miss in the crisscross of her dark hair.

A deep, ugly disgust filled my gut. How dare she say *she* belonged to Bannon? How could she, when Bannon was mine? Was there something between them that I was not aware of?

"What are you implying?" I growled.

A sly smile touched her lips. "So covetous and protective. Is Alaric Khan's personal witch so uncertain of her power over men, after all?"

I got to my feet, unceremoniously dumping Schala out of my lap. "I will fight you again *right now,* Mara, if you like. Let's go up to the weather deck. Would you prefer swords, or shall I beat you to death with my fists?"

"Sit down," she ordered.

At first, I resisted, snarling at her, unconcerned with the others around us, who now stared at me. The gallery had begun to fill up, and I recognized many of the soldiers assigned to row with us. Had she done this on purpose? Gathered her allies into the gallery so they could protect her, or even maybe aid her, in a rematch against me?

If that's the case, so be it. The beast within me surged for a fight. *This bitch is saying she* belongs *to* my *mate! I'll destroy that handsome face of hers and tear the braids from her head before I let her claim him so!*

"I said, *sit down,* soldier," Mara snapped. The tone in her voice cut through the red haze of my thoughts. Angry or no, I knew better than to try and pick a fight here and now.

Things between me and Bannon still haven't come right. Beating—or trying *to beat—his first lieutenant in a brawl right now would only make them worse.*

Scowling, I spat, "I am *not* a witch, and you know that by now."

"Yes, I know." She waved a hand dismissively. "I only wanted to make a point. You think you're in control, but clearly you need a better hold on your anger."

Narrowing my eyes at her, I sat. Schala immediately climbed back onto my knees, settling down and fixing an indignant sneer on Mara. As if

Mara had been the one to dump her on the floor. I loved this cat more and more every day.

"Well," I prodded. "What *are* you implying? Bannon has not taken a lover since his wife died, so don't tell me the two of you have a history."

"No," she admitted. "Not like that."

We were interrupted by a call from above, warning rowers to prepare for cast off. The last stragglers found their seats up and down the rows, and those in the inner position reached up to bring down the oar. Frowning, I watched the rowers in front of me, then did as they did, pulling the smooth, large shaft of wood down until it rested just above our laps. Mara took her end of it, resting with her arms draped over it.

"Do you know how the Red Bear got his name?" she asked me.

I nodded, as the drummer appeared at the far end of the gallery and made their way to the raised stage in the center.

"A battle with giants, from your northern mountains. He and his warband were captured and held prisoner, until he formulated a plan to escape."

"Aye," Mara said. She tapped the scar at her temple again. "He wasn't the only one with that warband. My brother and I both served alongside him."

Bannon's story came back to me. Several of the warriors had been tortured or killed. At one point, the giants had selected the sister of one of the other victims, and that was when Bannon launched his counterattack.

"Ah," I said. "It was you he saved from torture that day."

"Torture or death," she confirmed. "He proved himself a leader. The elders of our clans heralded his acts and named him Red Bear. From then on, he carried the axe not of a simple warrior, but of a warlord, donned with cords of crimson and black. And I swore to follow him."

"Hmph."

Another cry came down from above. The drummer lifted their hammers, and the first beat rang out. In answer, the rowers—all but me and Mara—answered with a loud and boisterous, "*Hoorah!*" and started up another lively, rhythmic chant. I struggled to match my motions to the beat at first, until Mara took the lead, and I lent my strength to hers for a smooth push and pull.

"I suppose I might have taken the captain as my lover," she said after a moment.

The red flicker of jealous hatred sparked in my chest again, but I kept it quiet, refusing to make eye contact with her and staring down at the wooden pole in my hands. Schala, discomfited by the rowing motions and the disturbance to her peace in my lap, slipped up to my shoulder and perched there.

"You're going to be too big to do that, soon enough," I grumbled at her. She thrust her head against mine in an aggressively affectionate head butt.

"I mean," Mara went on, "he is an exceptionally fine man, and fights like a true beast. I can only imagine he fucks like one as well."

The gall! I gritted my teeth, and right on cue, Schala issued a low, guttural growl and hissed at Mara.

Ignoring us both, she continued. "If he hadn't been so purely in love with Aileen, perhaps I could have shown him the true depths of my passion. Alas, though... he remained steadfast in his marriage, and I pined for him alone, even as I found others to keep me company at night and father three beautiful children I wouldn't trade for the world."

Another conversation with Bannon came back to me. *Mara has three children of her own and speaks of bearing another once we venture home.* I pictured the lieutenant upon their return, seeking out Bannon himself to lie with her and sire the new babe. Schala rumbled, claws pricking my shoulder. The brush of her stiffened hackles tickled my neck and ear.

Get a hold of yourself, Sadira. She is trying *to upset you. Don't play into her manipulation.*

I used to be so good at ignoring taunts and bullying. I could endure it from almost anyone— *except* Alaric. He could play my nerves as if I were a harp strung just for his hands, and he always knew exactly which points to pluck.

Because he threatened my only securities. Promised to give me away to the whoremonger or replace me with a more obedient slut. Shamed me for failing to please him and suggested he'd let one of the other sorcerers have me instead, his cast-off, thrown to them like a bone thrown to the dogs.

How could Mara play on those same fears so well? Did she know how painful these thoughts of abandonment were? How deeply it wounded me to think of Bannon tiring of me and my unique darkness, and moving on to a lover more... more *normal?*

Of course, she must. Is that not what she's telling you right this moment? That she *is the woman he passed over, in favor of* you?

"Even after Aileen passed," Mara said, "Bannon had no appetite for women. As though she'd taken every measure of love he'd ever have, for anyone else. Except of course, Ailsa. But that's different altogether."

"Why are you telling me this?" I demanded.

"So you understand why I will never leave Bannon's side."

Her knuckles on the wood blanched as she tightened her grip. A sense of danger prickled at the back of my neck, and all at once it occurred to me: I wasn't the only one infuriated by these revelations.

"I have a great deal of respect and admiration for the captain," she said. "And yes, even love. Passionate love, which I doubt will be matched by any man I *could* have in his place. I never, *ever* would have expected him to take another woman after his wife. Least of all a prisoner of war, who stood enemy across the battlefield, and in fact the favorite concubine of a twisted, sadist king. Of all the worthy bedmates he might have chosen, *you* were the last one I would have guessed."

"Perhaps you don't know as much about your captain as you think," I hissed. Already the rowing was taking its toll, making my arms sore and chest ache as I breathed. Or maybe it was Mara's infuriating tone.

"I know he had no choice but to bed you," she retorted. "Thanks to the savage customs of your horrible desert. Do you know how disgusted it made me, to know what he must do to you to cement our victory? I would have sooner broken with all those desert clans who fought with us and driven them back to their corners of the desert, than know my dearest friend must assent to *rape* to win his war."

"*Ha.*" I pushed the oar with perhaps a little more force than necessary, causing her to have to rein us in so we did not strike the oar in front of us. "What you don't understand—what *none* of you understand—is Bannon and I reached our own agreement that night. You claim to know him so well and yet still think him capable of rape? *I* saw something different in him, something dark and primitive and ultimately beautiful. I saw the *bear,* where you saw only a helpless man. How can you say you love him if you think him so powerless?"

Again, I'd pushed the oar too hard, fueled by my indignance, and she jerked it back, countering me. Now *I'd* infuriated her.

"Just because you agreed to be raped makes it no better!" she snapped. Other rowers looked back over their shoulders, expressions curious or puzzled or darkly disapproving.

"No." I seized control of the oar from her and took over the rowing, energized in my indignation. "Listen to me and listen well, Mara. *I* decided the outcome of that night. I *allowed* Bannon to claim me, because I desired him, because he showed me a strength and passion to satisfy my own. Perhaps you need it to be rape so you can believe it isn't real, or that I've ensorcelled him with my wiles. The truth is I have found my mate and master, and Bannon did not choose you."

"I *know* that!"

She shoved the shaft of the oar straight down, into our laps, arresting its motion entirely. I'd pushed my muscles too much and they gave up easily, offering her no resistance.

"I know my captain wants you," Mara conceded. "That is why I need you to understand how much he means to me, and to the rest of the horde. I don't like you, but I will tolerate you because *he* loves you. And because he loves you, we must find a way to work together, because I also know *you* will not leave his side."

"Oh?" The assertion, coming from her, surprised me.

"Yes. Because should you ever betray him, I will cut your heart out myself."

I peered at her, rubbing at one upper arm. I wanted to bite back at her, even remind her how our last fight had ended. But then, how could I? When all she'd done was promise to protect and defend the man I loved?

Even if she has the last word now, it is bittersweet comfort. It will not change things or give her what she genuinely wants.

Mara continued to row while I massaged sore muscles. Schala settled down with a soft, grumpy sound, and the stump of her tail thumped the back of my neck in an amusing gesture of annoyance.

After several silent minutes, I took hold of my side of the oar again and helped Mara row. It was my silent way of agreeing we must learn to tolerate one another, despite the deep distrust between us.

We'd just settled into a smooth, strong rhythm together when another cry sounded from up above. I glanced up, expecting perhaps a steering instruction, but no; another shout echoed the first, and soon a chorus of frightened cries drifted down to us from above.

"What's going on?" I asked Mara. She stared back at me, brows furrowed, and shook her head.

"Another fire?" one of the rowers asked his partner. The drummer had stopped their rhythm and half risen from their seat, while sailors up and down the gallery were abandoning their oars and heading for the ladderways.

"Come on," I told Mara, pivoting to climb off the back of our bench. We'd chosen a spot farther aft and could make it to the aft stairs before the others, avoiding the crush. Without waiting to see if she would follow, I slipped out of the gallery with Schala at my heels.

Others on the second and middle decks had also chosen the same stairs, but still we made it up to the open weather deck in minutes. I searched for smoke, letting out a huff of relief when I saw none.

"Goddess Sherida..."

Mara had followed me after all, and her mouth hung open as she looked up, overhead. I followed her gaze to the sails, and a surge of deep foreboding made my stomach lurch.

The wide, white canvas above us billowed in the breeze, soaked with the dark, crimsons stains of blood.

CHAPTER TWENTY-FOUR

MORE EVIL OMENS. More bad luck. If the sailors had seemed superstitious before, now they were downright fanatical.

"It's clearly a warning from the spirits of the seas!" one of them bellowed as Captain Arne took his place on the stern deck, overlooking the crowd.

"We must turn back!" another insisted. "We'll never make it to the next port alive!"

More shouts and terrible predictions followed, until Arne held up both hands and called for silence. The splattered red sails flapped overhead, as though in threat.

"We're not turning back," he insisted, and had to wait out a loud round of protests and boos before going on.

I hadn't had much time or reason to pay attention to Arne in the past, but as I watched him now, a sense of unease pricked at my instincts. A stout, self-assured man, he spoke with a booming confidence from deep in his barrel chest. The agitation buzzing in the mob around me felt far too strong for his calm, collected assurance, though. Maybe under other circumstances, it could have been effective, but at this particular moment, standing under the ruined sails spattered with blood as though from the scene of a murder, it rang of false and determined denial.

The same way he insisted the fire must have been caused by exotic spices and oils spontaneously igniting. They might have accepted it once, but this time...

"We will not be frightened off our voyage by pestering spirits!" he asserted. "A lot of nasty *skilggra*, that's all it is!"

"*Skilggra*?" I asked Mara.

"Sea hags." Her mouth twisted into a frown. "Old pagan folklore. A stupid claim, on a ship dedicated to Sherida, and with her own shrine right beneath our very feet."

"*Huh!* Sailors," scoffed a voice from beside me. Olson had arrived, with his usual partner Gregor beside him. Rayyan joined us too, but said nothing, staring up at the bloodied sails, face pale.

"They cling to many of the old beliefs in spirits and wild gods," Mara explained. The animosity between us seemed forgotten for now. "Some have taken up faith in the Goddess, but still these tales of *skilggra* and troll-cats and shapeshifters spring up."

I took another glance at the sails and twined my fingers with Rayyan's for reassurance. If the Goddess Sherida watched over this voyage, she hadn't offered her parishioners much favor.

"We'll need volunteers to mend the sails," Arne was saying. "Let's see hands, now. An extra ration of mead or wine for those who accompany the sail master up to the rigging."

"That's a job for days," Olson muttered under his breath. Rayyan answered with a slow nod.

An older sailor in neat clothing, with a white moustache twisted up into curlicues at the ends, made his way to the front of the crowd and turned to face us with a patient look on his face.

He must be the sail master. I stroked the end of my braid, watching and waiting for any of the crew to join the man at the front. Unhappy murmurs and nasty grumbling rippled through the group.

"I'll do it," I said at last.

Dozens of faces turned my way, many bright with surprise. I wasn't afraid of work, though. Bloodstained sails were an ominous portent, but it would be worse to leave them up out of fear. Better to dispose of them as quickly as possible.

I waded through the crowd to join the sail master at the front. He tipped me a nod of the head and extended his hand.

"Thank you," he said, in a comfortable, creaking old voice. "I am Jahn."

"Hello. I'm—"

"Sadira, I know." He gave me a patient smile. "Torv has spoken of you to me. Our resident *elathae* with her little feline companion."

The word shook me. "What? Did you say—"

We were interrupted as Torv pushed his way to the front. His pipe stuck out of his mouth at an angle making him look argumentative and ready for a brawl. The lack of courage among his crew seemed to have riled him up, and as many of them shouted out objections and urged him not to go, he waved them off.

"Shut up, the lot of you!" Taking a place beside me, he draped one big arm around my shoulder. "If this pretty witch can find the courage to climb up and handle the blighted mess, you sure as hell bet I can. And shame on the rest of you! Career sailors, letting a desert slave do your dirty work."

My mouth dropped open, and I was about to correct him—*please,* please *stop calling me witch, or slave, or whatever it was Jahn just called me*—when two more of the crew sheepishly came forward to join us. Arne clapped his hands for silence again.

I caught sight of Bannon at the edge of the crowd, leaning on the bannister of the steps leading up to the stern deck. He watched me with a look of appreciation, arms crossed over his chest, one brow cocked, as if he hadn't expected this of me.

But why shouldn't he have? I'd never shied from work before. I'd set out *determined* to make him and all the Sanraethi see I meant to earn my keep as more than a simple concubine or scheming prostitute, as some of them believed me. I'd served in any role assigned to me, ever since he set me free of my chains in the castle. What was so different this time?

"Can't go right up into the rigging yet, Captain," Jahn said to Arne, speaking loud enough so that the whole crowd could hear him. "Got to cleanse the shrouds and spars. Chase the spirits out of all the shadowy corners."

"We can't let these blood-soaked sails hang over us all night!" one of the crew shouted.

"I won't take a mending crew up there without first being sure the damned sea hags are gone," Jahn replied, regarding the sailor with a hard glitter in his eye. "I didn't see you volunteering to join my team, anyway. By all means, if you've changed your mind, *you* can take my knife and shimmy right on up there. I tell you, you'll put your foot down on a broken spar or a loose line and fall to your death while the *skilggra* cackle away above us all."

More unhappy grumbles made their way through the group. Jahn gave me a knowing smirk, though, and added under his breath, "They'll natter on about bad luck and angry spirits all they like, but they won't cross the *skilggra* if they can help it. Sea hags are some of the cruelest and most spiteful creatures beyond the veil."

"So why aren't you concerned about crossing them?" I glanced from one bloodied canvas to the next.

"Oh, to be sure, I wouldn't tempt the bitches either, as long as I had a choice. Jumping right into the rigging lines will only play into their mischief and end up with one or more of us strangled, broke-legged, or thrown overboard. That's why we're going to smoke them out, first. Got to burn lots of spice and tobacco to drive them off. We either do it right or have worse luck later, and farther out."

"Tricky work, smoking the bitches," Torv grunted. "Especially having just pinned up the holes in the ship thanks to fire. But we'll set up tin buckets with some pungent tobacco and keep a careful eye on them through the night."

He took his pipe from his mouth and blew a ring of smoke up toward the main sail. "*That'll* be the hardest part. Make no mistake. Keeping the flames low and watching for stray cinders. Once we have it out of the way and the hags clear, cutting down the canvas will be hardly worth a spit."

I grimaced and looked out across the deck at the crowd, full of nervous faces. Arne had already started issuing orders to the rest of the sailors, while Mara began gathering the soldiers for instruction. I moved in her direction, ready to report for whatever new tasks she'd have for us, when someone took gentle hold of my arm.

"C'mon, kitten." Bannon led me in the opposite direction. "You'll have your hands full enough tomorrow. The others can manage whatever is left tonight."

Wary unease filled my gut. "Sir?"

He put a finger to my lips. We slipped into the stern, unnoticed except perhaps by Jahn and Torv.

"I'm proud of you," Bannon said, guiding me past the first set of doors toward the aftmost cabin. I had thought it would house the captain's sleeping quarters, but when Bannon gestured me in, I found a brightly lit study, one wall covered in shelves of nautical tomes and atlases, and books I guessed to be Sanraethi tales of mythology.

Next to the shelves stood two desks carved of a dark and heavy-looking wood, with parchment tucked into neat stacks and quills standing ready beside inkpots. Across from these were a pair of couches and a globe. I drifted toward it, fascinated; I'd never seen a globe, even when I'd accompanied Alaric as his bodyguard in raids on foreign soil.

At the very back of the room, wide windows gave a glorious view of the sea, bobbing and sparkling in our wake. As I gazed out over the water, some sleek, blue sea creatures leapt from below, their smooth skins glimmering.

"Dolphins," Bannon told me, taking a place beside me. "Friendly things. Some of the crew think they're shapeshifters or mermaids in disguise. They keep away sharks."

"Sir?" I faced him, uncertain. "You said you're proud of me? For what?"

"Volunteering to go up into the sails."

He said it easily, as though it should have been obvious. Taking me by the elbow, he guided me to a soft, velvet-lined divan and bade me sit with him. He shifted me to face the window so I could watch the dolphins and the white lace of sea foam trailing behind the ship.

"All the upsetting experiences you've had on this voyage," he said, combing his fingers through my hair. "I know you fear dark magic is at work. Yet you were still the first to say you would face a terrible portent head on. I am proud because my kitten is brave, even in the face of unknown danger."

"It's getting worse." I twisted to face him again. "*Everyone* saw it this time. At first it only affected me, but now—"

He put his hands on my shoulder and pointed me back toward the windows. "I should never have doubted you, Sadira. You have an eye for the veil unlike any person I've met before."

"The veil?" My fingers came up to toy with the end of my braid. "Jahn mentioned that, too."

Bannon gathered back my hair, and then, to my surprise, he produced a small brush and began running it through the short layers.

"Where did you get that?" I asked, tone softening.

"I bought it from the innkeeper's wife before we left. I know this isn't as fine as one of the luxurious combs you had in Vashtaren, but—"

When he'd called me in here, I'd expected the worst. A scolding, or some cold proclamation he was through with our arrangement after all. Instead, after

263

days of uncertainty and awkward silence, he'd bought me a gift. He wished to pamper and praise me.

I closed my eyes, awash in warmth and sweet relief, and reached back to stroke his cheek. "It's wonderful.

"It's just a humble little thing made of plain wood." He chuckled. "I'll find you something nicer once we've reached Sanraeth."

"I don't care how pretty the brush is." I leaned against him as he combed. "I love this. Your touch... your affection. Your pride in me."

He kissed the top of my head. "Consider it a reward for such beautiful bravery."

We fell quiet for a few moments, as I basked in the attention, practically aglow with joy.

"What do you mean by 'the veil'?" I finally asked, hoping I wouldn't spoil the mood.

"The realm of spirits and devils. That which is unseen. Magic."

Reaching out a hand, I pressed my fingers gently to the cool glass of the window. As the sun set, it cast the ghost of my reflection back at me, and I stared at the lines of deep red, like blood, running over my skin.

"You seem to perceive it in ways the rest of us do not. I can't say I understand it. As I've told you, in Sanraeth, magic is rare, and belongs to the miracle workers of Sherida. They don't deal in ghosts, or summonings, or dark invocations like your Vash sorcerers. Theirs are the godly powers of blessing, of compelling evil to withdraw, and of healing the soul."

I grimaced, watching my reflection do the same. "It all sounds the same to me, Sir. The disciples of Sherida call upon blessings while Alaric and Rikhi

264

called it the favors of Akolet. I see little difference in calling up dark beings and ordering them out and about."

"Well..." he hedged. "Don't let Ailsa hear you say it."

"Perhaps in failing to manifest magic, I fail to properly respect it, as well."

"But you've sensed it, yet again, as it presses down on us. From now on, I'll take your counsel on the subject as golden, and never doubt you."

I didn't know if I wanted *that* much faith. If I sensed dark spirits and evil hexes, it seemed just as likely that again, *I'd* drawn it upon us, and we still had no answer as to why it had come, or what it heralded.

Alaric? I took my palm from the glass and touched the tattoo over my eye. The tattoo he'd given me with the promise it would hone insight and heighten perception. Bannon was certain the vicious king's last scrap of power had burned away when I broke free of my collar and we'd slayed the awful seven-headed beast he'd become.

But if Alaric truly was gone... what otherworldly presence had come to take his place?

And what did it want with me?

CHAPTER TWENTY-FIVE

I REPORTED TO the base of the main mast first thing in the morning, meeting Jahn before first light had broken through the thick blankets of fog. The acrid aromas of tobacco and alligator pepper made my eyes water; the smoke from last night's fires still hung thick over the weather deck, low and hazy. With close fog and little breeze, we'd be choking on it for a while.

The last of the night crew were just dousing the remaining pots and buckets of burning herbs as I found Jahn through the huddle of shapes and shadows. He greeted me with a prim bow—not a common greeting among the Sanraethi, as far as I'd seen. I returned the gesture, feeling stilted and a little foolish.

"Do you think the *skilggra* are gone?" I asked, glancing at the sails overhead, barely visible in the dark, ugly mire. If there really were hags, and they really were repelled by the dizzying reek in the air, I couldn't imagine there'd be any left within several leagues of us.

"For certain." Jahn nodded, twirling the end of his moustache while he watched the last of the crew douse the final pot and carried it away. "They'll be long gone by now and stay well away."

"The crew still don't seem very motivated to get up into the rigging."

I crossed my arms and leaned against the mast, glancing back and forth in deliberate gesture to the empty deck around us. Jahn gave a soft chuckle and rocked back onto his heels in a charming singsong way. I decided I quite liked him and offered him a smile.

"It's early yet," he said, "and too dark in this fog. We'll wait for the sun to rise higher and burn some of it away. By then Torv and the others will be along."

"And how do we do this?"

He drew his knife from his belt and held it out to show me. It wasn't a fighting knife, like Bannon carried. This blade had been forged in a hooked, almost talon-like manner, with a row of serrated teeth along the first part of the inner edge, close to the handle.

"The sails are made up of segments," he explained. "We'll cut away the damaged portions and save as much of the good canvas as possible. Then we patch the areas of missing sail with fresh sailcloth. It's a long process, mind you, and you'll be plenty sick of it by the time we're through."

I hesitated before asking my next question. "Do you really believe it was the work of evil spirits? Sea hags?"

Jahn glanced around us, a shrewd glimmer in his eye.

"You're pretty sure up in the ropes, aren't you? Yes, I've seen you climbing up in the ratlines before.

We can probably go up now without too much trouble, long as you're careful."

I cocked an eyebrow. Why the sudden change of tone? Before I could ask, he had turned and taken hold of the ladder rungs on the mast and begun to climb.

I stooped to give Schala a quick scratch before following him up. We reached the first spar and moved out onto the rigging lines, working our way to the middle of the sail. Jahn moved with a natural ease, as comfortable amid the ropes as I was, despite his age. As we reached the midpoint and he raised the knife to the canvas to show me the correct technique, he spoke in a jovial, conversational tone.

"Not so certain about the captain's conclusion, then, are you?" He grinned knowingly without looking away from his work. "Don't believe in flocks of *skilggra* catching up in our sails and taking out their anger this way?"

I couldn't decide if he was challenging me, offended by my doubt, or if he, too, thought the idea of *skilggra* unlikely. "I don't know. It's not the sort of spiritualism I'm familiar with. Sea spirits and vengeful fairies spreading havoc..."

"Right, *you* were taught to fear the great seven-headed serpent and his chosen sorcerers."

I narrowed my eyes. "Yes, exactly."

"And so, what does your faith tell you now, *elathae?*"

I reached out to take his wrist, stopping his cutting and making him look at me instead.

"What does that word mean? Why do you call me that?"

Jahn relaxed against the rigging, returning the knife to his belt and producing a pipe, similar to Torv's but with a much, much longer stem. Tamping a little tobacco into it and lighting it, he took a brief puff and eyed me with a shrewd, smiling expression.

"I'll tell you what *elathae* means," he said, "if you tell me what you think of these bloodied sails."

I wrinkled my nose at him and adjusted myself to lounge easily along the lines.

"I don't think it's mischievous or angry sea spirits." Bringing up a hand to my temple I closed my eyes and started kneading. "I think something else—something intrusive and malevolent—has found its way on board."

"Why would you think so?" Jahn drew on his pipe and blew out a winding silvery stream of smoke. How could he bear it, with the air around us already so clogged with such sharp, strong, unpleasant odors?

"I have dealt with a ghost before," I replied. Staring down through crisscrossing shrouds and waving canvas, I saw the morning crew beginning to mill about the deck, picking them out by the muted light of lanterns through the mists.

"Have you now?"

"Yes. He did not come because of hair cutting or spilling salt or because eggshells weren't crushed well enough. He came for me, out of jealousy and obsession."

I hesitated a moment before adding, "Many people died."

Jahn stroked his beard. "Well, no one on the *Drekakona* has met their end now, have they?"

"I might have. When the ropes caught me. And Mara could have when she fell overboard. If there *is* a

269

vengeful spirit on the ship—and I have *seen* such a being, I think, a shadow of a person with wide, white eyes—who knows what it is capable of. There's still a ways to go before we reach Sanraeth, I'm told."

"And if such a being has indeed attached itself to our ship," Jahn mused, "why do you think it has done these things?"

I nibbled at my bottom lip, staring out into the lightening grayness of the morning. When Alaric haunted us, his actions followed a pattern. We hadn't seen it at the time perhaps, but in the end, he'd revealed it to me: at first, he'd only been strong enough to possess an adolescent boy, not suitable for a long-term host; then, an injured soldier; then a herd of horses. Only after some time, and a greater gathering of his strength, had he been able to claim significantly powerful hosts.

And always, once he'd possessed his victims, he'd been compelled to attack women. Any woman. The closest woman. Until he'd managed enough control over his own dark emotions to target me directly.

Was there such a pattern to be discovered now?

The doors back at the castle. The mob in Olyb. Rigging lines attempting to twist me into a dangerous, maybe deadly, version of the suspension my former master once employed for his entertainment.

A shadowy creature lurking in passageways where only I could see it. Ship's corridors turning into a maze, leading me to a cargo hold that didn't exist. All to show me—

I stared at my hands, recalling the dreams I'd stumbled into. Temples and altars. Serpent worship? The last dream, leading me from my tent, taking me out into the woods...

Chased by a hunter. Caught by a lover.

It hadn't been Bannon, not in that vision. But I hadn't been Sadira, either, had I?

I was... primal Woman. *Wild and wanton, powerful and... and connected. The beast yearning within to be captured, dominated, subjugated. And it felt...*

"*Elathae,*" I murmured. In the vision, my unknown partner had called me *elathae,* just as Jahn had.

"What does it mean?" I asked him again.

Finished with his pipe, he tapped out the last of the tobacco ash and gave the bowl a quick wipe with a handkerchief, then stowed both in his pocket. He retrieved his knife again and went back to sawing through the canvas.

"*Elathae,* like the *skillgra,* are creatures of the old legends. Here, child, I think you get the idea now, so get out a knife and get to work."

I did as he asked, starting on a different segment of the sail. "Just spirits?"

"No. *Elathae* were spirit callers and enchanters among our ancestors. In times before the church of Sherida found its way into our land, and the Sanraethi people still worshipped the earth and its balance of forces, the *elathae* guided them in ritual and magic."

With an unhappy sigh, I stopped cutting and brought my free hand up to pinch the bridge of my nose. "You mean *witch.* That's what Torv said, too. When will people understand I am *not* a witch?"

"Are you not?" He gave me an innocent but incredulous look. "That cat seems to think so. They're good at recognizing spirit callers. And as I hear it, you whistled up a pack of black dogs scare off your enemies back in port."

"I don't know why Schala came to me, or those dogs. I spent most of my life with a sorcerer obsessed over finding magic in me, and in all that time I failed to display the tiniest spark of talent. I couldn't even manage sleight of hand for a laugh. I'm a soldier, not a spirit-caller or enchantress."

"Hm." He raised an eyebrow. "Perhaps it was the sorcerer who failed."

I scowled at him. "Let's just patch this sail, old man."

Jahn laughed, but he said no more about spirits or magic as we got down to the repairs.

Less than an hour into our work, the fogs had lifted just enough for Torv and the others to climb up on the other masts and begin their work as well. Torv waved to us from the spar of the forward mast, and Jahn waved back. The smell had begun to clear out now, but the mists lingered, even as I looked up to search for the bright hot spot in the clouds, telling me roughly where the sun burned in the big sky beyond.

The day passed slowly, and the work on the sails demanded a great deal of physical engagement. By midday, I was covered in sweat, aching from arms to ankles, and heaving like a bellows. On the other hand, being in the rigging exhilarated me, and I found myself daring to twist and hang in the lines with ever-increasing boldness, learning to swing and pull myself about, even working on a patch while hanging upside down from my knees. Jahn laughed at me while I experimented, calling me *rig monkey* and *squirrel*, and I decided to forgive him for believing I might be a witch after all.

Though the fog lifted from the deck, the sea around us remained shrouded in thick, rolling clouds.

Early in the afternoon I paused in my work, glancing out into the distance, frowning.

"We aren't going anywhere," I said to Jahn, who'd climbed up to the crosstrees above me to have another smoke.

"'Course not," he said, clenching the stem of his pipe between his teeth as he lit a match. "Fog like this, we could sail right into an island cliffside and find ourselves halfway to the sea bottom before we knew it."

"Isn't it strange, the fog hasn't lifted?"

"Not so much." Finally striking a flame, he lit the pipe and tucked his matchbox back in his pocket. He paused to take a couple gentle puffs, then gave a long, satisfied sigh, breathing silver smoke into the air.

"Some days are like this. Sea gods holding their breaths, putting sailors ill at ease for what comes next. Maybe sun'll burn it off, maybe rain'll fall instead."

I stared up, looking for a hint of the sun. "How long does it last?"

"Hard to know." He tapped the pipe against one leg, following my gaze. "One day isn't too strange. Two days, not unheard of."

"But if we're not moving..."

Jahn might be thinking of sea gods and signs from above. Or below, as it were. I, on the other hand, couldn't help but worry about a different threat entirely.

In Vash, it was a sandstorm. Here, heavy mists trap us in place.

Trapped—*For how long?*—with a lurking, shadowy entity, and its wide, white, glowing eyes.

CHAPTER TWENTY-SIX

THE NEXT DAY passed, and the fog did not lift. Another day, and still, no break in the dull, gray blanket upon the sea. We worked in the rigging, cutting and patching the sails, sometimes unable to see even each other through the thick, close mists, and each toll of the ship's bell deepened a growing, simmering sickness inside me.

What is waiting for us out there? Like Alaric's horrid, hateful spirit lurking in the sandstorm. What vengeful intelligence is doing *this to us?*

The *Drekakona* drifted, directionless. No wind filled the sails. We couldn't row, for fear of crashing up on some unseen reef or rocks. Restlessness and agitation hung over the crew like an awful smell, and everyone was more certain than ever the bloodied sails had been a terrible warning. Throughout the days, once the chores had been finished—what few there were on a ship at a standstill—the crew and the soldiers divided up into huddled knots, to drink or gamble or arm wrestle, or find some way to distract themselves from the yawning, empty hours adrift.

If I spent too much time thinking about our future on these seas, I found myself wanting to vomit.

Our team spent nearly a week repairing the sails patch by patch. Sometimes I looked up to find a spot in the clouds: the vague ghost of the sun moving across the sky. Other days, the chilly mists soaked through my leathers and left me shivering as I sawed through canvas and stitched up the gaps.

I lay awake at night in Bannon's arms, waiting for the knocking at the door. My moony-eyed shadow hadn't returned since the fire, but its conspicuous absence only set me more on edge. Certain it would come at any second, the very moment I closed my eyes. Exhaustion eventually dragged me down to sleep, and in the morning when Bannon shook me awake, I struggled to rise, always casting a glance out the porthole to see nothing but thick gray clouds again.

"What happens if we drift forever?" I asked him one afternoon, lying with my head in his lap as he stroked my hair. Again, we'd fallen into a listless, unspoken celibacy. I didn't know if it stemmed from the uncertain dread of the fog or from some lingering, wounded divide, keeping us distant and unable to say whatever it was we needed to say.

He said nothing. In a way, I thanked him for it. After what we'd been through, I didn't want him to patronize me with empty platitudes that everything would be all right. Maybe we'd drift until we died. At least our food supplies were still plentiful, and we hadn't yet had to discuss dwindling rations.

"Why aren't you sleeping?" he murmured in my ear one night as we lay in the darkness.

I reached for his hand, giving it a squeeze. "Waiting for *it* to come."

"I am here, Sadi. I won't let it hurt you."

He'd never seen it, though. He hadn't heard it that night, when it hammered on the door, when I screamed.

"And the cat," he added, guiding my hand to where Schala slept curled up by my abdomen. "Cats can see through the veil. She'll warn us if danger is near."

I stroked Schala, and she gave a deep, rattling purr as she stretched and rolled to give me her belly. I indulged her with a scratch. *Is that why she came to me? To warn me, and keep watch for me?*

She pushed her head against my hands, basking in my touch. I'd come to adore her so much, and so easily. I'd never known the deep, nearly soulful bond one could feel for an animal like this, and yet already I couldn't imagine being without her.

Is she a witch's familiar? Is she my *familiar? How?*

I'd told Jahn, as I'd told so many others, of Alaric's disappointing attempts to teach me conjuration and black arts. Like the desert itself, any part of me that might have harbored spiritual ability lay fallow and barren. Empty and dry as an old, worn wooden cup.

You have no power. I stole your power.

And even if I *did* harbor some talent... I had no understanding whatsoever on how I might bring it to my fingertips.

The altar with the serpent skull. My dream of the hunter... it was a sex rite, I know it. Haven't I been subject to enough of them to know?

When I did sleep, if I didn't dream of endless corridors and moony eyes, I dreamed of serpent worshippers. A new and different Order of Akolet, bearing knives with curvy edges, calling up raw, ravenous magic from the cold shadows.

Here are your people.

"What do you need, Sadira?" Bannon asked. I knew what he meant. He asked the same question whenever I grew anxious and tense. What did I need to ground me again, to help me find order through the chaos of my thoughts and fears? I didn't want to ask, though. He seemed too far away, divided from me by some strange electricity, cutting me off from his warmth, his breath, his life.

Cutting me off from everything... except *it.*

A WEEK PASSED. A week and a half. The first rumblings over rations and water supplies began passing from crewman to crewman. The vague, bright ghost in the sky showed itself less and less. The fog closed in, until we couldn't see from one archery tower to the next, or even the masts in between.

I stood at the deck rail, elbows resting on the wood left slick from drizzle. The sea had a smell about it today, an ugly and stagnant smell. The smell of dead things. All I could think about was death, lately. Starvation at sea, or sinking deep into the darkness when the ship wrecked itself on rocks jutting up from the water like teeth. Fire, kindling deep in the *Drekakona's* belly, which would not be extinguished no matter how hard the brigades fought it.

My bright-eyed apparition still had not returned. I wished I could take solace in that. Instead, my tension deepened until it throbbed and ached in my spine and left me too nauseous to eat.

Torv's voice startled me from my thoughts. "*Elathae.*"

I grimaced as he took a spot beside me, leaning on the rail exactly as I had. "Please, Torv, don't call me that."

"It isn't an insult." For once, his normally boisterous voice was soft, and he regarded me with a steely, somber expression. "Not so long ago, the *elathae* were our most revered seers and spirit-callers. Holy people, guided by the hands of the old gods."

I shook my head. "I know nothing about spirits or old gods. I have been hunted by one, yes. Maybe another hunts me now. But I have no insight to their ways, or how to be rid of them."

"No, no." He waved his hands at me. "I don't ask you to drive them away. I ask for you to *appeal* to them. Speak to them, as you speak to your little familiar."

I glanced down at Schala, as always seated at my feet. "I don't *talk* with her."

"You do. You just don't know it. *She* does, though."

He stooped down as though to touch the caracal, but she bristled and gave a high, whining rumble.

"Protective." He pointed a finger at her, wagging it to emphasize his point. "Fearless little guardian. Keep her well, and she'll never leave your side."

"I'm glad for her, I admit."

I scooped Schala into my arms and scratched her tufted ears. "One stray's adoption does not make me a spirit-caller, though. How could I talk to your spirits, Torv? How would I even begin?"

He shrugged. "I'm only an old salt, girl. I can't tell you more than my papa told me about the old stories and nature's ways. You, though... you can hear them. You can *see* them."

He gestured out, into the deep, dense fog.

"We *need* you to find a way to speak with them."

I put Schala down again and heaved a sigh, leaning over the rail again. I stared down into the flat, steely blue ocean, a hollow, empty sickness in my gut.

After several long moments, something in the water caught my eye.

"Torv." I pointed at it. "What's that?"

The quartermaster followed my gesture, narrowing his eyes with a gruff "Hmph?"

"There's another one," I said. "And there. What are they?"

Even as I spoke, the shapes resolved themselves, and as recognition dawned upon me, I staggered back a step, stricken. The color drained from Torv's ruddy face, and my immediate instinct told me to somehow keep him silent, keep him from alerting the crew. It wouldn't have mattered though: already, sailors and soldiers along the deck had noticed the shapes bobbing to the surface, and the workers in the rigging started to cry out.

Bones. *Human* bones. Skulls, ribs, whole skeletons. Bloated white body parts and drifting, floating scraps of disintegrating clothes.

I brought both hands to my mouth to stifle a scream. As though he'd somehow sensed it, wherever he'd been, Bannon appeared at my side, throwing his arms around me and turning my head to shield me from the sight. Up and down the deck, people began to wail, and I buried myself against Bannon's chest, squeezing my eyes shut.

"What does it mean?" I groaned. "Bannon, what does it mean?"

Before he could answer, the ship gave a sudden, shuddering thump, and swayed to one side. We braced against one another, keeping each other from falling. Schala gave a feline yowl and leapt up to my shoulder; all around us, the wails of the crew turned to startled cries.

"Did we hit something?"

"Are we damaged? Did anything breach the hull?"

Confusion swirled around us. I looked up into Bannon's eyes, frightened, and then the ship lurched again, her bow taking a sharp turn to the side. Beneath our feet, the deck tilted, and I found myself slipping from Bannon's grip.

"Sadi!"

He grabbed for my arms, but I lost my footing and tumbled to the boards, hitting my chin and rattling my teeth. Schala dropped down, wobbling as she tried to catch her balance, immediately whirling toward me, back arched, fur standing up in a stiff brush.

Sounds of splashes and cries of alarm sent a wave of fear through me. I scrambled for Bannon's outstretched hands. Another shuddering bump rocked the *Drekakona,* and a loud, wooden groan rose from below.

I had a flash of sudden memory: Mara, sliding and tumbling, thrown over the rail. I cried out, bouncing and rolling across the deck, tasting blood, and then came the harsh crack of the deck rail against my shoulder. I grabbed for it, but my fingers slipped and scrabbled against the smooth, wet wood, and then the world dropped out from under me.

I hardly had time to catch my breath before I hit the water and sank beneath the choppy waves.

Panic shot through me. A surge of adrenaline flooded my limbs and I reached up, searching for the surface. I sensed bodies in the water around me, and my hand closed around something cold and soft. A leg. A swollen, rotten green leg, ending in bone and gristle just above the knee. I screamed, sending bubbles of air out in a rush as I pushed it away from me.

The bubbles. Follow the bubbles up!

The water... so cold. My legs were pins and needles as I kicked and pushed. Bannon hadn't gotten around to teaching me to swim, not after the day at the waterfall. Moving on nothing but instinct, thrashing more than paddling, finally I found a rhythm with my legs and kicked upward.

Voices filled the air around me as I broke the surface and sucked in a breath of air. I whipped my head back and forth. More body parts and detritus floated around me. Several crewmates had fallen in too, and they splashed and screamed and called out to the others above.

There's something else here. Something moving in the water. Something—

A dark, smooth, shining shape humped up out of the sea just in front of me. Gliding, sinuous. Then it disappeared beneath the frothing waves again. An eerie, resonant cry sent a spike of fear through my body.

"Help!" I screamed, flailing my arms and desperately kicking to keep myself afloat. My foot struck something thick and solid, something alive.

Some of the others had caught sight of it, too. They pointed and clung to one another as a long, sleek shape surged up from below, and an enormous, green, tapering whip of a tail rose up, up, slicing through the air, and then came crashing down again, sending a massive spray into the air.

No... no, not a snake... please, *not a snake, not* him, *not* that *snake*—

Ropes came flying down from above. Voices called my name, and I twisted toward them in a halting, ungainly manner. The end of one of the lines floated a short distance from me. I reached out, stretching for it, kicking my feet. I'd almost reached it when that echoing sound came again, and a slithering length of the creature below wound up through the water, pushing the rope away.

"No!"

More bodies. Bones, bobbing against me in the churning foam. I couldn't keep my head up—my limbs burned with exhaustion—and the swirling sea threatened to suck me down once more.

I gasped in a lungful of air just as a fierce current pulled me under, and despite my struggles I sank deep into the dark, cold void.

That sound. What is that sound?

Again it came, a strangely curious peal, clear even through the water. I could only make out shadows and brief, weak flashes of light. Bubbles and foam swirled around me, nearly blinding me.

Then two huge, pale, shining shapes appeared before me. Wide, round circles of light—like bright, beaming moons under the water.

I stared in terror. The huge, white eyes cut through the darkness, aimed right at me. We looked at one another, and I forgot to kick my legs. I forgot to reach or pull with my arms. Cold down to my bones, I froze, caught in its burning gaze, stunned into total, mindless fear.

Something crashed into the water above me. Someone's arms wound around my midsection. I was pulled upward through the black, until we broke the surface. Someone's voice came, frantic at my ear, but I couldn't move. Numbness enveloped me. I couldn't shake my thoughts from those eyes, the horrible, familiar, wide, white eyes, enormous and shining under the waves.

What is it? What is it?

"Hold on tight, Sadi. Come on, now, get your arm around my neck—"

I was only vaguely aware of Bannon's arm curled around me while he swam, carrying me along. We were pulled up from the water like fish on a line; a team of soldiers hauled us up, over the railing, back onto the deck. The instant I felt the wet, slippery boards beneath me again, Schala pounced on me, butting my shoulder with her head, crying plaintively.

"Where did it go?" I whispered. Bannon leaned close to me, and I grabbed him by the collar of his soaking, clinging vest. "Bannon? Where... where did it go?"

"Quiet, Sadi. Catch your breath. You're shaking like a leaf."

At the rails, other sailors hauled the ropes, pulling soaked crewmates up over the rail. Lookouts were scanning the water, shouting back and forth. Arne and Torv stormed through the crowd, checking the survivors, demanding to know if they'd been hurt, bitten, bludgeoned. Ailsa had already gone to work tending to a man who appeared to have broken a leg.

I felt dizzy. So dizzy, and so sick, and so cold.

"Clear over here, Captain!" one of the lookouts shouted.

"Nothing over here, either!" another rejoined.

Bannon rested his strong, steadying hands on my shoulders. "There now, kitten," he soothed. "You're all right. It's all right."

"No," I managed through numb lips. One hand clutched Schala close to my chest. The other, tangled in Bannon's vest, gripped harder until my knuckles burned with pain.

Where did it go?

CHAPTER TWENTY-SEVEN

I FELL INTO a daze, hardly cognizant of the motion and voices around me, clutching Schala close and burying my face in the ruff of her gray fur. I couldn't shake the feeling of the cold, wet depths, a hungry, animal fear gnawing at my heart, as though I'd never been pulled up from the water at all, as if the ocean meant to devour me even now.

Someone—surely Bannon—brought me to our cabin and stripped me naked, then wrapped me up in a warm quilt. I lay with my head in his lap as he toweled my hair, and the only sound in the room was Schala's strong, ferocious purr, as she licked my face and the very edge of my wet hairline. A deep, terrible fatigue sank its claws into me to pull me down, making my whole body heavy. I wouldn't sleep, though. Sleep seemed far, far away, perhaps in another land altogether. Perhaps in Sanraeth, which I might never reach at all.

Those eyes... those enormous eyes under the water. Dark, waving, winding coils... and those eyes...

At one point, my thoughts returned to what Torv had said to me just before the attack. He'd asked *me* to beseech the spirits and call upon their mercy. Me? He wanted *me* to call upon gods I didn't know and didn't understand, and somehow guide us through this nightmare? I, who'd never even seen the sea before, who couldn't even swim, who froze in the face of—

What was *it?*

A snake. Somehow an enormous, icy snake from the deepest, darkest blackness below. I remembered the coils breaking the waves, slowly winding around me and the other thrashing crew. The tail, rising high into the murky sky and crashing down.

No one had been killed. This time. Bannon assured me of this as he brushed my damp hair, his voice a low and gentle tone, something for me to grasp onto. There were injuries, yes. Some quite serious. Everyone had been recovered from the waves, though, and everyone would recover.

"Will they?" I managed to ask in a tiny voice. "In the castle... during the sandstorm... Ailsa lost patients with only minor injuries, people she expected to recover. They... they just slipped away."

Bannon shushed me and planted a kiss on my temple.

"I'm here," he whispered, soothing me with each slow stroke of the brush. "You're safe now. I'm here, and Schala's here, and everyone's safe."

I pulled the cat closer to my chest and she obliged me, wriggling only enough to settle comfortably in the new position. Her cheek rubbed mine, the gentleness and affection bringing tears to my eyes.

"Hold me please, Sir."

"Of course, kitten." Bannon set the brush aside and slipped under the blanket beside me. He fitted his body alongside mine, wrapping his arms around my waist. "Like this?"

"Just like that."

I closed my eyes, sinking into a place of warmth and shelter between his body, the quilt, and the caracal. I huddled deep down, trying to bury myself and my fears, and find sleep.

The ghostly memory of the lights beneath the water—the moony, shining eyes—still followed me down.

I STAYED IN the cabin for three days, sick with fear. Bannon brought food from the galley and stayed by my side, nursing me day by day, saying little. I couldn't handle much in the way of conversation, really. So, he lay with me, or sat beside me to stroke and caress my hair, or my arms, or my back.

He told me about the activity above decks. The crew had started to set out nets for catching fish, to keep food supplies replenished and ensuring the livestock and the horses weren't the only options for meat. The hauls brought up plenty to keep the galley supplied, but water would be another matter. Torv and a few of the sailors had set up barrels and rags to capture moisture, but even with the fogs continuing to hang low and thick over the deck, it was a slow process, and wouldn't keep up with consumption.

The fogs. They still hadn't lifted. The *Drekakona* had drifted for nearly two weeks, and even the oldest of Arne's sailors, with the longest memories, had never endured such a morass.

Elathae. Speak to them. As you do your familiar.

On the fourth day, I stirred from my place, rising from the bed. Bannon, sitting at the small reading desk with an old, dusty book before him, looked up.

With the quilt still wrapped around my shoulders, I crossed to him and knelt, resting my brow on his knee.

"I need you," I whispered. "Sir... I am so lost in my head... I am so lonely. Please, my barbarian... help me."

He cupped my chin in his hands.

"How?" he asked.

The tone in his voice startled me. My Master, my *ruler,* sounded just as lost as I.

I opened my mouth, but no sound came out.

"How can I help you, Sadira?" His gaze searched mine. "You've been pulling farther and farther away from me this whole trip. Resisting my hold. Breaking away. Am I your master anymore? Or have you moved beyond my grasp?"

"I still need you." I laid one hand over his. Tears stung my eyes. "Bannon, I'm falling apart without you."

"Then why do you hide from me when you're afraid? Defy me, lie to me? How can I be your master if you no longer submit to me?"

I cast my eyes down to the floor, ashamed to look at him. "If the slave disobeys, it is the master's right to punish her. You could have beaten me for lying, or made me sleep in the livestock pens, or—"

"No."

He firmed his grip on me, making me look him in the eyes again.

"That has never been how this works, Sadira. From the moment we forged this bond, it has been a mutual agreement about trust and intent. I do not punish you for vengeance or for my own pleasure. I do it because you trust me to strengthen you through it. *You* give me the power to discipline. If you do not, then it is only violence between us."

I closed my eyes. "Alaric—"

"You are doing it again." His tone grew dark and displeased. "Hiding behind shadows, throwing excuses into my way instead of baring yourself to me, as we agreed. I am not Alaric Khan, and I have never been the master he was to you. Our bond is not his. *You* are not allowed to absolve yourself of responsibility by turning me into him."

I blinked, struck dumb as if he'd slapped me across the face.

Is that what I've been doing?

Holding back from him. Holding back my fears and my misgivings. Holding back my anger. Leaving it to him to beat it out of me and resenting him when he didn't.

I drew in a long, deep breath, and bowed my head.

"You are right. I should have recognized you would not rule as he did."

He stroked my hair. "If you still desire my domination, you must yield to me. Let me into that vulnerable place again, Sadira. Show me that raw, beastly beauty inside you."

I choked on a soft sob. "Sir... Bannon... please. I need you."

He rose from his seat, towering over me. For one horrible, fleeting second, I thought he would leave altogether. Instead, he slid the stool to me, and plucked a short length of rope from on top of the desk.

"Kneel over the stool."

I did as he said, gathering my knees under me and resting my elbows on the cushioned seat. He stooped to bind my wrists down, tying them to one of the wooden legs in a tight, twisting braid. Then he moved around behind me, lifting the blanket away and leaving me naked, on my knees, before him.

"Tell me you trust me."

"I trust you," I whispered.

The brief sound of shuffling came from behind me. He lowered a dark strip of silk—a Vashtaren veil—over my eyes, blindfolding me.

"Say it again."

I did as asked. He unsnapped a rivet on his belt, and a moment later the cold, hard tip of his hunting knife pressed into my skin just between my shoulders.

"Do you remember what you must say, if you want me to stop?"

"Atala," I recited.

"Very good, kitten."

I drew in a sudden, shuddering breath as the knife bit against my flesh. Not meant to cut; only to impart the threat and sensation of cutting, the sweet silvery edge of pain. Bannon drew the blade slowly, deliberately down my back, following just alongside the shape of my spine.

"*Mm,*" I moaned softly as he completed his first long stroke. Then I gave a startled twitch as the point of the knife returned to the place it had begun.

"Do you trust me?" he asked.

"I do, Sir."

He dragged the blade down my spine again, pressing it deep against my muscles, always just shy of breaking the skin and leaving a trace of shining, burning sweetness like a vein of deep liquor. Under the darkness of the blindfold, I sank into the sensation, able to focus only on the touch of steel, the heat of its fine pressure.

"Do you trust me?"

"I do."

He repeated the question with each new kiss of the knife, and I repeated back my promise. He drew lines across my back in rows and slants, careful to let each mark sink in before beginning another, filling my mind with beautiful, grounded order. I embraced each touch, bracing myself as my body quivered, holding my breath for every long, stinging stroke.

"I'm going to press harder," he whispered in my ear. "Don't worry. It's only the flat edge of the blade."

Yes. Just as I told him, in the torture room all those weeks ago. No need to draw blood. Just the kiss of the blade on skin.

I let out a moan, arching as the pressure deepened. He stroked back and forth, tracing the lines of my shoulder blades, the back of my neck, the swell of my hipbones. After a time, it seemed all I was, all I understood, was my skin, the shape of my body, the sense of touch. All else fell away, until his voice reached through to me again.

"Are you all right, kitten? You've been quiet for a long time."

"I'm all right," I murmured. I had no inkling how long I'd been kneeling, though my legs ached and my elbows, even on the cushioned stool, begged for relief. The thrill and sweet, sore lines upon my back sang to me like strong wine, and as I tried to find my balance again a soft, lacy dizziness teased my head.

"I think that's enough, then," Bannon murmured. Somewhere above me came the click of the knife being secured in its sheath. Bannon's hands warmed mine, and he untied them, then checked each of my fingers with a soft tug and a gentle, kneading massage. He didn't remove the blindfold, though, as he gathered me up in his arms and returned me to the bed, where he wrapped me in a blanket—a different blanket, not the quilt under which I'd hid for days but one of the lush, sweet furs I loved so much—and cradled me, stroking my hair.

A soft motion on the bed signaled Schala had joined us. She padded up to me and settled, purring, in my lap.

"Do you feel better?" Bannon asked after a long, quiet time. I couldn't summon up my voice yet, but I nodded, breathing in his wonderful scent of steel, and autumn, and fire.

"Do you think you are ready to come up to the open deck again? You need to stretch those legs and take in fresh air. Can you come with me for that?"

"Yes," I managed to mumble.

"Very well. Up with you, then."

He took of the blindfold, and I woke from my bliss as easily as if the dawn sun had broken through a window. Bannon kissed my lips, and I lifted a hand to stroke his cheek and the rough bristles of his beard, my heart brimming with desperate, joyful affection.

"Master..." I breathed.

He crooked a finger under my chin, gazing into my eyes with a fierce look of pride. We hung in a still, perfect, silent moment, sharing a deep understanding without needing words.

"Let's get you dressed," he murmured. With a nod, I obeyed.

Ten minutes later, we emerged onto the main deck, into the frosty drizzle of the gray fogs still crowding us. This time, though, as I inhaled the crisp, cold air, it invigorated me. I closed my eyes and laid my hand over Bannon's on my hip, smelling the fresh salt of the sea and the unique, fresh scent of rain.

"No scent of death this time," I told him. He made a sound of agreement, brushing a strand of hair out of my eyes.

But the *Drekakona* still drifted, stranded at sea. Who knew how far off course we'd gone by now? Without the sun or stars to navigate by, we were utterly lost.

"Some of the crew have started to wonder if we've drifted beyond the veil," Bannon confided to me as we walked the deck. Dispirited sailors and soldiers gathered in small knots or languished by themselves in lonely corners. Those working on their daily tasks did so with listless energy and frightened irritation.

"Arne sent out two lifeboats with some of the more experienced sailors, to seek out aid, or an end to the fogbank," he went on. "But I question whether they could find their way back to us, even if they did come upon an answer, or a haven where we might land."

"Torv?" I asked.

"He led the first boat. They've been gone since the day before yesterday."

"And the creature in the water?" A flurry of fear touched my heart, but along with it, a spark of intrigue. "Has it been seen again?"

"Not a trace. Plenty of the others who fell overboard with you have been keeping an eye out. Every unexpected bump or lurch of the ship makes people jump, though none have been nearly so powerful as that day."

"Not only that day," I said. "Remember, Bannon, when Mara fell over the side? The ship lurched then, too. At the time, I think we all dismissed it as a freak swell or a patch of rough water. But it was the same, wasn't it?"

His mouth twisted into a grimace, and he scratched the side of his head. "I suppose you're right. But that happened before the fire below decks, and before we made port for two weeks. Could it be—"

"That creature has been *following* us?" I finished for him, my eyes going wide.

We'd nearly reached the bow of the ship. I opened my mouth to say more, when I spied Rayyan sitting near the forward deck, by the catapults and ballista that were rarely ever manned. Now, a member of the crew had been stationed at each, and two on the ballista, no doubt in case the rounded, winding coils of our sea-snake were spotted again.

"Rayyan!" I slid from Bannon's arm and crossed to my brother's side.

He hadn't been assigned to the weapons, it seemed, and he crouched on the balls of his feet, peering into a bucket. He didn't glance up as I neared him, and deep furrows of concentration lined his brow.

"Rayyan..." I tilted my head as I came close to him. "What are you doing?"

"It's a trick my uncle taught me," he mumbled, chewing his lip in thought. "I don't know if it will work... I've been trying to get the needle to point straight for days."

"What do you mean?"

He'd filled the bucket with water, and on the surface bobbed a rough round of cork—probably the stopper for a bottle of wine someone had claimed during the long, empty days. I cocked an eyebrow, studying the nail he'd perched flat on top of the cork.

Bannon joined us as I crouched down beside Rayyan. "What does it do?" I asked.

"If I've done it right, the needle should point north." He prodded the cork, nudging the tip of the nail to one side. It rebounded when he withdrew his finger, returning to its previous orientation.

I glanced up. To our left, where the nail pointed, a rigging line anchored to the deck rail had been marked with a scrap of bright red cloth.

"I did that," Rayyan explained without looking up. "To make sure it keeps pointing the same way. I think we've probably drifted a little bit since I started, so it's not pointing directly at the cloth anymore... but it's close."

"How did you do it?" Bannon asked, stroking his beard.

"My uncle used a lodestone, stroked against the edge of the nail." Rayyan pulled his knife from his belt. "I used this. At first it didn't work. I wasn't striking the nail correctly. You have to repeat it a hundred times, striking it the same way, before it will point north."

"How do you know it's north?" I asked.

He shrugged. "In the Vashtaren river valley, we knew because the river flowed south, and at night you could judge by the stars. As for now... I suppose I don't know for sure."

"It's pointing in a straight line, though," Bannon said. "That should be enough. If Arne sends out a pair of scouting boats, tied to the bowsprit, we could steer ourselves accordingly and at least know we were on a steady course."

"Yes!" Rayyan jumped to his feet. "That was exactly my thought, sir. Do you think Arne will agree?"

Bannon clapped Rayyan on the shoulder. "I think it's the only chance we have."

CHAPTER TWENTY-EIGHT

I STOOD AT the ship's bow, gripping the rail until chips of wax finish came up under my nails. Captain Arne wouldn't allow me onto the guide boats since I couldn't swim. I would have defied him outright if Bannon hadn't agreed with the man and instructed me to stay on the *Drekakona*. He'd gone out ahead though, with Rayyan and Ashe, and Jahn and others in a second boat. Each carried a version of Rayyan's needle and cork, and a third needle—the original—sat on the deck between the catapults, with Mara keeping watch over it.

The lines tying the guide boats to the *Drekakona* had remained steady and tight for hours, and in the thick fog ahead, voices called out to one another, confirming information. I couldn't make out the words, but the tones at least kept me at ease. I worried about a sudden change, a scream of terror or the crunch of wood, indicating one or both of the boats had suffered some deadly fate.

"Stop fretting," Mara muttered. "It's useless and disruptive."

"Well, how do you suppose I stop?" I snapped at her. "My brother and the man I love are down there, with some sort of monster lurking about in the fog."

She scoffed. "Well, wringing your hands and fussing and pacing won't do them any good, now, will it?"

I narrowed my eyes at her and dug my nails deeper into the wood. "I am not doing any of those things."

At my feet, Schala gave a little growl in Mara's direction. Mara rolled her eyes and flicked a hand at the caracal in dismissal.

"Go find something to occupy yourself elsewhere," she told me. "We're at work here and we don't need your distraction. That's an order."

I cringed at the word, wrinkling my nose. I hated taking orders from Mara, and she knew it very well. Unfortunately, as Bannon's lieutenant, she held sway over me in his stead, and I must obey.

I stooped to pick up Schala. "Please have me summoned if anything happens."

"Of course," she replied. Despite our tenuous, unfriendly relationship, I believed she would do as she promised.

Stroking the caracal in my arms, I left the bow, tossing a glance over my shoulder to reassure myself the tether lines were still taut and pointing in the right direction.

My first thought was to go downstairs to our cabin and wait for him. Perhaps on my knees. Perhaps with an implement of torture from among our secret chest of treasures held up for him to consider. For the first time in a long time, I had a racy desire to have my thighs and ass thoroughly flogged,

298

and to return the favor with a long, lustful session of pleasure giving.

At the same time, though, I should remain nearby in case anything did happen. If all at once the sea began churning, or the guidelines snapped or went slack—

And what would you do about it? jeered a snide voice in the back of my head. *If anything attacked the guide boats, you'd be powerless to stop it anyway.*

I gritted my teeth, hiding the unhappy grimace behind a nuzzle of Schala's fur.

I chose instead to go to the stern and revisit the study Bannon had taken me to; the quiet, private place where he'd brushed my hair and said I'd made him proud. The room held a sense of peace and quiet, a familiar hushed repose where I might be alone with my thoughts. The library at Alaric's castle had been such a place to me, before. Maybe I'd find one of the Sanraethi books to read and learn a little about the land I was traveling to.

As the stern door shut behind me, a sense of disquiet, an awful nagging at the corners of my mind, settled around my shoulders. I forced the feeling down, burying my face against the cat in my arms. Despite my determination, the hairs on the back of my neck prickled. *Something* was in the passageway with me. I knew it.

The low murmurs of Arne and his officers drifted out from behind the door to his meeting room. I passed it, walking quickly, focused on the room ahead. My hand found the doorknob in the darkness. It creaked as I turned it then swept us into the cool, still study.

The room looked different, with close, dark fog pressing in at the windows. If there were dolphins playing in the ship's wake, I wouldn't know. None of the lamps were lit, leaving the desks and shelves in a dismal, shaded darkness, like a house hidden in the shadow of a great peak. The ship bobbed and rocked, silent and slow and gentle.

I let Schala down and she padded off to explore this new place. I moved to the first writing desk and picked up the lantern, striking a match from the box beside it and lighting the candle within. Carrying it with me, I moved to one of the velvet couches and took a seat.

The comfortable cushions welcomed me, and I sank down into them with a sigh.

"I'll take a look at the books in a moment," I told Schala, as if she might object to my lounging upon the sofa. Closing my eyes, I inhaled the sweet scent of pages and leather hardcovers around me, and of polished wood and old fabric, clean but dry and dusty in the nooks and crannies.

After a moment, with a husky *mrrp,* Schala bounded up onto the couch with me and stretched herself out on my lap. The weight of her pressing me down sent a gentle feeling of shelter and safety through my mind. Without opening my eyes, I stroked her, scratching her ears and cheeks, all the way down to her stub of a tail.

How long as it been since I had a real sleep?

The question came from nowhere, it seemed, and the answer was beyond me. I'd been drifting between a faint, razor-thin sleep and a desperate, waking panic for weeks now... maybe even a month. Fearing I'd once again wake up far from my bed, somewhere in a forest thick with moss and cold with rain. Fearing the great serpent would seize me in my slumber and plunge me deep into an icy blackness. Fearing the moony-eyed shadow on the other side of every door and at the end of every hallway.

The heavy weight of my exhaustion lay upon me like an enormous blanket. Schala's reassuring presence soothed me.

"A nap won't be so bad," I whispered to her. "And if there's any change in the situation outside, I'll hear it when they come get Captain Arne."

Schala purred. I let my eyelids sink closed.

Then I opened them wide, a jolt of panic jerking me upright again and jostling the caracal.

Something changed.

I searched back and forth through the gloomy, mostly lightless study. Nudging Schala aside, I rose, lifting the lantern and scanning the desks, the table, the walls.

It's the maps.

I took a careful, steady step forward, raising the light to peer at a framed map above the reading desk. Seconds ago, it had hung in its place, immaculate and austere, a beautiful work of cartography.

Now it hung upside down. The *frame* had not been disturbed—only the map within.

I brought a hand to my mouth and backed away. I swung the lantern to one side, over the other desk, to an oil painting of a cherubic, naked woman upon the seashore. She, too, hung upside down.

I searched the whole study. Every portrait, every map, upside down inside their frames. Panic throbbed inside my chest and Schala would around my ankle with a troubled complaint.

"It's all right, Schala, all right." I mumbled through nearly frozen lips.

A squeak came from my left. I spun and the light fell on the divan by the rear windows. It stood straight up on its side, steady as the ship rocked. A scrape sounded behind me, and I swung the lantern to reveal the couches, too, standing on end. The chairs stationed before the desks now perched atop them, upside-down, and the globe—

With a whirring, chirping urgency, the globe spun on its spindle. Schala gave a low, uneasy moan as it picked up speed before our eyes, moving faster and faster as I stood, dumbfounded.

Snap!

The spindle broke and the globe flew at me, striking me in the shoulder and knocking me to my ass. The lantern flew from my grip and shattered somewhere out of sight, leaving me and Schala in gloom. A humid, thrumming vibration seemed to shake the air around us.

Making a grab for the caracal, I lunged for the door. Books flew from the shelves to hit me in the back and the legs. I deflected one from striking me in the head and skidded to a halt just before the exit. My heart leapt, certain when I tried the knob, I'd find myself locked in, imprisoned with my ghostly stalker, the being with the moony eyes. Schala yowled in my arms and I fought the urge to glance behind me, certain I'd see the dark silhouette there, slowly making its way across the study to me—

The door clicked and I stumbled through, slamming it shut behind me. I raced on, past the door to the meeting room and out onto the deck. By the time I reached the mizzenmast and slapped my hand to it, bringing myself to a stop, Schala struggled in my arms to be let go.

I loosened my grip, allowing her to drop to the deck. Bending over double, I heaved air in and out, covered in sweat, shivering even in the bright golden sunlight.

Sunlight?

I glanced up and had to raise my arm to shield my eyes. The last, lacy tendrils of mist streamed away from the masts and the sails, creeping back over the stern deck to disappear behind us. Overhead, the late afternoon sky stretched out, deepening blue, scudded with fluffy white clouds drifting away toward evening.

"The... the fog..."

How had it retreated so quickly? After weeks of lingering and burying us under cold, heavy misery?

A flash of outrage ignited in my chest. *How could it be so... so simple? After all that!*

All around the deck, sailors were talking brightly, even whistling. As I straightened, it occurred to me: with the fog cleared, the guide boats would be visible from the bow.

"C'mon, cat!"

Shaking off my encounter in the library, I snapped my fingers for Schala to follow and kicked into a trot, making my way through the knots of crew toward the bow. Halfway there, though, I came to a rough stop, a gathering of several soldiers of the horde catching my eye. They stood on the port side, by the small crane-like devices I'd learned were called davits, where the ship's boats were raised and lowered. One of the guide boats had already been hauled up, and as I watched, Rayyan and the other members of its tiny crew were helped back onto the deck.

"Bannon!" I crossed to meet him as he stepped from the tiny boat back onto the *Drekakona*. "How? But... you returned so quickly! And the fog—"

Mara, standing to one side, gave me a quizzical look. I glanced toward the bow, where I'd last seen her, then to Bannon again. Eerie understanding crept up, raising goosebumps along my arms. I glanced up again, at the sun standing well across the sky...

"Mara." I nervously stroked the end of my braid. "How long ago did I leave you on the bow?"

The lieutenant blinked at me. I had the distinct impression she'd dismissed me entirely from her mind after our conversation and now had to scour her memory to recall when it had been.

She shifted her halberd from one hand to the other and shot a quick glance at Bannon. "I'm sorry, Sadira. I thought you'd gone to your cabin to sleep and didn't want to disturb you. I haven't seen you on deck since yesterday."

CHAPTER TWENTY-NINE

THE HEAVEN STAR shone overhead, a welcome sight to everyone on the crew. Below, on deck, Arne and his navigators were engrossed in maps and star charts and calculations, trying to determine how far off course the *Drekakona* had drifted, and how we could return to our proper route.

I sat in the lookout, with Schala as my only company, gazing up at the constellations and the bright, colorful swirl of celestial lights. I'd volunteered to take the watch for the night and should have been keeping a keen eye out for rocks or shallows or land in the distance, but my mind wandered from the task over and over, and I lost myself in the awful, unnerving darkness of my memory.

More than a day? I was alone in that study... for more than a day?

I remembered sinking into the velvet cushions, meaning to rest my eyes or even to nap, if I could manage it. But something had startled me immediately from any rest. I'd risen right away without even drifting off.

Hadn't I?

Is there any difference between sleeping and waking anymore? When I sleep, I walk, just like Bannon and Ailsa said, and when I wake, I find creeping shadows and those eyes waiting for me around each corner, abducting me to times and places I do not know.

I ran my hand over Schala's flank, and she gave a deep sigh, stretching and curling her front paws over her face.

"If only I could find rest so easily," I murmured at her. Making a quick scan of the horizon, I found nothing but empty water.

Bannon had wanted me to go with him to the study and show him the paintings and the furniture, but I couldn't stomach going back in. He'd asked if I wished to stay with him, in our cabin or some other place I felt safe, but in truth, I didn't feel safe anywhere. I could have gone with him to our small bed and let him hold me, or begged for the flogging I'd been yearning for earlier, but I feared if I let myself return to the small, closed-in bunkroom and let him comfort me, I'd sink into another three- or four-day episode, as I had after falling overboard and nearly being devoured by a sea snake. I might not manage to pull myself out and face the danger again.

Instead, I asked him to allow me time and space to clear my mind of confusion. Granted it, I climbed to the highest place on the ship, above everyone else, to sit alone and stare up at the stars.

There is a malevolent creature on this ship. What is it? What does it want from me?

I hugged my knees to my chest and closed my eyes. My thoughts returned to the vision of the altar and the seven-pointed ritual design before me. Smooth hands—and gnarled hands—and tattooed hands, moving over the arrangements of objects and tokens arranged for wicked ceremony.

The snake's skull.

Visions of serpent worshippers, playing out before me.

I didn't think I could stand the implications: leaving the land of Akolet's disciples and their poisonous cruelty, only to find *more* agents of the snake ahead?

Ahead, I scoffed at myself. *Here. Here on this very ship, somehow. And in the depths below.*

Where did the sea snake go? Where did it wait for us, in the days ahead? Certain we hadn't seen the last of it, I pictured it winding and weaving through the blackness of the deeps, following the *Drekakona's* shadow from above, waiting for its next opportunity.

I rested my head on my knees with a soft groan. I hadn't felt sick during the first days of our voyage, as Captain Arne expected. Now, though, the rock and sway of the boat made me so dizzy, so... overwhelmed.

You must crush the eggshells to prevent angry entities from following you.

Even if it worked, could I ever crush enough eggshells into small enough pieces to drive away the ghosts and ghouls—and *snakes*—determined to lurk in my shadow? Torv thought me a spirit caller. Perhaps I was a spirit *magnet*, drawing their awful, stalking presence to me wherever I went. Maybe Alaric's machinations, whatever they'd been intended to do, had kept me safe from notice.

I took your power, he'd told me. *As a Master does.*

I wrinkled my nose and rubbed at one temple. I hadn't really thought back to my last confrontation with Alaric—the *man* Alaric, rather than the grotesque monster that had been, at least in some part, him as well. I'd tried to drive the memories from my mind, too gutted by the juxtaposition of Alaric and Bannon in one body, to think too much about it. When I imagined it now... when I thought of Alaric's eyes staring out at me from Bannon's face, or the way Bannon's dusky skin and rich, red hair had leached of color...

I closed my eyes and forced myself to take a long, deep breath. Thoughts like those had turned my passion to panic when Bannon had taken me down to the forge to play.

I took your power.

Alaric meant my power to resist him, my power to deny him.

Hadn't he?

Or perhaps he'd meant my power to move on and love another. Because he'd helped shape my every development, taught me the ways of twisted and beautiful pain, maybe my bond with Bannon—or with any other lover—would never be safe.

No, some part of me whispered. *Think harder. There was more to it than that. What else did Alaric say?*

Swallowing back an ugly taste in my mouth, I pushed myself to remember.

Nothing is yours, remember? You belong to me. Your body, your loyalty, and any scrap of magic you manage to conjure for me.

I touched the place where my collar had been. His symbol of ownership, and his conduit to me even when his body had been destroyed. Bannon, who briefly shared a mind with my dark tormentor, had said it, too. Alaric stole from me. More than I could ever know.

With a sigh, I wrapped my arm around my knees again and leaned my head back against the mast. *Maybe I should have stayed with Bannon after all. Let him take the brunt of this worry from my shoulders and fill my head with sweet passion instead.*

"Then you should go to him."

I jerked to attention, startled by the unfamiliar voice. Schala came awake with the sound of agitated confusion, hackles raised, and I scooped her into my arms to guard her against my chest.

A woman stood before me, her back turned to me as she stared out at the water. A cold frisson traveled down the backs of my arms and a sharp heat dug at my gut; I hadn't heard anyone arrive on the lookout with me.

"Who are you?" I demanded.

Her short, blonde hair drifted back on the breeze. She said nothing. In my arms, Schala trembled, and a low growl ticked in her throat.

I rose to my feet, pressing my back to the mast. The stranger had dark marks on her arms: familiar, winding red tattoos. Deliberate scars feathered across one shoulder. I followed them up to the back of her neck.

A mark in the shape of a winding serpent—what Bannon called a lemniscate knot—showed in dark contrast against too-pale skin just at the nape.

The air rushed out of my lungs. Violent trembling seized my limbs as she began to turn my way.

Unwilling to see the stranger's face I spun for the mast, grabbing the rungs of the ladder one-handed while I helped Schala up to my shoulder with the other. I scrambled down as fast as I could, nauseous with the awful sense of an icy, creeping gaze upon me. Several feet above the main deck, I jumped down, and Schala's claws dug into my shoulder. If she weren't still a baby, she might have cut me down to the bone. Unfazed I sprinted down the boards to the stern and the ladderway leading down to the middle deck and our cabin.

Please let Bannon be there. I need to tell him—I need him *to tell me I'm not* mad—

I pushed past deckhands and crew, refusing to stop even when Rayyan's voice carried to me from across the deck and Ashe, in front of me, attempted to take me by the arm. I made it to the ladder and slid down the rails rather than climb.

Schala bounded down from my shoulder to run alongside me. My heart raced and my breaths came in short, heavy huffs as I reached the door to our bunk. I'd just laid my hand upon the doorknob when Mara's voice came from within.

"—one thing when she was still under the black magician's power, Bannon, but with his influence far behind us her behavior is *still* erratic and inexplicable. You can't believe she'll be any better once we reach Sanraeth."

Mara? Mara, alone with him, in *our* cabin?

Bannon spoke next. "Were you any better, after we emerged from the battles at Caspan? I seem to recall you struggled with night terrors for months."

"But I never lost an entire day's worth of time," Mara insisted. "I didn't grow disoriented and become lost in a simple set of corridors, or wander away from my camp in the middle of the night, or—"

"I should never have told you about that. Stop troubling yourself with Sadira. She isn't your concern."

"Of course she is!" A thump sounded from within: a stomped foot or a fist brought down on one of the shelves or on our trunk of belongings. "How am I to serve you if your mad harem girl is running amok in the ranks, threatening me and the rest of the horde with her hysteria?"

A flash of fury replaced my earlier fear. It burned under my skin with a draconic rage.

"Bannon." Mara's voice again, soft and personal. "She does not belong with us."

My mind buzzed; a fierce, primordial possession filled my chest, raked by that soft tone, the *intimate* undercurrent. At my feet, Schala bubbled into an angry snarl, arching her back, baring her savage teeth.

Bannon was saying something else, but I'd heard enough. I thrust the door open hard enough to make it slam against the wall. Mara and Bannon whirled, startled at the intrusion. He'd been turned away from her, staring out the porthole before my entrance, but all I could see was her closeness to him, her presumptuous nearness to *my* Master.

"Get out of here," I snarled. She opened her mouth to retort, but I shouted over her, "Get *out!* Or I will cut *your* heart from your chest and feed it to my caracal!"

Mara took a step back, eyes wide, expression contorted in a mix of outrage and fear. I liked that. I advanced on her, a crackling sense of energy and vindication swarming inside me.

"Sadira!" Bannon snapped. He lunged for me, but before he could I reached a hand toward Mara, closing it into a tight fist.

I hadn't exactly meant to do it. I didn't even know why, or what I expected it to do. To my horror, though, a flickering mass of shadow coalesced between Mara and I, taking a shape I recognized. Though it seemed amassed of pure darkness, I could peer through it to Mara's face, a face gone pale with fear.

I could see its wide, white, moony eyes.

The vision thrust its own fist into Mara's chest. It passed right into her, disappearing up to the forearm. She seized and choked, eyes bulging wide, and I realized the thing had closed its fingers around the very part of her I'd just threatened.

Her heart.

Bannon and I stood frozen as Mara made a hitched, pitiful mewling sound. She grasped for the apparition's dark arm, fingers moving right through it, like mist. Where she touched it, the blackness swirled away, shimmering into a faint, silver glow instead. The gleaming traveled up the creature's arm, and patterns emerged: red tattoos. Ritual scars.

The light ate away at the dim gloom, turning the nightmare into a ghostly, flickering woman. Short, blonde hair. Lemniscate knot.

My knees wobbled and my stomach turned to ice.
It's me.

"Stop!" I shouted.

The silvery apparition withdrew its hand. Mara crumpled to the ground, clutching her chest, and lay still.

Then—without actually moving—the figure was facing me, and I looked into my own face, bright and dusted with misty starlight, shining brilliant white eyes at me like the heart of the heaven star.

And in those eyes... I *saw*.

It's me. It's been me. All this time…

"But it can't be," I groaned, hiding my face as the apparition loomed over me. "I have no magic. I have never had any magic!"

I sensed it reaching out for me. Its desire washed over me.

I whirled and lunged for the door. Bannon reached out for me, but I shoved him away, racing into the passageway. Reversing my earlier course, I charged for the ladderway, grasping the rungs and fleeing for the open air.

The first savage bump hit the ship as I climbed. I gave a short cry and clung closer to the ladder, until the sway evened out. Another lurch sent us the other way almost immediately, and above, I heard voices swearing and calling for the archers and catapult crew.

It's back. The sea snake. Now, of all times?

It was all connected, though. The doors in Alaric's castle, the black dogs, the rigging ropes around my neck, the fire. The snake. It was all connected, and the common thread was *me*.

Beast inside. Poisonous. Snake. The daughter of serpent worshipers.

I scrambled onto the weather deck. A crash sounded from off the port side of the *Drekakona*, and a droning, fluting cry filled the air. Blue-green coils rose on my right, higher than the ship's own enormous flank. Water sprayed over us, gigantic waves crashing over the deck.

The sailors screamed back and forth. Cries of "*Sea serpent!*" and "*Leviathan!*" filled my ears. The deck seemed to rise, cresting another huge wave, and crashed down into the water again, dark green swells and roiling masses of foam washing people off their feet. I stumbled hard to one side, slipping and sliding, finally catching myself against the rail.

"Stop!" I screamed again, but my voice flew into the wind, unheard. The serpent's rumbling, echoing cry rolled over us, and the *Drekakona* tipped perilously starboard.

It's come because of me. It's come... because I called it here.

I had one thought. Violent and horrible... and deadly.

I must make it go away.

"Sadira!"

Bannon had appeared at the top of the ladderway behind me. I faced him, taking a long, silent moment to study his face. His beautiful, brick-red mane. His kingly features.

"I love you, Master."

Without waiting for him to come for me, I climbed up, onto the railing—

—and flung myself into the sea.

CHAPTER THIRTY

I SANK INTO cold water, curling tight into a ball. The sea serpents' enormous coils wound and undulated around me, glimmering in the rays of starlight dancing beneath the surface. Fins of glorious teal and blue and violet flowed like pennants off its sides, and gleaming, jagged shards, like spearheads, marched down its spine.

It's beautiful.

The musical cry came to me through the churning water. The creature's attention pivoted on me. Just as I had gambled it would. It zipped through the water toward me, and without any other choice, I grabbed onto one of its fins and let it draw me down.

As long as you leave them alone. Let the Drekakona *go. You can have me.*

The descendant of serpent worshipers, dragged under the waves by the greatest serpent of all. Not Akolet—this gleaming blue monster, this killer *beauty* dwarfed the seven-headed serpent in every way. Though I knew I would die clinging to its scales, I couldn't relinquish my grip.

It's the most beautiful creature I've ever beheld.

Deep into the darkness we plunged. The water, like ice, numbed me head to toe. My lungs burned, holding on to my last breath.

Another sweet, melodious note seemed to emanate from deep within the serpent, resonating along its flanks. I closed my eyes. Bubbles drifted from my mouth and air left my lungs. I surrendered to the cold, to the darkness, embracing the voice of the monster, welcoming it into my soul.

Our descent slowed. The sleek dive softened into a gentle, floating ease. Movement in the water stirred me to open my eyes again, and I beheld its colorful fins drawing close around me.

The serpent drew itself into a protective coil. I couldn't orient myself within its grasp, until it found me with its shining, white eyes.

As its gaze fell upon me, a blessed relief seized my chest. Like a lungful of fresh air, it eased the pain and desperation clawing inside me.

How? Have I frozen? Have I died after all? What other reason could there be, that my lungs are no longer screaming for air?

Shining white eyes. Just like the eyes of the shadowy apparition. Like my own ghostly face, staring back at me.

But so much bigger.

We drifted in the flow of subtle currents, looking into one another. A calm, rhythmic movement passed between us, something as natural and comfortable as breathing, though breath was a thing of before. Of above.

In the welling, ebbing silence, my mind settled into an easy peace.

It has *been me This whole time. Everything stemmed from me.*

Doors slamming... when *I* closed them, slamming them on a life I left behind. Ropes twisting around my limbs and neck... when *I* had been thinking of Alaric's hard, heartless ropes around my throat.

The shape in the shadows only appeared after Ashe warned me about angry spirits. The fire ignited below decks when I was angry at Bannon, and the woman in the marketplace, when I was thinking of strangers and mobs coming after me. The bodies in the water... when I feared death had come for all of us at last.

Every strange occurrence, the product of my conflicted heart and mind. Filled with fear as I left my old world and old ghosts behind; filled with awe and curiosity for what lay ahead. My lost life. The faraway beach and the woman crying my name.

Seren! My sweet Seren!

Somehow, I'd called out—just like Torv said, like a spirit-caller, the *elathae*—and something new had answered.

But I have never had magic.

As though in answer, the sea serpent blinked its beautiful eyes. Could it sense my thoughts? Could it *understand* me?

I didn't think so. It, too, had come when I called out. Like Schala had come. Like the black dogs. Somehow, when anger or fear took over, my soul called out to it and it had come, thumping and bumping at the ship to find me. Growing more and more agitated as I grew more distraught.

How do I do this? How long have I been able *to do this?*

Was this the real power Alaric stole from me? *How?* How could he have?

Over a lifetime, and across my whole body. The sinister truth of his bondage. My tattoos, my chains, my collar, each one leashing me closer and closer to him, and his great reptilian monster.

So they both could feed off my soul.

How funny. I brought up a hand to my face, covering a silent chuckle that wasn't really there. *My serpent could eat the seven-headed golem of Alaric's final curse easily. Perhaps whatever unknown cabal of serpent worshipers I really belong to, they know more about Akolet than Lord Khan ever did.*

No. This was not a sea serpent.

I reached out to lay a hand upon its scaly, serrated muzzle. I looked deeper into its eyes, willing it to somehow tell me more.

You are no mere serpent. You are the devourer *of serpents. You... are a* dragon.

I bent my head to it, resting my brow against the smooth, glimmering scales of its head. It fluted softly at me, a song resonating through my mind and my heart.

You are beautiful. Beautiful girl. Beautiful beast.

Such wild power. Such dangerous strength and deadly loveliness. Nature bowed before this dragon and her voice.

And she... is me. We are the same. We are—

Somewhere far away, above and beyond us, the deep sound of thrashing water rippled through our floating world. Something from *outside* us. Something separate, and different... but not dangerous. I couldn't bring myself to break away from the creature's gaze, even as arms encircled my waist from behind and strong legs kicked. Someone tried to pull me back, pull me up toward the surface once more.

No. Not yet.

I raised a hand. I found Bannon's familiar, bearded cheek, and willed him to understand. I wanted him to see the dragon with me, look into her eyes. I needed him to *know.*

He relaxed, his grip around me softening. The great sea dragon gazed at us, and we gazed back. The world, the water, the waving reflections of light and deep shadows of the depths seemed to slow.

I took Bannon's hand, twining my fingers with his. He gave me a tight squeeze, and I knew he, too, hung in awe of her.

Then the spell broke. The burn in my lungs returned, and Bannon tightened his hold around my waist. He kicked, propelling us upward, but I'd already gone too long without breath. A sleepy gloom crept in around the corners of my mind, and all I could think was—

I have beheld the most sacred of serpents. Devourer of serpents. The dragon, upon whose altar snakes are laid to waste.

Was that what my vision meant? The snake's skull in the ritual circle? Not an implement of worship, but an offering to the *eater* of snakes.

Bannon kicked harder. Then, without warning, the sea dragon streaked past us, ascending like a knife. My barbarian nearly released me, startled by the great predator's movements, but I put out one hand, searching for its fins again.

Looping my arm around Bannon's, I caught the dragon's fin, and we shot upward along with it. We broke the surface with a fantastic spray of sea water and dazzle of colors in the starlight, and I heaved in a desperate breath of air, losing it again almost instantly as I cried out in mingled pain, rapture, and relief.

Tears filled my eyes, and I hugged Bannon close to me as the dragon crested and descended again, this time turning it into a shallow dip. We bobbed at its side, dripping and gulping in air, clutching tight to one another and to the dragon's graceful fin.

"What were you thinking?" Bannon demanded, covering my face and mouth with salty, cold kisses. "You idiot, you incredible idiot, *what* were you thinking?"

"It's me, Bannon." I brushed wet tendrils of hair from my face. "This whole time, all the strange things happening, it was *me*. I don't know why, or how—"

"It's all right," he assured me. "We'll find out what it all means. For now, let's just get back on the—"

"*Mara!*" I covered my mouth with one hand. "Oh, Eye of Akolet... Bannon, did I kill her? Please say I didn't!"

Bannon looked down at me, brow furrowed, then up again, searching the sea around us. The *Drekakona* floated just ahead. The sea dragon skimmed along the surface of the water toward it at a sprightly pace. Bannon's expression darkened as we neared the boat. "I'm sorry, Sadira. I don't know."

CHAPTER THIRTY-ONE

THE CREW LINED up along the starboard rail, a mob of faces staring overboard at us as we approached. Some peered through the portholes and the open sides of the rower's gallery. Ashe and Jahn held gathered lengths of rope, ready to throw them over to us, and Arne stood beside them, gaping.

The sea dragon gave a curious chirrup of a sound that echoed over the water, and dipped briefly below the waves, taking Bannon and me along with it. Then it arced its slender body upward and rose gracefully alongside the *Drekakona,* spreading out a series of lovely blue and green and violet fins. The sailors gawked, wide-eyed, letting out breathy *oohs* and *ahs* as the starlight glimmered along its body.

Bannon and I, still holding tight to one of the smaller fins further down the creature's side, slid ourselves free and dropped to the deck. The crew backed away from us, giving us plenty of space to catch our breath and gather ourselves. Appearing as though from nowhere, Schala butted her head against my side, miaowing and purring, pawing at my hands, licking the seawater dripping from my face.

When I felt steady enough to stand, I gathered the feline up in my arms and gave her a long, grateful squeeze, dripping cold sea water all over, making her fuss. Then I turned to behold the dragon again.

Risen from the water, gilded in a silver gleam, she gazed back at me, eyes like shining pearls. In her full splendor, she teemed with majesty: just below her elegant, angled head and sloping, smooth neck, her first four huge fins appeared more like wings, muscular and elegant, feathered with shimmering, membranous scales. From this vantage, no one could mistake her for anything so common as a snake—even a seven-headed one risen from the desolate, dead sands.

"Thank you," I whispered to her.

She made a rumbling, voiceless sound like wind rushing through reeds. I reached out to lay one hand on her sleek, scaly belly, before she wheeled away and plunged back into the water.

"Mara," Bannon reminded me, even as I gazed wistfully after the winding, skimming hint of scales just below the surface. He took me by the arm and guided me away, though, through the crowd of stunned crew, down to the ladderway and the surgeon's quarters below.

Rayyan waited in the hallway, next to Ailsa's open door. He straightened when he caught sight of us and rushed to greet me with a hug and a string of ugly Vash epithets.

"You idiot!" he shouted, squeezing me so tight Schala wriggled to get out from between us. "What were you thinking, throwing yourself to that beast? Have you completely lost your mind, Sadira?"

"It was... a gambit." I shrugged. "How is Mara?"

"Can't say." He tossed a grim glance over his shoulder. "Ailsa hasn't been able to rouse her. Her pulse is..."

"Weak," I finished for him, voice heavy with shame.

Rayyan gave me a quizzical look. At the same time, Ailsa appeared in the entryway to the surgeon's quarters, arms crossed, her curly, red hair falling out of a hastily gathered knot at the back.

"I think she will live, Da," she reported to Bannon. "But there will be lasting effects. She... may never serve in the horde again."

The words sank like stones in my mind, weighing heavy enough to make my heart hurt and my stomach grow weak. My anger at Mara left her nearly dead. In an instant of raw, unchecked emotion, I'd cursed her, maybe forever. I didn't even know how I had done it.

Worst of all, though... I didn't know how to *undo* it.

"Can we go in and see her, Sir?" I asked.

Bannon and Ailsa exchanged a silent glance and the healer stepped to the side, gesturing us in. Bannon rested a hand on my shoulder and together we entered.

Mara was not the only member of the crew bunked in the surgeon's ward. Others rested in hammocks or on pallets, bandaged and probably sedated for pain. A few remained awake, murmuring quietly together of the sea dragon's attack on the ship—an attack I now understood as the creature's instinctual response to me. It hadn't had any desire to destroy the *Drekakora* at all. It attacked to free a kindred spirit in distress and protect them.

Ailsa had delegated Mara a bunk at the very back of the ward, surrounded by empty beds and a behind a quiet buffer of clean white sheets. Mara's skin appeared dull and ashen, clammy with sweat. Dark blue bruises sunk deep under each eye, and the lines across her brow and at the corners of her mouth— barely perceptible before—had deepened slightly. The change might look negligible to the casual observer, but I noticed.

Worst of all, one beautiful, glossy braid on the side of her head had turned a steely, iron gray. It stood out against her marks of honor and battle like a terrible scar.

Like my scars. Like my tattoos. Something she'll never escape.

I knelt beside her bunk, resting my hands on the edge of sheets, not daring to touch her directly.

"I did this to her," I whispered. "If she never fights again... it is because of me."

Bannon said nothing.

We hung in silence for several long moments. Desperate thoughts raced through my mind as I grasped for a solution, some understanding of how to heal the damage I'd done, wishing I could go back and simply *not make that decision.*

"I must make this better," I finally said. "I *will* make it better."

Bannon moved closer to me, resting his hands on my shoulders.

"If it is true," he said, "and you have found the spiritual power Alaric believed you possessed, perhaps there is a way."

I withdrew my hands and folded them in my lap. "My people will know. If they are still out there... if we really can find them... someone among them will know, and they can help her. Show *me* how to help her."

"Mara won't like that," Bannon said with a sigh.

"She'll have every right. But I owe it to her to find a way."

"There is a custom in old Sanraethi ways." He straightened, widening his stance and folding his hands stoically before him. "When one saves another's life, they form a bond unbreakable, even by the will of God. When one *takes* the life of another unjustly, they become obligated to that person's family, to do what the victim cannot."

"Then I am obligated to her. So she may keep her honor. So I may make amends and restore her. So be it."

Perhaps I imagined the twinge of pain in my chest. Perhaps it had something to do with the newfound power kindled within me. A tiny shiver of nausea wormed its way into my gut, but none of it mattered. I'd trespassed against my fellow soldier and nearly stolen her life. The debt must be repaid.

"Will you tell the others?" I asked Bannon. Only he, me, and Mara knew the truth of who had rendered her so low.

"No. There is no need to make them fear you again, or make you stand before them to be judged. You have already admitted your guilt before the captain of the horde and submitted yourself to the consequences. See out your sentence, like the good girl I know you are, and there will be no reason to make it known to anyone else."

He paused, seeming to mull things over. "I can't promise Mara won't speak of it."

"If she does, then so be it. I can't begrudge her that."

I stared at Mara for another long, silent moment. We would never be friends. Now, though, we were bound by a strange fate I didn't understand. I'd lived for thirty years, never once showing any glimmer of magical talent, even under threat and torture by Alaric Khan. Now, all of a sudden—

My hand rose to my throat, where once I would have found my leather collar and the ring I toyed with so often in times of anxiety. No, it had not been all of a sudden. It had begun the moment my collar—and my connection to Alaric—was severed forever.

My fingers brushed the thin scar just under the right side of my jaw, where the knife had nicked me when I cut the collar free.

Cut the collar. Revealed the mark of the lemniscate knot beneath it. The one Bannon had described like a coiling snake.

Snake? Or dragon?

A mark left by Alaric before he bound me? Or something I'd carried all along?

The mark of a spirit caller?

EPILOGUE

I STOOD ON the bow of the *Drekakona,* Schala perched on my shoulder, staring out at the torchlit port below us. The last port before we sailed on to Sanraeth. In a week's time, given good weather, we would disembark at last in Bannon's home country. *Our* new home country.

I reached up to scratch under the caracal's chin. She stretched out her neck to accommodate me, purring right beside my ear. I'd come to the conclusion she'd answered some primal call from my heart, just like the sea dragon, and come to protect me when I needed her. I was more than happy to have her now, my self-appointed guardian angel. She, like me, would be a stranger in Sanraeth, but we would have each other.

I glance over my free shoulder at the tock of boots on the boards. Bannon joined me, resting one hand on my hip as he, too, gazed at the warm golden lights.

"You were talking in your sleep again today."

Since the coming of the dragon, I'd found sleep much more easily, though spates of exhaustion came on me at strange hours. Rayyan had discovered me sound asleep on a hay pile by the livestock pens, and Arne and Torv—whose scouting ship had rejoined us three days ago—had found me curled up on one of the divans in the ship's study, just after breakfast yesterday morning. I'd been warier than ever about my new, untrained magic, and of allowing myself to become frantic or anxious. The heightened precaution tired me out faster. At least I didn't fear what I might see while I slept.

There'd been no more sightings of a shadowed silhouette of me, anywhere on board. Mara had woken the day before yesterday and evidently did not recall the exact circumstances which put her in a sickbed at all. From the way she grimaced and glowered at me still, I gathered she still knew *something* about it.

"What did I say?" I asked, leaning into him, closing my eyes and basking in his warmth.

"You called out for your mother. And you said..."

He furrowed his brow. "*Dae Catori.* I think I've heard you say it before."

"You have." I straightened, looking out at the lights again. "Back in the castle. I saw it in one of Alaric's books, too. *Dae Catori, Dae Caedon.* I don't know what it means, though. Even in my dreams, I can't... I can't quite seem to find those memories."

"We're getting closer, though." He stroked my hair. "And now we know why Alaric wanted you. You really do have power."

"In the end, he said something about taking that power. I think he knew all along, and the collar—the black magic he put on the collar—blocked it all away from me. It must be why I had those headaches. He would push, and push, testing my limits, triggering the energy, and stealing it, through our bond. He owned me, so he owned my magic, too."

I stooped to gather Schala into my arms. The caracal purred, rubbing her head up under my chin, her front paws flexing and kneading with delight.

"It's like a story," I said. "Like a myth I read from one of the books in the study. Something fanciful and impossible, that happened to someone else, far away. Not me. I'm changing, my barbarian, and it scares me."

"That is why we face it together."

He drew me closer, wrapping his arms around me. "Whatever your powers are, Sadi, it is clear to me they stem from some primal well. You have a ferocious soul within you. A she-cat indeed. Queen of the she-cats, my golden lioness."

"But it's too much! I feel it in me, as you say, like a wild beast. The monster I've always suspected inside of me. It rattles its cage and shakes the locks—"

"Perhaps you were never meant to keep it in, love."

He tilted my face to his, to give me a warm, reassuring kiss.

"You've always known there was a force within you. Something volatile and untamed. Isn't that why you crave pain and subjugation? Isn't that what you spoke of when you told me you needed someone to hold you down and possess you, to exercise the control and give you no choice but to obey?"

He brushed a loose strand of my hair behind my ear. "Isn't that why you trust me to rule your heart, and possess your body, as violently as you can withstand?"

I brought a hand to my lips. "I... is that why?"

"It seems as likely a reason as any. And I would have it no other way. In your heart you are a strong woman, a wild woman, and one unafraid of her passions."

"Thank you," I whispered with a smile. "No one has ever... understood it so well."

Not even me, perhaps.

"What will we do once we reach Sanraeth?" I asked.

"Well..." He stroked his beard. "It's more important than ever that we find your people, and delve into this magic you have unlocked, whatever it is. Perhaps they'll know more about why Alaric's father and the Order of Akolet wished to have you killed, and why Alaric himself would resist such a thing. First, I think we should go north, and seek a Sanraethi soothsayer for more. The northern clans still retain some observance of the old ways."

Something nagged at me. My lips twitched into frown, and I toyed with my braid as I tried to remember. Something about these Sanraethi old ways... something one of the refugees said, something I'd forgotten...

"Oh!" I dropped Schala unceremoniously to the boards, and she landed with expert graceful ease, flicking her bob tail. "The skull!"

Bannon cocked an eyebrow. "The... *skull?*"

I took him by the hand and pulled him along after me, making way for the stern deck and the ladderway to our middle deck.

"It was a snake's skull. I saw it in one of my visions, the day I got lost in the corridors, and found the cargo hold with the apples. I saw the skull on a ritual altar. I thought it was... an offering to Akolet. I was afraid it meant my kin were worshippers of the seven-headed snake, like the Order and Alaric were. I see now, though, what it really was."

"What's that?" he asked as we reached the ladderway and descended.

"It *is* an offering, but not to Akolet." I paused long enough to turn and meet his gaze. "An offering to something *greater* than Akolet. Something like the sea dragon!"

"And you saw this in a vision? So..."

"Come on, Sir." I smiled. "I will need your help."

We reached the door a scant moment later, and once inside I went immediately to the bag in which I'd hidden the serpent's skull. Digging it out again, I inspected it. Yes... just the right size. How had I not seen the intention before?

"My braid," I told him. "Calla said Sanraethi warriors once wove trinkets and trophies into their braids to commemorate their battles, and that I should find and kill a snake as soon as we reached Sanraeth, to commemorate my battle with the golem. It was right after that I found this in here. I thought it was evil, carrying the memory of a serpent cult."

I paused, studying the skull. "I... didn't want to discover my people were worshippers of that monster. I didn't want to face that possibility."

"But now you think it's something else?"

"It's my token."

I slipped the small reptilian skull into his hands. "Will you attach it to my braid, and accept me officially into the horde?"

He beamed at me. "Of course, kitten."

He slipped the end of my braid through the serpent's hinged jaw, sliding it up until it found a place to naturally rest. We would have Calla manage it later, to be sure it didn't slip from my hair. It made me Bannon's in more than just one way, though. Now I belonged to him, officially, in the bedroom and on the battlefield.

I didn't know who my true people were, but Bannon accepted me as one of his own. Now I was part desert girl, and part Sanraethi foundling.

One more week. Then we could begin the search for my people in earnest.

Then I could find my mother—and the fading blue light she called me toward—at last.

The End
***

Return home.
Reunite with the past in Book Three:
Beauty's Power

ABOUT THE AUTHOR

When she isn't visiting the worlds of immortals, demons, dragons and goblins, Brantwijn fills her time with artistic endeavors: sketching, painting, and working on graphic design. She can't handle coffee unless there's enough cream and sugar to make it a milkshake, but try and sweeten her tea and she will never forgive you. She moonlights as a futon for six lazy cats, loves tabletop roleplaying games, and can spend hours penciling naughty, sexy illustrations in her secret notebooks.

Brantwijn is the author of *The Chronicles of the Four Courts, Shifter's Dawn,* and *The Dark Roads* series, as well as many short stories and novellas. Follow her on

Facebook, Twitter, or visit her website at www.brantwijn.com.

Join Brantwijn's newsletter for a free book! Get updates and special offers from Brantwijn and other indie authors.

https://www.brantwijn.com/newsletter.

THANK YOU FOR READING

Please help indie authors and their books be seen!
Take a moment to leave your honest review at your
regular book purchase site,
and share with friends.

The author thanks you kindly.

#WriteOn
#IndieBooksBeSeen